7

FIRE

Rosie Scott

Dedication

Many thanks to the readers who have followed me over to fantasy from *The New World* series. I hope this is another world I have built that you can be immersed in.

I also dedicate this to anyone who is adopted and/or had a soul-searching experience in regards to their parentage. I was adopted and thus, this book became a personal journey for me. If you have chosen to search for your biological origins, may you be at peace with what you find.

This book would not exist if it weren't for the many dedicated men and women who have created video games for the enjoyment of millions over the past decades. Gaming is the top entertainment industry for a reason. Thank you all—your worlds and characters inspire me daily.

Most importantly, this is to my husband, Tim. My writing inspires your hobbies, and you inspire my writing. It is a fantastic cycle that I hope never ceases. I am immensely grateful for your love and support.

Other Books by Rosie Scott:

Dystopian

> The New World series:
> *The Resistance*
> *The Betrayal*
> *The Acquisition*
> *The Insurrection*
> *The Calamity*

Fantasy

> The Six Elements series:
> *Fire*
> *Earth*
> *Water*
> *Air*
> *Life*
> *Death*

> The Six Elements Origins:
> *Rise of a Necromancer*

For More Information:

Publisher's Website:
www.amazon.com/author/rosiescott

Author Blog:
www.rosiescottbooks.wordpress.com/

Business Inquiry Contact:
rosiescottbooks@gmail.com

Important Terms and Characters

Alderi – Casually referred to as *dark elves*. Blue, purple, or blackish in color with black eyes. A brutal and crude race suited to the underground and sly dealings.

Alteration magic – A school of magic dealing in the altering of material objects. Used for practical purposes and for battle support. Includes spells like telekinesis, detect life, and shape shifting.

Ancients – An ancient race of beings that not much is known about. Possibly based only in myth.

Arrayis – The world, consisting of all continents and oceans.

Bjorn Berg – A general of the Seran Army and a member of Sirius Sera's court.

Cel Mountains – A mountain range between the Seran Forest and the forests of Celendar, containing the dwarven city of Brognel and the secluded Whispermere.

Celdic – Casually referred to as *wood elves*. A peace-seeking race not prone to battle. Most have light complexions and stand slightly taller than humans. Most reside in the tree city of Celendar.

Celendar – One of Chairel's four major cities, made of nothing but trees that date back to the time of the Ancients. The pearl-white bark of these trees is found nowhere else on Arrayis, and the trees rival the nearby Cel Mountains.

Cerin Heliot – Kai Sera's childhood friend, come to learn life magic at the Seran University from the fishing village of Thornwell.

Chairel – A rich country mostly known for its four major cities of Sera, Comercio, Celendar, and Narangar. A land of forests, grasslands, and mountains. Known for its strict magical law system.

Comercio – One of Chairel's major cities and its central trade hub. A city of merchants and fortune seekers. In the center of Chairel and connected to each other major city via Caravaneer Road.

Dark Star – The season of winter. 90 days in length. Last season of the year.

Dual Caster – A mage capable of wielding two elements.

Elemental magic – Sometimes referred to as destruction magic. Deals in the elements of fire, earth, water, air, life, and death.

Eran – The first, smaller moon of Arrayis. Shows itself in the sky all year round.

Fortnight – A period of two weeks.

Gods – An immortal race of creatures said to have been created by the Ancients. The source of most of the religions on Arrayis. While many claim they actually once existed as tangible beings, none have been heard from in hundreds of years.

Golden Era – An era spanning 5782 years before the current Mortal Era, said to be a time of discovery, including the forming of most major nations of Arrayis. An era of which little is known for sure, given the mix of myth and history passed through the generations.

Glacia – A continent that also serves as its own country, home to the Icilic elves, at the northern most point of Arrayis.

Half-breed – A person who carries the blood of two separate races and contains traits from both.

High Star – The season of summer. 90 days in length. Second season of the year.

Human – The weakest of the mortal races, and the most common race to populate Chairel.

Icilic – Casually referred to as *snow elves*. The oldest lineage of elves in all of Arrayis, known for their magical abilities and disdain for other races. Extreme isolationists.

Illusion magic – A school of magic dealing in the creation of illusions for entertainment or nefarious purposes. Includes spells such as charm, frenzy, or invisibility.

Kai Sera – Wielder of the six elements. Adopted daughter of Sirius Sera.

Kilgorian Law – Named after its discoverer, Arturian Kilgor, it is a scientific law which states a mage's magic energy is pulled from reserves in a natural order: environment, weather, self.

Material element – Another way to describe the elements of fire, earth, water, and air, due to magic energy being used for creating a material rather than being used as the actual element (as is the case for life or death).

Meir – Arrayis's second moon, and the largest. Only appears above Chairel twice a year, and for weeks at a time.

Moons – Another word for *seasons*, as in, there are four moons in a year. Sometimes used as a method to describe the passing of time.

Mortal Era – The current era, directly following the Golden Era, said to belong to the mortal races of Arrayis given the disappearance of the *immortal* races such as the Ancients and the gods. Any dates referred to in *The Six Elements* are of the Mortal Era, unless otherwise specified.

Nahara – A poorer country known for its giant beasts and vast deserts. Just south of Chairel.

Narangar – The dwarven capital in southwest Chairel, nestled deep in the Golden Peaks just above the Chairel/Nahara Border.

Necromancy – Another term for death magic, and the only element that is banned across Chairel. Deals in the reanimation of the dead, the leeching of energy from life, and the decomposition or plague of living forms.

New Moon – The season of spring. 90 days in length. First season of the year.

Nyx Sephtis – Kai Sera's Alderi best friend. Former assassin.

Orders of the Mages – The name that encompasses all of Sera's mage armies, broken down into different Orders.

Queen Edrys – The ruler of Chairel. Has a regent in each of the four major cities. Resides in Comercio.

Red Moon – The season of autumn. 90 days in length. Third season of the year.

Sera – A rich, mostly human city that was built on the edge of a mountain. Attracts tourists and seekers of magic services. Home to The Twelve, and the famous Orders of the Mages. Ruled by Sirius Sera, who also serves as headmaster to the Seran University.

Seran University – The only place in Chairel that officially teaches magic and grants magic licenses to prospective mages.

Servis Ocean – The ocean which separates the continents of Arrayis.

Silas Galan – Kai Sera's bodyguard and former lover. A Celdic elf of royalty from Celendar.

Sirius Sera – Headmaster of the Seran University and regent of Sera. Wielder of air and life magic.

Terran Sera – Biological son of Sirius Sera, and heir to the Seran throne. Wielder of earth magic.

Theron Boa – A human mercenary hired by Kai Sera. A ranger and tracker. Alchemist. Wielder of a longbow and dual swords.

The Twelve – A prestigious arm of the Seran Army, consisting of twelve of its highest ranked soldiers, utilized for reconnaissance missions and to serve justice in the name of Sirius Sera. Each is awarded her or his own griffon mount.

Whispermere – A secluded village high in the Cel Mountains. Isolated and secretive.

Fire

Creatius les fiers – Create fire

Creatius les fiers a nienda – Create fire that sticks to another spell (i.e. air)

Earth

Creatius la terra – Create earth

Creatius el roc – Create rock

Air

Creatius le air – Create air

Generat le funel – Generate tornado

Generat la bolta – Generate lightning bolt

Water

Creatius la agua – Create water

Creatius la agua a friz – Create frozen water

Life

Givara le life – Heal

Givara la mana – Give energy

Promotus le imun – Promote immunity

Sheel a phisica – Shield for physical damage

Sheel a mana – Shield for energy damage (ward)

Death

Enflic le plague – Inflict plague

Corpa te risa – Raise corpse (singular)

Corpa te risa a multipla – Raise corpses (area of effect)

Absort la mana del life – Leech (translates to "absorb energy from life")

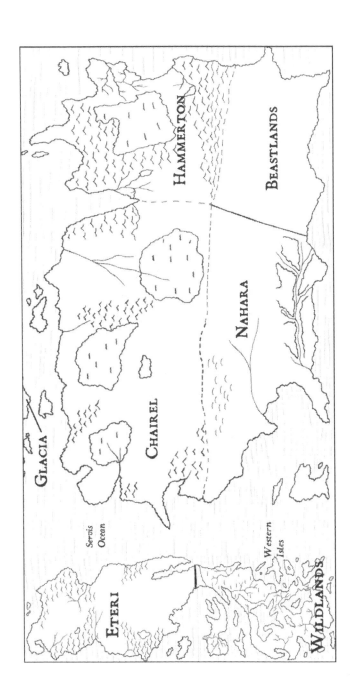

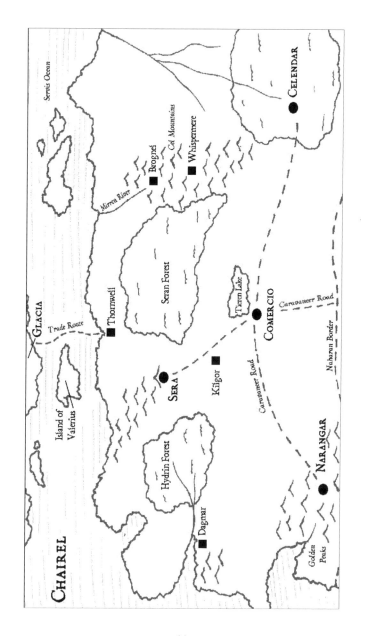

The dark blackness of night pulled a curtain over the city of Sera, inviting the stars to twinkle seductively overhead. The firelight of sconces and the magic lights of the illusionists kept the cobblestone streets visible from the high window of my bedroom in the Seran University of Magic. Below, people of various nationalities walked along the streets, either visiting the famous city or possibly perusing its services of healing magic, which were rarely found elsewhere.

From my window in the highest tower of the university, I could see the entire city and beyond its walls for a couple of miles. It was one perk of being the daughter of the university headmaster. They treated me like royalty here. Magic was a rare weapon to wield and had to be taken seriously; the harnessing and use of energy took its toll on mortal bodies, slowly chipping away at life forces until the mage herself died an early death. It was a rare occasion to find someone who not only accepted this and still wanted to wield magic, but was good at it. At the Seran University, there were hundreds of us here from all over the world. It was because of this rareness that magic was a commodity. Kingdoms took advantage of what few mages they had, particularly healers. Getting a healer to even attempt to cure the illness of a loved one was an expense few people could afford even if they could travel all the way to Sera to try.

I turned from the window, my thoughts on my studies. Being only fourteen, I had only just learned what elements I could wield. Out of all the magics, elemental magic, comprising six elements—fire, earth, water, air, life, and death—was the most challenging and dangerous to wield, and most mages were

17

only strong enough to wield one. Few wielded two elements, and no known mage in Arrayis's history could wield three or more. I was lucky to be a dual caster.

I walked up to the lone candle holder on my wall that was not lit, intent on practicing what little magic I knew. I lifted my right hand, palm up, toward the candle, and whispered words I studied intensely over the days before.

"Creatius les fiers." With a crackle of heat, a ball of flame conjured over my palm, warming me. The intense heat of the flame was kept safely tucked away from burning me with a protective energy barrier between my skin and the fire that was part of the spell. If I were to mess up the spell, it was possible it wouldn't be there, and I could burn myself to death. It was little wonder why an entire university was necessary to teach these magics.

I directed my attention to the wick of the candle, and the fire in my palm transferred to the wick in a tunnel of heat that dissipated a moment later. The candle was now lit like all the others.

Again, I lifted my palm. *"Creatius le air,"* I whispered. If it hadn't been for feeling the swirling air above my palm, I wouldn't have seen it there. Once more, I directed the energy to the wick, and the oxygen fed the flame. The fire burst upward and out, and I stepped back, a little in shock at the strength of its response.

"Kai." The rough voice called my attention to the door, and I spun. My father stood in the doorway, having seen the last of my practice, his eyes still on the candle. If I'd impressed him, he said nothing of it. As always, his eyes held authority and distance, a cool gray compared to my own golden pair. Silver speckled his dark hair from the stress of his responsibilities. He looked so different from me. Of course, I wasn't his biological daughter, and it wasn't only our physical differences that reminded me of this daily. "Your power is not to be played with like a toy."

My eyes fell to the ground, and I nodded. "Yes, father. I was only trying to practice."

"Remember what I told you?" He waited a moment for my answer, which did not come. "Kai?"

"You've told me many things, father."

"The day you become a mage is the day you become a woman. A woman wields power. A girl plays with toys."

I nodded.

"You are a dual caster, Kai. Do not disappoint me by spending time on frivolous things."

"I'm sorry."

"Apologies are words, not actions. Get to bed. You have class in the morning."

He was out of the room again before I had time to respond. It was times like these when I wondered why he had ever bothered to take me under his wing. Someone had dropped me off as an infant to the front steps of the Seran University, as if my parents had known I would be a mage. That was why my father had taken me in; he assumed I would have skill. Now, after years of worrying I wouldn't live up to that notion, my abilities as a dual caster had been discovered. Yet, he still wasn't happy with me.

The next morning, my older brother Terran stopped by to take me to class. He was my father's only biological child, and the obvious pick to be the headmaster and regent of Sera in my father's place when that time came. Terran was a nice enough sibling, I supposed. I was a good seven years younger than him, so we had little in common, but when we would socialize he treated me much better than father ever had. It was his work ethic that bothered me. Terran was an earth mage, and while he was skilled, he did not take his position very seriously. For having a future as the headmaster of the university and the regent of Chairel's richest and most prized settlement, he didn't seem to have a care in the world.

It made me a little bitter if I were honest with myself. Terran was not as talented as I was, nor as serious at his job, but he had father's approval and could look forward to a prestigious future.

Terran's long, dark brown locks were kept back in a lazy ponytail as he walked with me through the long stone hallways of the university. He looked fatigued and smelled of ale. I knew then that he'd been out the previous night partying with his group of friends. Terran was well-known in Sera's taverns, and his good looks and royal position made him popular with fortune-seeking women.

"Did you hear I can wield both fire and air?" I asked him because we hadn't yet spoken of it. Terran's face brightened and he grinned over at me despite the circles beneath his eyes.

"Yes, sister, I did. Don't let it get to your head, now." He turned around a corner of an intersection of hallways before we continued down another. The university was bigger than even the castles of the nation, and could be a maze to anyone who walked through it and didn't live there. "I wouldn't want to dual cast, myself. I love life. Want to live as much of it as I can."

"Do you think dual casters live even shorter lives than other mages?" I asked, morbidly curious.

"No, I don't think it, I know it. The more magic you wield, the bigger the toll. And you're no elf, sister. You have a short enough lifespan as it is. I wouldn't be using your powers fruitlessly."

His last words reminded me of father catching me practicing the night before. "Did father tell you of last night?"

"He did," Terran replied, just as shortly. He stopped, then, because we had reached our destination. My first class of the day sat in the room ahead. I could already hear the students within chatting and giggling amongst themselves. My brother took one last look at me and said, "Magic is serious business. Please be careful with it."

Please be careful with it. I could have asked Terran to follow his own advice, but I knew he was only looking out for me. "I will. Thanks, Terran."

He nodded with a boyish smile before turning and heading off to wherever he needed to go.

I made my way into the classroom a moment later, avoiding stares and whispers. For the few years I'd been going to classes at the university, I was used to my classmates keeping me at a distance. Perhaps they were uncomfortable with going to class with the headmaster's daughter. Days before, when I'd found I was a dual caster, things had gotten even worse. Now the tinges of jealousy were in the glares of my peers.

I sat in my usual seat, at a table in the far back with only one other occupant. His name was Cerin Heliot, and he was tall, pale, with eyes of the sharpest silver and hair long and as black as an abyss. He had no friends, which gave us something in common. He was also the only classmate I'd ever tried to become friendly with. Despite his dark and foreboding looks, I found him oddly warm and welcoming given his quiet nature. I was also biased; I found Cerin to be beautiful, and had pursued friendship him since he moved to Sera to learn magic from the small, northern fishing hamlet of Thornwell.

Until the past few days, I'd worried that Cerin would have been a natural with death magic. He certainly looked the part, and as most elemental mages had found throughout history, their physical appearance resembled the elements they were predisposed to. It was why wielding fire and air hadn't come as much of a surprise. My hair was a fiery deep red that shone gold in the light, so unique in color that many thought I dyed it with the expensive dyes imported to Sera from the desert nation of Nahara to the south. I was also quite pale, a feature that was a common attribute among air wielders. Due to Cerin's dark features I'd assumed he would have easily learned death magic; it was an element as powerful, if not more so, than the others, but the art of necromancy was a banned practice in all of Chairel and much of the world. Bringing the dead to life, wielding plague and disease, and leeching the life and energy from others were all practices considered too savage for warfare. They had no place in a modern society, according to our queen and the Seran University. The moral and ethics implications of the element were far too complicated and vast to keep the practice legal.

Regardless, Cerin had found life magic to be his calling. He was lucky in this respect. Healers were the most sought after of mages and became the wealthiest. Alchemists could often heal sickness, and surgeons could often mend broken bones. But life mages could do both, and more accurately, while taking a fraction of the time.

My ears picked up on whispers, and I glanced up to the table beside ours just in time to see a classmate use his air magic to blow a gust of wind in Cerin's direction. Cerin's notes from the day before blew off the table, scattering and skidding across the tiled floors. The boy and his friend burst into laughter, while Cerin wordlessly moved out of his seat to gather the papers.

"Your powers aren't to be used so needlessly," I hissed at my peer, getting out of my seat to help gather the papers.

"Or what, girly? You gonna tell daddy and get me sent back to Kilgor?" he sneered back at me.

"No, I'll tell Ms. Ply about this so she makes it known you're not taking your studies seriously," I retorted, taking the stack of Cerin's notes and handing it over to him.

"Thanks," he offered, his voice nearly cracking. He looked away in embarrassment.

"Oh, I'm shaking in me boots," the bully replied to me carelessly.

"Kilgor's not so bad, mate," his friend teased him, as Cerin and I sat back into our seats. My table mate had an arm protectively over his notes now. "Not if yer lookin' for the farmer's life."

"Yeah, but I ain't. Why the hell else do ya think I'm here?"

"Because the only girls in our town are goats," his friend replied with a snort of laughter.

The classroom door opened a moment later, and our professor Beatrice Ply hurried in. As always, she was late and disheveled, her thick mop of curly red hair refusing to be tamed by a few oddly placed hair pins. She carried a stack of old texts to the counter ahead of us before turning to the impatient class.

"Good morning, everyone. Sorry I'm late." As she said it, her eyes met mine. She likely thought I would tattle on her to my father. Unbeknownst to her, I never would. I didn't like talking to him more than I had to. "Please get out the spell books you were assigned yesterday. We will continue where we left off, learning various words for each of your elements and how they connect between spells. Remember, don't conjure, just read and study. We don't want any accidents."

I retrieved my two spell books from my pack, bringing them to the table before me. Cerin eyed them both with admiration. He was impressed by my ability to dual cast.

"Now, who can tell me what *creatius* means?" Ms. Ply continued, looking over the class.

I raised my hand, and when she chose me, I said, "Create."

"Very good."

"Very *easy*," the bully from earlier seethed. I ignored the comment.

"And who can tell me what *givara* means?"

Cerin hadn't raised his hand, but he was called on anyway. Perhaps because he was the only one in the class who knew a spell where *givara* was relevant. "Give," he offered.

"Correct. Give, as in give life. Create, as in create an element, using the energy in the air around you and harnessing it to your will. Does anyone know what would happen if you were to say a spell incorrectly? Suppose you said, *givara les fiers?* Or even, *creatius le life?*"

I raised my hand again, but Ms. Ply called on another student.

"Nothing. Nothing would happen," came the response.

"Correct. To give fire is an incorrect statement as is create life. Even in necromancy, the spells are not stated as you *creating* life because you are not. You are using energy to reanimate the dead. Even if you have a corpse standing before you, it is not living, because it cannot. It is only existing and acting upon your will because you are commanding the energy animating it. Does this make sense?" A few of us nodded, and she continued, "Now would be a good time to remind you all that if you see any student—or anyone, for that matter—using necromancy, please report it to your nearest professor or guard. Necromancers are enemies of Chairel and are often put to death."

"Ironic," I heard a student muse.

"Now, using the words you know, I want you all to attempt to write new spells using these words. Spells that you think could work. To use magic effectively, you not only need to wield it, but understand its language." She paused, looked around the room, and finished, "I'll be coming around the room to guide each of you. Please begin."

Cerin and I were silent for minutes afterward, using our spell books for reference and writing down ideas. Ms. Ply took her time moving from table to table, helping other students with the language, telling them when they were wrong about the usage of a word and why.

After a while, I looked up to Cerin, deciding to attempt conversation with him as I often did. "Cerin, have you ever tried to wield another element?"

His silver eyes rose from his book, meeting mine with a stare that felt oddly distant. "Why would I do that? I'm no dual caster like you."

"How would you know if you've never tried?"

"Are you saying I have?" The question was weird and defensive. I wondered if I annoyed him.

"No. I'm sorry. I meant nothing by it. I just wonder what would happen if you tried, you know? Once you have designated elements, you're not supposed to branch out. But what if you did?"

Cerin hesitated. "I've heard nothing happens. You can attempt a spell of a different element, but it doesn't work. If you're a dual caster, anyway. If you only cast one element and casting another works, well...I guess that's how you find out you're a dual caster."

The beginnings of a smile spread on my face, for his distance faded and left only warmth and soft curiosity. "Yeah, I guess so," I admitted.

"Do you want to try it?" Cerin offered, pushing his spell book over to me. "Let's see what happens."

"Oh, so I get to be the guinea pig?" I teased.

"I doubt it'll hurt you. It's life magic, after all."

"How will I know if it's working?" I asked him, reading the beginner's healing spell. I wasn't injured. It wasn't like I would be able to tell if it was working by mending a cut that didn't exist.

"You'll feel a warmth. Put your hand to your skin, and you'll feel warmth from your hand, and tingling from what it's touching."

"Okay." I put my right hand to my left arm, and recited low, *"Givara le life."* There was a rising heat in my palm. Slowly, I felt the warmth transfer to my other arm, leaving it numb and tingling like it had fallen asleep. I looked up to Cerin, a little in shock. "It's working."

He stared back in disbelief. "It can't be. You already know fire and air."

I reached across the table to him, grabbing his hand. In normal circumstances, this would have embarrassed me. But I needed him to feel it. I repeated the spell, and Cerin realized I was right. He jerked his hand away before staring at me like I was some kind of god. "That's impossible," he whispered, rubbing at his hand.

"Then how am I doing it?"

Cerin only stared back. He had no answer.

Ms. Ply was at our table a moment later, asking about the spells we'd attempted to create. I barely heard her. I turned to her and asked her the first question that came to mind.

"Why can I wield life?"

She watched me for a moment before chuckling. "You can't, Kai. You wield fire and air."

"I just used Cerin's spell." It was stupid of me to admit. We weren't supposed to be practicing spells, only writing them. My excitement overcame me.

"Kai...it is impossible to wield more than two elements. You know this." She appeared uncomfortable and confused by my ramblings.

Risking much, I grabbed the professor's arm, reciting the spell. A moment later, she, too, jerked back from it like it was hurting her.

"I saw you wield fire and air yesterday," she said, her words a rush.

"I know. I've done both. And I just wielded life."

She stared at me, in a state of shock. After a few seconds of silence, she stuttered, "Then—then do this for me. Lift your palm, like you will wield simple fire." I did so. "Now repeat after me. *Creatius la agua.*"

I repeated the spell, and just like that, water formed from the energy particles in the air, the water splashing slowly up against the protective circular energy barrier just above my palm. Both Ms. Ply and I stared at it as if it shouldn't exist.

"Dispel it!" she exclaimed, almost as if in fear. I did so with a wave of my hand. The water fell to the classroom floor, splashing across the tile and dampening my shoes.

Now, I had the attention of the class. Everyone was quiet, watching history unfold before their eyes with me at its center.

"Repeat *creatius la terra.*"

I did so. Instead of water, or fire, or even air, I harnessed even more energy within my hand, and a ball of earth hovered where water just had, swirling with minerals just like I had dug up a shovel full of the earth in the university's courtyard.

Ms. Ply stared at the earth, swirling around within its barrier and waiting to be used, and pointed toward one of my peers closest to the door. "You," she said, her voice a frightened, hushed tone. "Get the headmaster. *Now!*"

One

34th of New Moon, 417

Towering stone walls rose above me on both sides as I trotted along one hallway of the university, on my way to see a good friend. An employee of the university nodded toward me in greeting as he lit the candles along the wall that had died overnight with quick bursts of fire magic.

At the end of the hallway, the walls opened to a large gathering room. With polished wooden floors that reflected its occupants and ceilings as high as five stories, it was a sight to behold.

Halfway across the room, a friendly face came into view. Silas Galan was an old friend. Born among Celdic royalty in the great city of Celendar, he was given a free ticket through the Seran University to learn earth magic in exchange for his service as my personal bodyguard through my teenage years. At just a year over forty, he was extraordinarily young for an elf, as elves had an average lifespan of hundreds of years. Elves were mostly known to only die prematurely by battle wounds or extreme heartbreak. Celdic elves were not fond of war or battle and favored peace whilst living tucked away in the great Cel Forest.

Silas was a handsome sight, as were most elves. Because of the delayed aging process elves were known for, he appeared to be only twenty or twenty-one, with a mop of sienna brown hair that swept over the points of his ears, and stunning, sharp green eyes. He was taller than most humans, built for speed and agility with practical muscles and a knack for attention to details. His trusty bow sat perched on his back along with a quiver of white arrows. The weapon was a beautiful one, made of the pearl-white bark of the trees only known to grow in the forests of Celendar.

"On your way to see Bjorn?" he questioned, spinning to seamlessly go from a standstill to walking by my side. He spoke of a general of the Seran Army, and one of the few authority figures I was completely comfortable around. Bjorn was like a father to me. He was loving, caring, and interested in the happenings of my life while Sirius usually avoided spending time with me.

"Yes," I replied, my voice holding a slight tremble. "I'm a nervous wreck."

"You have your supporters. The only person standing in opposition to you is your father."

"I know," I acknowledged. "Sometimes that's the hardest fact to accept."

Silas remained silent. I knew he agreed with me, but he was also intelligent, probably already thinking through how verbally acknowledging my depressing statement would only make me feel worse.

We walked together toward the front exit of the building, passing by an entire room full of people waiting to meet with members of the university to discuss magical services. Despite not knowing what they were here for, I knew most of them would be disappointed. Most were poor and could not afford the services. Others had trekked seasons from Nahara and would be told that Seran mages dealt in gold, not trade, like many of the Naharans were used to.

I had never agreed with Chairel's methods of holding its mages above the heads of ordinary folk. The only thing I was ashamed of as a mage myself was being an unwilling participant to the monopoly Sera held over magic. It was illegal in Chairel to practice magic without a license from the Seran University, which, of course, didn't mean that no one practiced it without licenses at all, only that they were imprisoned or executed if they were caught. Because healers were so expensive, many civilians of Chairel died from simple illnesses or wounds that didn't need to be fatal. Many rebellions had arisen in my home country in the past, but none had ever changed Chairel's strict magical laws. Not only did my home country hold magical knowledge above the heads of those who could not afford an education from Sera, but it also had the largest and most diverse army in the world. Few could hope to rebel and win against such odds.

Silas and I exited the university, and the bustling city of Sera opened before us. Sera was built on the side of a mountain and set up in tiers. At the uppermost point of the city was the Seran University, the city's prized possession. Beneath that was the sector in which the tourist attractions, merchants, and prestigious class of citizens lived, those who either had family members who were mages, or could simply afford our services. Beneath that near the bottom of the mountain was the poor sector along the edge of the outer walls. This is where most of the people who kept the city fed and serviced lived. The poor even spilled over to the outside of the walls, where small farms scattered over the surrounding plains.

From the northernmost point of Sera, the view was incredible. From the courtyard of the university, the rest of the city sloped downward for a few miles, before the plains and view beyond opened to the horizon. It would be an easy city to defend if there were ever a need. The view allowed defenders to see for miles, attacking the city would be an uphill climb, the wall was gigantic and sturdy, and Sera held one of the best armies in the world. Not only did we have the Orders of the Mages, we also had the Seran Army, an army of rank-and-file soldiers armed with the best armor and weapons available to humankind. And at the very top of that army was Bjorn.

"Hit him like ya mean it! Is this a training field or a little girl's playroom? Bloody hell!"

I chuckled at the sound of Bjorn's voice bellowing out from the training fields behind the barracks. Raised by dwarves in the neighboring country of Hammerton, Bjorn had picked up a bit of their dialect and accent despite being human. Turning the corner with Silas at my side, I found the bulky man behind the voice, yelling at two frightened men who were in a dirt arena, both wielding wooden swords.

Bjorn was my father's right-hand man regarding the Seran Army. He was the best general we had, and took a front seat in training the non-mage soldiers, putting himself in charge of melee fighters. Bjorn was a large, towering, and muscular man, with light reddish hair that held stubborn grays he kept back from his face in a short, messy ponytail. His face was usually covered in facial hair of some description, though he wasn't fond of keeping it tidy. His skin was a natural tan, and his muscles stuck out in sharp angles from his body from years of training and fighting.

In comparison with my father, Bjorn was frightening in appearance. He reeked of strength and power and jovial confidence. On the contrary, my father was thin and pale, and if one were to glance at him without knowing his name, they could be mistaken in believing he was not a threat. Yet, it was my father I feared and with Bjorn that I took solace. While I was

32

raised as the daughter of Sirius Sera, it was Bjorn that I looked up to and admired the most.

"Bjorn!" I called. Despite being in mid-training, I knew he would call off the day's events to make time for me if he had to.

Bjorn turned from the sparring match, his eyes brightening when he saw me. "Ah! There ya are, my girl. The word from the messengers is that your father's already looking for you."

My heart sunk into my stomach, attempting to hide within its acidic bile. I said nothing for fear that my sudden nausea would overcome me.

"Listen, Kai, I know you're scared. Your father makes me shit my pants sometimes, myself."

I couldn't help but chuckle from the unexpected humor. I could always count on Bjorn to make me feel better.

"You have my support, and that will help. Your father sometimes listens to me as much as he tries to pretend otherwise. I've already told him of your plans, and I've told him I agree."

"What'd he say?" I asked quietly.

"Well, he had a few choice words for me, to be honest, but that's neither here or there. Just remember, you've swayed your father's opinion before. You remember how much he resisted siding with you on Nyx."

Nyx. In a quick distraction, I wondered where she was. She knew today was important for me, yet I hadn't seen her. There had to be a reason for it. As stubborn and even arrogant as she was by nature, the Alderi held a deep respect for me after my pleas kept her from execution. Five years ago, when both of us had been sixteen, we'd met under unusual circumstances. I had been sleeping in my bed and woke up abruptly to find a girl standing over me, a dagger in hand.

She had noticed I had woken up and said delicately, "I am here to assassinate you."

I'd heard how young her voice was, as young as mine, and had replied through fear, "Then why are you hesitating?"

She had responded, "Because I don't feel like it would be right if I did."

Nyx and I had spent hours exchanging stories and simply talking. It had gone from me talking to her to keep her from killing me to actually finding a lot in common with her and wanting to befriend her. She'd come from underground, where the massive cavernous cities of her race were hidden discreetly from the rest of the world's view. Like most Alderi, sometimes referred to as dark elves, she was raised to be heartless, brutal, and vengeful against the races of the surface world. She had been employed as an assassin from twelve years of age, and though she enjoyed both the chase and the brutality of the job, she'd been searching for reasons. When I was her target, instead of adding someone high profile to her list, she had finally found someone who understood what it felt like to be raised with certain expectations while desiring something different.

Nyx had been caught in the morning when we had still been in mid-conversation, and thrown in the dungeon of the Seran University, as it also served as the city's castle. As with all caught assassins, she was to be executed for her crimes within the fortnight. With much pleading and compromise with my father, I had gotten her pardoned. We had been best friends ever since.

"You'll no doubt hear some rough words from your father today," Bjorn went on, pulling me out of my thoughts. "Don't let him get to you. You are your own woman, and you will do grand things with your life, whether or not he has planned them for you."

I nodded, wishing my father felt the same way. "Will you be disappointed in me?"

"Are you kidding? You couldn't disappoint me if you tried, child. I feel lucky every day just to be a part of your life."

I smiled wide before pulling the big man into a hug. His muscular arms surrounded me, squeezing lightly. Bjorn kissed me on the top of the head.

"Thank you," I said to him.

"I'm here for you, Kai. Always will be." Bjorn pulled back, nodding behind me. "You're being summoned again."

I turned to see a teenage boy running toward me. I recognized the messenger from the earlier times he'd come to me.

"Kai, your father requests your presence immediately," he said, slightly out of breath.

I tried to ignore the anxiety that traveled up my esophagus from that statement. I nodded, before turning back to Bjorn. "Call upon the Priests of Hades, Bjorn."

"Why, my girl?" he replied, curious.

"They will hold my funeral a few days from now," I said, attempting to jest in my nervousness.

Bjorn only chortled at my words. I turned back to the messenger who listened to our conversation with a mixture of curiosity and unease. "Where is he?"

The boy turned back toward the university. "Follow me."

*

Silas and I ambled into my father's office. It was a large, dark room with floor to ceiling bookshelves filled with spell books and informational texts about various kingdoms. A large map of the entire world of Arrayis hung on the wall to my left, free from markings. A single window made of stained glass allowed little sunlight in on my right.

Father's desk was an organized mess of texts, papers, and letters from the day's mail. A candle holder sat on his desk, allowing a much needed orange glow to wave along the walls. Beneath my shoes was an expensive woven rug my father had received as a gift from the king of Nahara in the capital of T'ahal, an expansive city in the sand dunes of the Arobe Desert, as part of a trade deal from the somewhat recent past.

Since my father's chair faced away from us, I let my eyes wander around on the rug, taking in the deep red dyes of the thread. After a few moments, I focused on the candles instead, watching melted wax roll slowly down toward the candle's holder, my mind trying to stay off the impending conversation.

The chair turned, and my father's eyes immediately fell upon Silas.

"I trust you can separate yourself from Kai for the time I need to talk to her," he said. It was an explicit command.

"Yes, sir," Silas said, bowing slightly before turning to leave.

36

It hurt to hear my father talk so shortly to someone so dear, but I said nothing, for I was as used to it as I would ever get. The door softly closed behind me, my father's eyes unrelenting on my own.

"I have secured you a place in the Seran Army," he announced, his stare unwavering as he watched me for a reaction. "The Fourth Order of the Mages will be in town in a few short weeks, and you are to join them. They have plans for you. Plans I expect you to handle."

"The Fourth Order, father?" I asked.

"You didn't expect to get a promotion before beginning your career?"

"I don't expect a promotion. I just expect a taste of combat, and as far as my knowledge goes, the Fourth Order deals in nothing of the sort."

"Each army is critical to the success of the entire unit. The Fourth Order is currently working on escorting diplomats from Dagmar to T'ahal."

I hesitated. "How much combat does this involve?"

"*Damn* it, Kai, get your mind off of combat. Very little, if any. What's important is that the money involved is better than most, since we're dealing with dwarves. They're gullible bastards."

"No, they're just more willing to trust," I corrected him.

"Yes. As I said. Gullible." After a slight pause, my father went on, "I trust you have no objections to these plans."

I swallowed hard. "Actually, I—"

"Speak up, Kai. I don't have time for your stuttering."

"I heard you've talked to Bjorn."

"Bjorn has absolutely no relevance to this discussion," my father replied sternly.

"He *does,* actually, because he spoke to you on my behalf."

"What are you, a *child?* Sending men who have much better things to do to me because you're too lazy?"

"That's not what happened. I didn't send him to you. I expressed my concerns, and he took them to you of his own choice."

"Hmm. Well. In either case, I cannot see how his words to me about you have anything to do with your plans with the Fourth Order."

"His words to you should have outlined exactly what I felt about your plans for me and your army."

Anger slowly creased the skin of my father's forehead. "You would *waste* your life? This university trained you, and I expect you to show respect for your upbringing by serving in its army. I fail to see how you believe this is up for discussion."

"Father, *you* are the one who wishes for me to waste my life. Sending me to the Fourth Order is not a good use of my skills. It borders on insulting."

"How stupidly arrogant of you to assume your skills are any more valuable to the army than any other mage," he seethed.

"How absolutely blind of you to assume they can't be," I retorted. "I know I have no experience on the battlefield. That's why I desire it. Why waste time sending me on escort missions? Aren't you aware that I might not have that much time to be of use to you?" I spoke of the fears I had of my own mortality. Because no mage had ever before wielded all six elements, it was untested. I was a guinea pig in the studies of magic. My existence should have been an impossibility. I had the unwelcome knowledge that any day could be my last.

"What time you have left is of no concern to me," he retorted, unaware of how badly it hurt for me to hear him say it. "Regardless, before you are ready for combat, you must be trained in being part of an army, following the orders of your superiors. It is something you have failed at time and time again, so before I can trust sending you into combat, we need to see if you are even capable of following simple directions."

His statement was insulting and followed too closely to the hurtful words I'd endured from him just before it. Anger sizzled and popped within me from the pit of my stomach.

"I trust your silence to mean that you have no further questions," he stated.

"You trust wrongly, then. I reject your plans for me, father. I have something else in mind for my future."

My father sat stiffly in his chair, unmoving save for a nerve beside his right eye. "Such as?"

"It doesn't matter, does it? Regardless of what they are, my plans differ from yours. You won't agree with them."

"You are naïve and juvenile, Kai. Words cannot express how disappointed I am in you."

"I accept that. Your approval has not been at the top of my hopes and goals list ever since I found it was impossible to obtain." I turned, opening the door to the hallway beyond.

"I did not excuse you," my father called from behind me.

I closed the door behind me, calling back, "Yes, I know. I excused myself."

Two

Silas opened the door and held it for me, and I thanked him in a mumble before I walked through it and into the Howling Wolf Tavern. I quickly scanned the room for familiar faces, finally finding who I was looking for.

A thin but shapely figure sat at the bar, clothed in light black leather armor and a hood. A belt with several sheaths hung from her hips. After the tavern keeper whispered some words to her, Nyx turned, her deep, blackish-purple face looking up at me from under her thick hood.

"I was wondering if you'd ever come," she greeted, motioning for Silas and me to take the saved stools from beside her. Nyx's hair escaped the sides of her hood from around her face in dark wisps, and she watched me with concern swirling in her entirely black eyes.

"We didn't have plans to meet here," I replied in defense.

"No, but your talks with your ass of a father usually end in a hefty tavern bill, so I figured I'd wait for you here." Nyx grinned at me, before glancing over at Silas to judge his expression. "I'm paying."

"Nonsense. I can vouch for myself." I raised my hand at the bartender.

Nyx called to him, "Anything this woman orders is on my bill. Don't let her tell you otherwise."

With a resigned sigh, I ordered a mug of ale before crossing my arms on the bar, banging my head onto them.

Nyx laughed heartily beside me. "I cannot *wait* to hear this story."

I told Nyx the same story I'd told Silas about the conversation with my father. She listened with enthusiasm, as usual, laughing as I told her the final moments.

"Well, no shit, you told the old man off, did you?" Nyx glanced at the bartender. "Bring us a pitcher!"

I shook my head in response to her antics before taking a few swigs of my ale.

"So is that it, then?" Nyx asked, intrigued. "Are we leaving Sera?"

"I don't know. What do you think?"

"I think it's about time! I'm tired of having to live in this dump of a place. There's barely any work for me here. I have to take cuts in pay to serve the poor, and the holier-than-thou upper district wouldn't dare hire me, the racist bastards. There's coin to be made elsewhere, I'm sure of it."

I looked to Silas, whose only concern at the moment seemed to be keeping a close eye on how much ale I was consuming.

"What about you?" I asked him.

"I'd come with you wherever you decide to go," he replied.

"How *sweet,*" Nyx teased, though she cut it off at that out of respect.

"But how will we make our livelihoods?" Silas pondered aloud.

"I have enough coin to last us for a few years as it is," I admitted, my voice low as a precaution against any potential thieves. "Though some people can make a fine living off of being a mercenary, and they don't come from the same background I do. We'll be able to do it. The three of us."

41

"We have to decide where to go," Silas mused. "We can't leave the city with no direction or clue where we're going."

"Why not?" Nyx retorted, before taking another swig of ale.

"Because that would be *unwise,*" he replied evenly.

"Does dear brother know about all this?" Nyx asked, a quick change of subject, but a relevant question.

My thoughts went to Terran, and my stomach soured. "He knows I am unhappy here with father's direction. He has advised me against disobeying him multiple times. His main concern is my..." I trailed off, staring at the swirling gold of the ale below me. "...lifespan."

"Terran would rather you stayed here and wasted your life being unhappy than to leave and find happiness in what little time you may have? Smart one, that." Nyx ran one dark finger around the lip of her mug.

"He knows my life will be shorter if I use the powers I have, that's all."

"Yes, but you *have* them. You are the first in history to wield six elements. Live a little, right?"

I'd often thought the same. I had come to terms with the death sentence of being a mage long ago before I'd even known I was more skilled than most. Still, we were talking about how long I had to live, here. Part of me was uncomfortable with that. I was only twenty-one and still waiting for life to begin. Looking over to Silas, I found him avoiding my gaze. Our vastly different potential lifespans had been the source of much turmoil for us.

"So, when are we leaving?" Nyx asked once I'd said nothing. She was eager to leave Sera. Much of the pretentious, mostly human populace were judgmental against dark elves, given they were a rare sight in the city or above ground at all. Just the appearance of a female Alderi could be frightening; they were known for their murderous and crude ways. If it weren't for her being friends with me, Nyx would have left years ago.

"I don't know. Give me a few days, maybe a few weeks. I need to talk to Bjorn about it. See if he has ideas for us. And to...say goodbye." Saying goodbye to those I loved who would stay here would be the hardest part about leaving, but Sera was not where my future was. I'd been flirting with the idea of leaving ever since I realized long ago my father would not take my skills seriously. I should have left years ago. Most mages began fieldwork at eighteen. Here I was, three years past, with a shorter lifespan and still no battle experience. It flabbergasted me that my father was so afraid to put my skills to the test.

"Ugh. Please make it closer to a few days than a few weeks," Nyx mused teasingly, before ordering another pitcher of ale.

It was a plan we finally decided on. After quite a few more mugs of ale and hours of talking, the daylight faded outside and turned to darkness. The tavern held a golden glow from the various candles and the fireplace, and a lute player came into the bar, setting up a seat in the room's corner, a small cloth pouch on the ground at his feet for tips. He played his instrument, and the music soon swirled lovingly with the effects of the ale in my head.

"All right, I think you need to be leaving," Nyx said to me a few hours after the darkness had fallen outside. "You look like you're ready to pass out."

"It's been a long day," I replied.

"Are we going back to the university?" Silas asked from beside me.

"I'd rather not."

He nodded. "I thought you'd say that. Let's get a room here, assuming they have a vacancy."

Nyx lifted an eyebrow but said nothing. Silas called the tavern keeper over, paying him for one room for the night. Nyx waved us off with a friendly goodbye.

Silas held my arm as he led me up the stairs to the tavern's second floor, the room key in his hand.

I tugged at his hand. "I can walk," I protested.

He kept his grip. "You've had one too many mugs of ale."

"Pfft." Despite the disagreement, I didn't pull away again. Silas unlocked the door before us, leading me within a room that smelled as if it hadn't been cleaned for weeks.

"Well," Silas commented matter-of-factly, as was his personality, *"that* stench is quite interesting."

I laughed louder than I should have at the statement. "How eloquently put," I said, collapsing onto the bed without a care.

Silas closed the door behind him and turned to face me. He looked at me for a moment, his eyes portraying words his mouth resisted saying.

"Maybe I should ask for a second room," he suggested, suddenly uncomfortable.

"Oh, *Silas,"* I groaned, rolling on the bed so it made enough room for him on the other side. "I expect nothing more than a good night's sleep. Let the past be the past."

"It's not a problem. I'd pay for it out of my own pocket. I simply figured you'd want to save the money."

"Stop your bickering," I replied, readjusting to be under the covers, lying on my side. "I have respected your wishes for over a year, haven't I? All I want is sleep. Promise."

Watching me as my eyes fluttered close with fatigue, he replied, "As you say."

*

Nyx was waiting for us at a small table the next morning, her hood uncharacteristically off, allowing her to show off her dark purplish-black skin and even darker black hair. The tavern was nearly empty at this hour so she dodged fewer stares than usual. Despite the thick heat of the air, she was in full leather armor again. It served as more than just protection from elements and weapons; because she was Alderi, her skin was made for thriving in dark and moist environments. She constantly avoided direct contact with the sun and always carried around lotions that she bought at an alchemist's shop to keep her skin from peeling.

I hadn't remembered making plans the previous night to meet her here, but then again, I couldn't remember much about the night before at all. The pain that permeated through my stomach reminded me that my coping techniques for dealing with my father were sorely due to be revised.

Nyx wiggled her eyebrows at me before making a crude gesture with both her hands about the night before.

Glancing back behind me, I saw Silas hadn't appeared in the stairway yet. "*Nyx!*" I hissed.

She shrugged, a grin on her face. "I figured maybe Silas had finally come to his senses," she reasoned.

"He's allowed to have his opinions," I mumbled. I wanted to leave it at that. Silas had been my bodyguard since not long after someone had hired Nyx to assassinate me, so we had been inseparable for years. It was only inevitable that we would form a friendship, if not more. After a year of a fulfilling romantic partnership, Silas had abruptly broken it off and asked to revert to the friendship we'd had. He was uncomfortable with our vastly different lifespans and found it easier to cut things off with me than to love me and lose me in what would be a blink of an eye in his own life. His opinions on the matter didn't entirely make sense to me, but he was entitled to them. I just didn't have to be happy about it.

"Okay, so you're allowed to have some wild fun on our adventures, then, right?" Nyx went on, pulling my thoughts onto other things. "We'll find you some *fine*-looking man in some city far away, and we'll keep your identity a secret from him so he doesn't charge you extra for a night, eh?" Nyx patted me on the back. "One night, passionate action, and you'll never have to see him again."

"You think it's that easy, huh?" I asked. Who was I kidding? Of course she did. Nyx had never been in a relationship, but she'd had her taste of plenty of men from many races. The Alderi were an extraordinarily sexual and non-monogamous race, and she was no exception.

"It's the oldest profession of them all, my friend, and a woman is entitled to partake in it."

"True enough," I replied with a sigh. Nyx was trying to get me to feel better and look forward to something. I just didn't think doing something like that would make anything better for me.

Footsteps on the stairs alerted me to Silas, and he came over to us, oblivious to our previous conversation, his bow on his back. "Are we off to see Bjorn, then?" he asked.

"Ready," Nyx replied, pulling her hood over her head to leave her face in shadow. "As long as I don't have to get close enough to the university that I start picking up on its pretentious stench."

"Just to the barracks. Bjorn will be training again today until dusk," I explained. I had always respected Nyx's wishes not to get too close to the university; within it, after all, were the dungeons in which they had imprisoned her. And despite my father having released her years ago, he still abhorred her, and she returned the feeling with equal passion.

Nyx led us out the tavern door and into the cobblestone streets. We made our way through crowds of citizens and tourists alike, stopping only at a merchant selling whole turkey legs so Nyx could pick up a few with her incessant hunger.

"You want one?" she asked, holding out one drumstick.

"Sure, thanks," I replied, taking it from her. It smelled delicious and fresh. I knew not to ask Silas. Celdic elves, while not all strictly vegetarian, believed in certain rituals of respect for hunting animals and eating their flesh. Silas did eat meat occasionally, but only if he had hunted the beast himself, and only if he could use the entire carcass for materials and give it a proper death, as he called it, with a prayer of thanks and respect toward the animal that had given its life for a different being's consumption. I greatly respected Silas for having such firmly held beliefs, but I did not share them.

"You don't think Bjorn will have me kicked off the property, do you?" Nyx asked, just before tearing a piece of bird flesh from its bone. Years before, it had been Bjorn who had arrested her. In the time since the two had rarely seen one another. Bjorn's work kept him near the university, and Nyx was usually as far from it as she could be.

"No," I replied quickly. "Trust me—he's come around. I wouldn't be taking you there if I thought otherwise."

The three of us made our way uphill, the massive stone gate separating the Seran University grounds from the top tier of the city intimidating before us. Just beyond, the clangs of training weapons clashing and parrying echoed off the massive university walls. I kept my face at a downward tilt as we passed the gate and neared the training grounds. After my argument with my father the day before, I couldn't be sure he wasn't looking for me.

We hurried onto the training grounds and past the small stone wall that separated it from the university courtyard, my eyes on the lookout for Bjorn.

"Kai!"

I spun, finding Bjorn jogging toward me from a building I'd already passed.

"Where have you been, woman?" Bjorn asked, grabbing me into a bear hug. I melted in his embrace. I longed for the physical intimacy of others, and Bjorn was one of the rare people who'd ever given it to me. Perhaps my desire for it stemmed from the way my father had never shown it to me. He'd never hugged me or kissed me, even as a small child. The most he'd ever done was grab me on the wrist when he was impatient, and even then his touch was cold.

48

Bjorn pulled away from me, his eyes glazed. It was the closest I had ever seen him be to tears. Glancing back at the university in all its glory, the stone walls and towers rising upward to rival the clouds, he told me, "Come with me."

The three of us followed Bjorn into a nearby armory. We waited to speak until Bjorn led us into a side room from there.

Nyx pulled back her hood in the shadows of the indoors, happy to be free of her cover if only for a moment.

Bjorn blinked at her a few times, surprised to see her. "Nyx?"

She smiled awkwardly, lifting a hand. "Bjorn," she acknowledged.

"I haven't seen you in years."

"I assure you, my absence was intentional."

Bjorn laughed heartily, which was odd considering he was concerned just moments ago. "No need to be uncomfortable around me, my dear. I was just doing my job."

"The same excuse didn't work for me, you lucky bastard," Nyx replied in jest, speaking of her assassination attempt on me.

Bjorn chuckled once more. "I like your spunk, woman. Just real quick, before I get into the thick of things, let me tell you that you've proven yourself, at least in my eyes. You've become a great friend to Kai, and you started out as her enemy. The decision for that change was yours, and I thank you for makin' it."

"I appreciate you saying so, sir," she replied. It was odd to hear her use the word *sir* in respect. Nyx was definitely a product of her rough, brutal, and crude race, but she could still surprise me from time to time in the classy ways she could handle things if she wanted to.

"And so polite," Bjorn grinned, before turning back to me. "Your father is outraged."

Even though I'd expected as such, I still cringed. "Yes. I suppose he is."

"He claims you disrespected him and left his office without waiting for him to excuse you."

I hesitated. "Yes, I suppose I did."

Bjorn snorted a laugh, surprising me. "By the gods, Kai, you have balls made out of the finest brass."

"They're about this big, too," Nyx said from beside me, holding her hands about two feet apart.

I laughed at the two of them, though I felt conflicted.

"How I wish I had half the audacity you do in your dealings with him," Bjorn went on.

"He definitely provoked it. He told me that the time I have left alive is of no concern to him."

Bjorn's amused smile faded. "He *said* that?"

"Yes. I told him I wasn't sure how much time I had and that because of my abilities he should put me into combat as soon as possible. That's when he said that and told me that the reason he was sending me on an escort mission was that I consistently failed to follow the orders of my superiors."

Bjorn's jaw tensed, and a vein rose in the skin of his forehead, a telltale sign of his anger. "Let me tell you something, Kai. You—or your father, I don't know which—came to this world at the wrong time. Sirius is undeserving of you. You are a walking contradiction to all the studies we have ever done; the limits to our magical abilities and our simple abilities as human beings are being tested by your very existence. *You* will be remembered throughout history, even if you never accomplish *anything*, if only for being a living phenomenon. But you *will* accomplish many things, I am sure of it. And your father? He is *no one* compared to you. He is but one of many generic headmasters in a long, boring lineage of Seran royalty. The world will forget his name. Not yours."

I said nothing, overwhelmed by his praises.

"Your father is a bitter and jealous man," Bjorn added.

"You think he's jealous?"

"Are you kidding? Sirius once thought himself special for being a dual caster who could cast the coveted life spells as well as a material element. He worked for decades to become respected. You arrive, and other countries request *your* attention, not his."

I stared at Bjorn. "What do you mean, they're requesting my attention?"

Bjorn hesitated, confused. "Ha. I suppose I shouldn't be surprised you don't know. Sirius shares nothing with you."

"Know what?"

"Do you truly think you'd gone unnoticed?" He hesitated. "News of your abilities spread across the world like wildfire when you were a teenager, despite your father's best efforts to keep it a secret. Leaders across the world have offered outrageous sums to get you in their armies."

This news should have been enlightening. Instead, it baffled me.

"Why doesn't he take the money and send me elsewhere, then? He'd likely enjoy the funds more than my presence," I added dryly.

"You are the greatest asset of war that exists," Bjorn reminded me carefully. "Armies may have mages, they may even have dual casters, siege weapons, and other inventions, but many of all of them exist. There is only one of you. We have no reason to believe there will ever be another just like you. Your father is keeping you within the confines of the Seran Army to prevent you from being used against him, either in war or within negotiations.

"It's why keeping you in Sera is important to him. He is outraged not only because he feels you disrespected him, but also because he's trained you throughout your life to be the greatest asset of his army, and you're not keen on the position."

"Why would he act like I'm incompetent if he thinks I am so important?" I asked, confused.

"My personal opinion is that he's trying to keep you dependent on him. He wants you to think your abilities aren't marketable simply because he wants you to feel your options are limited. That, and he's an ass."

I took all of this information in for a few moments, sensing Silas and Nyx do the same. Finally, I asked, "Is he searching for me?"

"Yes," Bjorn replied. "That's why I hurried you in here. Among other reasons."

"You're risking your job for it," I replied.

"So be it." Bjorn paused, searching my eyes with his. "I have no reason to believe your father would ever intentionally hurt you, but his selfishness and arrogance are limitless, and you are defying him. I have no doubt he might try to use intimidation tactics to get you to stay within the university."

"I am leaving soon, Bjorn," I blurted then.

"Leaving? Sera?" He cocked his head slightly. "Already?"

"Soon," I repeated. "I can't stay here. I can't let him control me anymore." Even as I spoke, Bjorn nodded, understanding. "Silas and Nyx are coming with me. I don't know yet where we'll go, but I want to see the world. Use my skills. Make a name for myself."

Bjorn smiled. I could tell it saddened him that I would leave, but he wished me nothing but happiness. He'd often told me growing up that my motivation and drive would take me places, and that was even before we had known of the extent of my skills. "And you will, my girl. You will. Oh! That reminds me." Bjorn straightened, glancing toward the door of the armory as if he could see through to the other side. "There's a messenger here for ya. He's been waiting for you since early this morning. Claims he's from Whispermere."

I frowned. *Whispermere.* The word was familiar, yet somehow distant; I knew I had heard of it before, but it must have been far away because it didn't come up very often. "Whispermere is...in the mountains, correct?"

Nyx glared at Bjorn. "I think you have the location incorrect. Whispermere is a long way from here. It's only accessible by a terrible uphill trek through the mountains, and its populace is very exclusionary."

"No...Whispermere is correct. He looked very fatigued and said he left two moons ago."

Two moons? Then whoever the messenger was, he'd been carrying his message for half a year. It must have been important, or someone paid him a worthy sum of gold for the trip.

"Did he say anything about what his message was or who sent him?" I asked, intrigued.

"No, my girl. He refuses to speak to anyone but you. He's in the university waiting for you. I'll have someone retrieve him for you, so you don't have to take a step in there."

I nodded. "Okay, that would be best."

Bjorn did just that, leaving the three of us in the armory for a few minutes while he made the arrangements. We made small talk while he retrieved the messenger.

"Maybe we'll have a destination in mind after this," Nyx commented, wiggling her eyebrows in excitement.

"Yeah, no kidding," I mused, anxiousness foggy in my chest. "Now that we know my father's been turning down requests for me from other countries, perhaps it's a message from one of them that they wanted to make sure got through to me."

"We can hope so, but that'd be rather convenient timing, wouldn't it?" Nyx mused.

It wasn't long before the armory door opened, and Bjorn hurried in, a middle-aged human man behind him, with skin made of a tan so unique in hue it appeared gold. I had never seen someone with skin of such a color. I wondered if it was due to the environment in which he lived, or perhaps it was even a dye or fashion from his hometown. Other than his skin, it appeared he'd lived roughly since he'd left Whispermere. His long, dusty brown hair was matted and oily, and he had an unruly beard that had grown onto the top of his throat.

The man glanced at the three of us, but zoned in on me, like he somehow knew I was the one he was looking for. He bowed as if he were approaching royalty. Of course, if he knew where to find me, he probably knew I was an heir to Sirius Sera. The messenger did not meet my eyes again.

"I bring you a message from Whispermere, Kai Sera," he spoke, his voice one of relief. After having carried his message for so long, I could understand why. "But I'm afraid that in order to deliver it, you must be completely alone."

I hesitated, glancing over at Silas. He was never happy to leave me alone with anyone. Sure enough, he was already staring at the messenger with deep suspicion.

"It appears to be a letter, messenger," he pointed out. "Surely, she can read it quietly and receive the message alone and in the presence of good company."

"I apologize, sir, but my direct orders were not to deliver the message in the presence of anyone but her. It is crucial she receives this information alone." The man's voice wavered, almost as if in fear. I had the feeling that if his given orders weren't followed, his livelihood was on the line.

Silas was already replying to the man, but I interrupted, "No, I understand. I'm powerful here, and you know that to try anything would mean your death. You wouldn't request this if it weren't the case." It was true. I was fully capable of defending myself, but the fact remained that the messenger might not be aware of this. In either case, I'd just warned him. "Come, we will discuss this in the other room."

The messenger nodded and allowed me to lead the way. I headed to Bjorn's office. With Bjorn still standing alongside my friends, it would be unoccupied.

An ache of uncertainty settled warmly in my gut as I closed the door behind us a moment later. I felt no hostility from the man, but whatever his message was, it was undoubtedly significant.

The messenger nodded again despite my silence and handed over the letter, keeping his eyes on the floor. "Please," he offered, "read it, and I will attempt to answer as many questions as I can."

Even as I broke the red wax seal on the envelope, I watched the messenger, concern in my eyes. Pulling out the letter within, I let my eyes finally fall to the paper and read the few words available to me.

41st of Red Moon, 416

My dearest Kai,

It has come to my attention that you are causing quite the stir in Sera with your unique skills. Because I care deeply about your safety and well-being, I would love to finally meet you and discuss these powers and how you can best utilize them. Many wish you dead for the simple fact that you exist—and, may I say, I am pleased that past attempts on your life have failed or fizzled out. Regardless, my dear, you have such immense power because you are an anomaly, and the fact you exist defies the gods. I would love to explain more, but it is much too dangerous to put everything in writing. Therefore, I must request that you make your way to Whispermere with haste. I will try to explain everything to you when you get here. There are more options available to you than you may have ever dreamed, and you would be of more use taking one of them than to be killed because of who you are.

I have instructed my messenger to destroy this letter upon delivery. I am sure you understand, and I trust you will make the right decision.

Sincerely,

Your Mother

My eyes stayed glued to the last two words, my heart slowing its pace to meet the stilling of my thoughts.

"My...my mother sent this?" I looked up slowly, finding the messenger nodding. "Who is she?"

"I...cannot answer that," he admitted apologetically. "Only she is permitted to tell you. I assure you, I can say that she is very important, and you would be best listening to her requests."

"How can I find her if I do not know her name?" I asked, the tone of my voice laced with desperation.

"If you come to Whispermere, we do not allow many people within. Simply tell them who you are, and someone will take you to her."

Take you to her. It all sounded so...formal. So business-like. "How do I find Whispermere?" I asked the messenger next, my voice barely more than a murmur.

"I have a map made just for you," he replied, pulling out a small, folded piece of paper from a satchel at his side. "This details the best routes for the least resistance. Nevertheless, the path is hard, and the weather in the mountains can be finicky. I suggest you bring an entourage of people you trust and enough supplies to last you a year. It took me two moons to get here, but Dark Star was harsh. If you leave soon, you may get there after only one moon or so."

I nodded slowly, trying to wrap my head around everything. "And you...can't tell me *anything* of my mother? Nothing? I've spent twenty-one years not even knowing if she was alive."

"The only thing I can tell you is that she has many people dedicated to her, Miss Sera."

I swallowed, frowning at him. "*Dedicated?* Why?"

"She's very important. Very protected. Going into public would cause a stir. It is why we built Whispermere for her." The messenger hesitated, and his cheeks reddened. "I have already said too much. I am sorry—"

"Whispermere has existed for hundreds of years, has it not?" I protested, confused. "It couldn't have been built *for* her!"

The messenger shook his head furiously, looking down at the ground and backing away. "I have said too much. I apologize, Miss Sera. Your mother will explain everything. Please, come to Whispermere."

I was silent for a few moments, watching the man desperately for answers. I was so frustrated. To know more than I ever had about my true parentage, and yet it still wasn't enough to answer any of the questions I'd never thought I would get a chance to ask. I was good at reading people, however, and I knew by the looks of the man that no more would be said.

"Very well," I finally murmured, my words barely more than the hiss of an exhale.

"Oh, thank you. Thank you." The man reached out a hand for the letter. "Please, Miss Sera, I must destroy it."

"May I read it once more?" I requested. When he nodded, I did so, trying to memorize as much of it as I could to discuss later with Nyx and Silas. Regretfully, I handed over the letter. The messenger took it, folded it, and pulled a small box from his satchel. When he opened the box, I saw a green, fine powder inside. He put the box on Bjorn's desk, before pulling out a small bottle of what appeared to be water and pouring it into the box. As soon as the liquid hit the powder, it thickened and sizzled as if it boiled. Then, without further words, he put the folded letter within, closed the box, and gave it a shake. I heard nothing but a dull fizzling for a few seconds, and then silence. He opened the box again, and there was nothing visible within as if it had never had contents.

"What matter of magic is that?" I asked him, intrigued.

"A mixture of alchemy and alteration magic is all," he explained shortly, as if in a rush. I knew of alteration magic but had never learned it. It was a school of magic much like illusion or elemental though it was much more focused in the altering of matter to suit certain needs. Alteration spells existed for telekinesis, or even to reshape objects or to detect life from through walls and other physical objects. I wondered what kind of spell he'd used. Perhaps the remains of the letter were transported elsewhere.

"May I have the honor of knowing an estimated date for your departure from Sera, to relay back to Whispermere?" the messenger asked as he prepared to depart.

"I will leave within the fortnight," I replied because I knew that was possible. It gave me enough time to plan my trip and to say goodbye to Bjorn and Terran.

He bowed toward me one last time. "Very well. I will report as such back to your mother. Thank you for meeting with me, Kai Sera."

"Thank you," I replied, watching him leave the room. I did not follow for the moment, my mind swirling with thoughts and possibilities. I'd had no idea just how much one simple message could affect me until now.

Bjorn and the others came looking for me a few minutes after the messenger had left, concerned when they found me in such a pensive state. It took a while for me to finally relay what little information I knew about the letter and the upcoming trip. There wasn't much we knew, but the one thing we certainly could count on was that Nyx's earlier comment was right.

We had a destination in mind for our adventure.

Three

A plate of uneaten baked partridge sat before me, the bird surrounded by a variety of buttered vegetables. It looked and smelled delicious, but was turning cold. I wasn't hungry enough to eat it yet. I had too much on my mind.

Nyx, Silas, and I were staying at the Howling Wolf Tavern once again. Now that I knew my father was looking for me, we would probably be here until we left Sera. I watched absently as a few tipsy patrons danced with glee to the small band of musicians set up on the tavern's stage. The music was happy and catchy, but it was dull in my mind, having been relegated to the background.

"Whispermere is old," Nyx said, eating her own meal and downing it with ale. She was the only one drinking tonight. Silas didn't drink, and I had too much to think about. "It was built in the Golden Era. I keep trying to figure out why the messenger would have said it was built for your mother."

She hadn't needed to say that. I was already wondering the same. The Golden Era ended over four hundred years ago. According to history and legend, it was an age of discovery, a period when gods walked amongst mortals. It was an age when dragons and wyverns ruled over the lesser races, exterminating entire towns and enslaving the survivors.

History and legend often melted together into one mishmash of conflicting statements, so I didn't know how much of that to believe. Many prayed to one god or another, but I was loyal to none. I didn't believe they existed. They hadn't shown themselves for hundreds of years according to legend, so I felt they deserved no attention even if they were alive. Most dragons and wyverns had been exterminated, but stories varied as to how or why. Some still existed, and this I knew for sure due to the stories that mercenaries sometimes touted of fighting and besting them. But they were arrogant and greedy creatures that would rather hibernate in deep caves amongst ill-gotten loot than to mess with the lives of mortals.

"How do you know so much of Whispermere?" Silas asked Nyx, before taking a bite of his own dish. He had ordered a marinated mushroom. It was so large that when it was served, I could barely tell it sat on a plate. The sharp scent of vinegar wafted from his dish from a dark sauce that drizzled over it and the bed of lively greens beneath. I had to admit, his meal looked more appetizing than mine.

"There was a man who visited Sera a few years ago and claimed he came from there. After I bedded him, we got to talking. He was a pretty interesting guy, but it was of Whispermere that he was most secretive."

I nearly rolled my eyes. Most of Nyx's knowledge of the world came from the men she had been with, as she had lived exclusively in Sera for the last five years.

"He seemed to tell you enough about it," I commented, poking around at the buttered vegetables on my plate.

"Well, I can be very convincing," she chuckled, before taking another swig of ale. "After all, what little he did tell me wasn't all that helpful and left me with more questions than answers."

"He didn't happen to say anything about a powerful woman there? Or why the city was built?"

"No. He hinted at having a reason he went to live there, but after a few years he became unhappy and left. Whatever pulled him there also convinced him to leave."

That wasn't the most welcoming news. I stuck my fork through a carrot before just moving it through the excess butter on my plate.

"What if the letter writer wasn't really your mother?" Silas asked.

I frowned, watching the carrot gather oil on my plate. "What would be the purpose of writing to me, then?"

Silas shrugged. "Isolating you. Perhaps to make an attempt on your life or to take you hostage to use your powers for themselves."

"Then I guess their fishing tactics have worked because I'm taking the bait." I finally brought the carrot to my mouth to eat it. It felt dry and tasteless in my mouth. "But we'll be careful. I'll have you two with me, and we'll overcome them."

Nyx held up a finger to interject. "Can I suggest something?"

"Sure."

"I think we should hire at least one or two more people. Mercenaries. Don't get me wrong, all three of us are fully capable people, but it's been years since either Silas or I have gone on a trip this long or far, and your spoiled little ass has never left the city."

"I agree," Silas added.

"Where do you suggest we go to hire someone?" I asked, before a hesitation. "And what would I pay them?"

Silas shrugged from beside me. "As for the latter question, pay them a little upfront and promise them a cut of all money made from anything we run across. Offer them another sum when we return to Sera, or at least nearby to it."

"Why would they work for us for a cut if they could work by themselves for the full amount?" I asked.

"Most jobs require more than one mercenary," Nyx replied. "We rarely work for the full amount. You'd also be promising them security for two moons, assuming they're good at what they do. Job security is always a plus." After a short pause, she added, "As for where you can hire these mercenaries, I'd suggest keeping your eye out for people who look useful and see if they're for hire, and I can take you to the Lounge tomorrow. I have someone in mind for us *if* he's available."

"What's the Lounge?"

"It's where mercenaries gather to wait on work while they're in town," Nyx replied, with a shrug. "That's where I've been picking up jobs recently."

"Okay. We'll go there tomorrow," I decided.

"This letter..." Silas began hesitantly, as if something was on his mind but he was anxious to bring it up with me. "Did it mention any reason as to why your mother would have dropped you off so far away from her if she knew your powers would endanger you?"

I shook my head slowly. "She really only spoke of my powers and coming to see her. The reason she wrote is that she heard I was causing a stir. I don't even know how she could know *that*. I have never seen a true battle."

"Maybe she's royalty," Nyx suggested. "Bjorn said other countries have requested you."

"Then why drop her off at the university?" Silas countered. "Why not just raise her as royalty from the get-go?"

Nyx shrugged. "It was just a suggestion. I know no more than you do."

The door of the tavern opened then, distracting me. A man hiding much of his face beneath a hood stood in the doorway, the darkness of night behind him. He was mostly covered, but I recognized him, his clothes and stature a dead giveaway. I wasn't sure why Terran was here. Perhaps he wanted to say goodbye to me since I hadn't been in the university over the past day or so to do so myself. Or he could have wanted to convince me to stay.

I looked away with a sigh, knowing he'd seen me and would come over. And sure enough, within moments, a shadow fell over the table as Terran came to stand beside my chair.

"Sister, why are you hiding?" Terran's rough voice betrayed his concern and confusion.

Without looking over at him, I replied, "Terran, you know very well why I am in hiding. Father—"

"Father wants what's best for you," he interrupted. "He's been concerned for you since you walked out. He fears you leaving."

"He fears me leaving because he wants to keep me cooped up and abiding by his will forever," I retorted, finally looking up at him. My brother was a handsome sight, his face made of the hard lines and sharp angles that adorned many earth mages. His dark brown hair teased its presence from the bottom of his hood, and his piercing green eyes portrayed his inner demons with the current situation. It saddened me that I'd had something to do with that, but I wasn't budging on my stance.

"He is a regent, Kai," Terran protested. "I am also obligated to him. You are not alone in this."

"Yes, but he takes you seriously. Not me."

"Your lack of fieldwork is proof he takes you seriously. Father knows you could die after only a handful of tasks."

I blinked at him, understanding his concern, but becoming angry at the fact this was brought up again and again. I was sick of hearing it. "So *let* me die, Terran. Why prolong the inevitable? Let me die in battle because it is what I have trained years for. At least I will die with satisfaction."

Terran nodded slowly, coming to terms with my opinion, though not liking it. "Let me talk to him, Kai. I can tell him how serious you are about this."

"He *knows*, brother, and having people talk to him has never worked. He is not budging. Besides, I have plans to leave. I have received a message from my mother, and I am going to meet her."

Terran watched me intensely. "Your mother is *alive?*"

"Yes. And she wants to help me understand why I have the powers I do."

"It doesn't *matter* why you have the powers you do, Kai. Your place is here. Father has raised you here with me. *We* are your family." I could sense he was a little hurt by my admission.

"My place is wherever I want it to be," I corrected him. "Going to see the woman who gave me life does not erase the years I've spent with you. You will always be my brother, even though we don't share blood."

Terran hesitated. Perhaps he realized he couldn't win this argument. I hoped my reassurances gave him a little bit of peace. "I wish I could change your mind," he finally said.

"You cannot," I replied.

"I see," Terran said, resigned. "Can I at least get a hug from my sister before she leaves?"

I stood from my chair. I said nothing; I just hugged him because I longed for it. I loved Terran. He had been the one tie to my father who had ever been sympathetic toward me. Despite our differences, we had always pulled through them and shared the common thread of being siblings.

Terran's warmth was comforting. He smelled of ale and sage, as he often did. He squeezed me tight. Terran knew if I were to see a battle on my journey, it was possible this was the last time he would see me.

"I remember," he murmured into the hair beside my ear, "when I was seven, and they dropped you off at our doorstep. Father said he would raise you, and I was so happy. Before mother died, she always said she wanted as many kids as possible, even though we all knew a second pregnancy could kill her before it did. I always wanted a little sister. I am so happy it was you."

My eyes burned with unshed tears, and I patted him on the back. "Thank you, Terran. I appreciate you saying that. I've always felt like a disappointment."

"I am the disappointment," he replied, pulling back and holding me at arm's length. "I could never live up to what you offer."

A slice of pain cut my stomach in half at his admitting that.

Terran left the tavern after promises he would say nothing to father about my departure until after I left. I knew I could trust him in that respect. His loyalties were split between my father and me, but with something as simple as withholding information until I was out of my father's reach, I knew he would follow through on his promise.

We stayed the night at the tavern once again with plans to head to the Lounge in the morning to hire a mercenary. Nyx mentioned she had someone in mind, and I hoped he would be available. I wasn't willing to wait around for very long to hire a particular person. I wanted to leave as soon as possible and make the trip to Whispermere while the weather was nice and warm.

The next morning, Silas and I followed Nyx through the busy city streets, past street vendors and magicians using illusion magic to awe small children and extort money from parents. After a good twenty minutes of walking a zigzagged path through the cobblestone streets, we followed her to the door of an unmarked building. Had I not known its purpose, I would have just walked past it. It baffled me why they didn't have a sign, and I was sure they lost potential customers with their apparent secrecy.

Nyx led the way inside the building. Curious eyes glanced up at us as we walked in, though Nyx's presence seemed to sate their interest, as they most likely thought we were all mercenaries. The building was run-down, with a floor of dirt and a stench of body odor. People of all shapes and sizes sat at various tables, some drinking mysterious liquids from bagged bottles, others chatting with their peers. I glanced over to a corner, watching a grungy, shady looking man exchange a bottle of what I assumed was rempka, an addicting and life-altering liquid drug, for a handful of gold coins from an eager customer.

I followed Nyx down a short hallway and into another room much like the first with Silas on my heels. He would most likely be uncomfortable in such a place. I wasn't too enthusiastic to be there, either.

I felt a nudge on my side. Nyx leaned close and whispered, "He's here. Back right corner. Male human. Attractive as hell. Long brown hair, scar on his face."

I couldn't help but chuckle a bit at her description as my eyes found the man she spoke of. "He's good?"

"He's always one of the first to get hired. I'd interview him if I were you."

"Noted," I replied, walking toward the man. "I've got nothing to lose."

The mercenary noticed my approach and watched me with eagle-like eyes as I made my way toward him. When he realized I wasn't looking for work, he sat up straight, clasping his hands on the table as I sat across from him.

"What can I do for you?" he asked.

"I've been told you're good at what you do, so I want to know what exactly it is that you do," I said, noticing it was an awkward statement only after it had come out.

He huffed a laugh. I eyed the scar on the right side of his face. It looked like he'd narrowly dodged a sword swing that had aimed to cut his head in half vertically. He had dark brown hair that hung shoulder length, and stubble on his jawline. Slight creases on his face gave away he was in his early forties and had spent many days in direct sunlight. His eyes were a few shades lighter than his hair and gave away the man's intelligence.

"Someone told you I'm good at what?" he questioned.

I jerked my thumb back at Nyx. The man nodded in understanding. "You get hired before the others. There's probably a reason why."

He pondered this. "Yeah. Probably."

"What's your name?"

"I am Theron," he replied. His eyes lowered to the table, taking in my many rings. "You are a mage?"

"Yes," I replied.

"What could a mage want with a mercenary?"

"I'm looking to add to my crew," I replied. "We have an ex-assassin, archer, and a mage between the three of us, and we're looking for someone to diversify our abilities before we leave Sera. I have somewhat of a personal quest."

"Where will you be going?"

"Whispermere," I replied.

"That is quite far," Theron mused.

"I will pay you well. We'll split any loot or profits equally along the way, and I will give you a payment upfront and a payment when we return."

Theron thought about this for a moment. "How long do you think this will take? Once we get to Whispermere, what business do you have to take care of?"

"I'm currently uncertain, which I know is inconvenient to hear. If it takes me a long while, I will pay the remainder to you there. It's even possible that if we work well together, I would want to keep you with us for permanent mercenary work. It's an option I am considering for myself."

"This seems a bit hard to believe," Theron said, his eyes judging me. "Why would you offer me this without knowing what I do?"

"I'm not offering it to you yet. I'm explaining my plan because you asked."

"That's fair," he admitted. "Well, to answer your inquiry, I fancy myself a man of many trades."

"What are your skills?"

"I fight with a bow and dual blades, depending on the situation. I'm a good ranger and scout, trained in the ways of both prevention of attacks and hunting down targets. I know weather patterns, and I can judge landscapes well, figure out the best path to take in the case of trouble. I know wildlife inside and out and can keep you alive if tragedies befall us in the wilderness though I'm sure your Celdic friend here is well-rehearsed in such things."

"What kinds of survival techniques do you know?" Silas asked from just behind me.

"How to make salves to prevent infections or rid the body of poisons. What types of plant and animal life are poisonous, what kinds are edible. How to keep frostbite from taking a limb. Wound care. That sort of thing."

Theron sounded useful. I decided to ask him a question tailored to figuring out his beliefs. "Let's say I wanted to hire you to kill a target and I just told you the location. Would you accept the job?"

"Is this a theoretical question, or a real question meant to sound as such?" he questioned.

"Answer it honestly and I'll tell you."

"I could complete the job, but I normally want reasons for killing."

"What if I gave you none?" I questioned.

Theron shrugged. "It would depend on how desperate for money I was, and I haven't been desperate to eat in a long while."

Theron seemed to follow his own neutral moral compass. I liked the sound of that. "It was a theoretical question."

"I respect that," he replied.

"Are you interested in working with us?" I asked.

"The job sounds tempting," he said. "The only thing keeping me from saying yes is not knowing how much you're offering."

"That's understandable. What are you asking for upfront?"

"A couple hundred gold," he said, before a hearty laugh.

"Done."

Theron's smile faded. "Either you're joking, you're desperate, or you're stupid as hell," he commented.

"I'd hope I was none of those things. I won't be paying you the money until we're ready to set off, which should be in a few days, so I know you can't run off with it."

"That's not the reason I said that," he replied. Eyeing me suspiciously, he went on, "Why are you considering working permanently as a mercenary if you have a few hundred to spend on me upfront? You can't possibly be hurting for money."

"I'm not hurting for money, my friend, but for purpose."

Theron surveyed me. He looked back down at my rings, studying them closely. "I don't believe I caught your name."

"I'm Kai," I replied. "Kai Sera."

Four

The day we were to leave Sera was quickly upon us. Silas, Nyx and I had stayed at the Howling Wolf for the last two nights we were in the city. The tavern keeper became friendlier and friendlier to us over the couple of nights we had stayed, enjoying his constant stream of room income. He'd served us mugs of ale on the house the last night, and after getting to know us on a first name basis, he told us that the next time we looked for a room and ale to come see him. We had heartily agreed though it was unlikely we would ever stay in Sera again.

Silas and I met Nyx in the downstairs tavern, and we left together for the Lounge, where we had set to pick up Theron. I planned to pay him five hundred gold today as per our agreement. It was a hefty sum, but the man would spend at least half a year with us.

The skies overhead of Sera were overcast, and the usually warm and colorful weather of New Moon gained a chill, taking advantage of the bashful sun. I hoped it was not an omen of things to come.

The streets of the city were still crowded as they often were. My home city rarely slept, and most tourists and locals alike would wait until an absolute downpour to seek shelter. I was leery of most of them today in particular after Bjorn's warning words and my suspicion. I pulled my thick hood over my head to limit others' view of me.

Theron waited for us outside of the Lounge, his head under his own hood, leaning back against the building with one boot against the wall. As we approached, he opened his eyes like he'd been resting. Pushing off the wall, he walked over toward us, a large satchel hanging by his side.

"Good morning, Theron," I greeted, immediately getting to business and pulling out a coin purse with five hundred gold. I'd counted it multiple times the night before to ensure its accuracy, and I told Theron as such when I handed it over to him. "You can recount it before us if you'd like."

Theron shook his head as if he found that unnecessary. He smoothly put the coin purse in an inside pocket of his satchel. "I can count it later. I can already tell it's more gold than many in the slums will see in a lifetime. I know you will pay me."

I nodded, relieved to hear he trusted me professionally. I wasn't sure if it had to do with who I was or not. It was evident by our conversation the other day that Theron understood my importance, whether he'd heard of my skills or simply related my last name to that of the city and its university.

"Are we ready to leave, then?" Theron asked, his eyes down the slope of the city and toward the walls.

I nodded, though Bjorn and Terran came to mind. We had said our goodbyes to both, but somehow, it didn't feel like enough. I'd never left the city, and while that was mostly a burden to me, it also meant I had never left those I loved.

The city of Sera was a beautiful and overwhelming sight. I had always known this, yet once I was outside of its walls for the first time, it truly hit me. It was a masterpiece of a city, taking up at least half of the mountainside with its tiers of buildings and architecture.

The mountain the city sat upon was the last in the range of the Seran Peaks, surrounded by valleys of deep green. Lush fields of grass would blow in methodical artistic patterns throughout the day by breezes, which was something I'd gotten used to viewing with admiration from the window of my bedroom high above the rest of Sera. Little plant-life other than grass existed in these valleys, for the land was a reach for the seeds of trees from the Seran Forest. Despite this, the valleys were unusually clear of grazing animals. Legends stated that early in Sera's history the once rare dragons and wyverns had a population boom. Before that led to their attempts to take over mankind, any animals that saw fit to graze in the valleys around the city were preyed upon by the beasts with nowhere to hide. It was for this reason that the valleys alone were viewed as just something else magical about Sera, for it was a lush landscape uninterrupted by any animals save for the tourists and caravans that traveled along Caravaneer Road.

"They say that the building of Sera was commissioned out to dwarves by the settling humans back in the Golden Era," Theron spoke up after a long silence between us, knowing all our minds were on Sera's beauty. "Only dwarves could build something so complex and significant, for they can mold mountains like no other mortals." After a hesitation, he added, "I mean no offense, Miss Sera."

The people of Sera looked down upon the dwarves for their focus on the earth and hands-on work with mining and architecture, so Theron had reason to worry. "Little offends me," I told him. "I want to learn the truth of the world, not an altered version. And call me Kai."

"Very well," Theron replied, his voice a little more comfortable.

Sera was so large and pronounced on its mountain that even after a day's worth of travel, it was still in our sight as we set to camp along the border of the Seran Forest. The lights of the city made of both magic and fire lit the night sky in a halo glow.

"Do you think we'll be able to hunt a deer this close to the valley?" Theron pondered aloud to Silas. The walk through the valleys was so uneventful and quiet that it was awkward to talk to one another when we'd trekked through them, like interrupting the majestic silence would corrupt nature.

Silas looked deeper into the forest. "We'll find one."

Theron and Silas had talked amongst themselves from time to time throughout our first day. The two men had found common ground with their similar skills and interests. I was glad for Silas, as his acquaintances always coincided with mine, and he had very few people he spoke to regularly that weren't my friends first. Theron, while intelligent and willing to answer questions, was a bit intimidating to me. He had a gruff edge to him, along with obvious experience in his field that put me to shame. Theron acted distant with me. It was likely a mixture of being the only hired member of our group, and me being such a prominent figure from the city he worked in.

"We'll set up camp," Nyx offered to the two. "You guys go ahead and get dinner."

Theron and Silas wandered off together into the woods, bows in hand. The two seemed to be happy to get out of helping to set up camp. Once alone, my best friend and I unpacked supplies and prepared to settle for the night. Though it would have been easier to use my fire magic to start a campfire, Nyx was kind enough to start one with a match and tinder. I didn't want to use my magic unless I had to in battle.

Before long, Nyx and I sat on a makeshift log bench, our eyes gazing over the miles of the Seran valley we'd trekked through and to the distant skyline of the city. A light evening breeze whistled low over the valley, rippling the grasses like the waves of an ocean, the sides of the long blades reflecting the moonlight of the double moon.

This was so peaceful, so relaxing. It was also the first time I'd ever felt a true taste of freedom. In Sera, I wasn't being held hostage by any means; that didn't mean being held down by obligations never felt restrictive. Perhaps I'd never known just how restrictive it was until I was free. I wondered what Bjorn, Terran, and my father were doing and if they were thinking of me. Maybe it was a selfish thought, but I was thinking of them.

"How's it feel to be out on your own for once?" Nyx asked, leaning back on her arms to get a reclined view of the landscape.

"Beautiful," I replied, my voice whimsical. I glanced over at Nyx. She had taken off all of her armor save for an undershirt. In the cool darkness of late evening, she was finally comfortable enough to relax.

"Normally, I'd argue with you that *beautiful* isn't a feeling, but I get what you mean," she mused. "I'm so glad to be out of Sera. I'm also glad you decided to actually leave. Part of me thought you never would."

That surprised me. "You know how tied down I felt. I needed to get out of there."

"Yes—but you also felt, as you said, tied down. Some never break out of their ties. I'm happy you did."

"And I'm glad you're here with me," I admitted, my eyes focusing on some blinking lights in Sera. I wondered if an illusionist was having trouble lighting the street lamps with a spell. I wasn't able to tell from this distance.

"Wouldn't have missed it for the world, friend."

My mind floated back to the subject of the letter, and something that had been bothering me about it that I'd wanted to ask Nyx when we were alone. "My mother said in her letter that many would make an attempt on my life because of my powers and that she was happy to hear none succeeded."

"I wouldn't worry about that. You're surrounded by people who can fend off pretty much anything," Nyx replied, seemingly taking my statement differently.

"Well—I'm glad for that, but the reason I'm bringing it up is that they sent you to assassinate me."

"Oh." Nyx chuckled. "I'm aware."

"Do you remember anything about *why* you were sent to kill me?"

"I thought we'd talked about this before. You're not second-guessing me, are you?"

"No," I answered quickly, because I wasn't. I trusted Nyx with my life. Other than how we'd met, she had shown nothing but gratefulness for my keeping her from execution, and genuine selflessness with looking out for me. "I just thought that now that all of this has come about, you might have a new perspective on it, looking back. Maybe you could remember...something. Anything."

Nyx didn't like to talk about the life she had before the assassination contract. She had her qualms with the Alderi culture, but she also felt she'd betrayed her own people by settling for a life above ground. Her past didn't come up very often because it was a source of introspection for her, something Nyx wasn't fond of.

"They raise assassins to be as cold-blooded as possible. When we were given a target, we weren't told why. To tell us why could give us a reason to form an attachment to the target. I knew nothing about you but your name and your general location. I figured out as I worked that you were very important, given how hard it was to get to you in the tallest building of the most pretentious human city in existence. That's all I knew. Anything else I knew about you I found out as we became friends."

"You didn't know who ordered my death?"

"No." Nyx hesitated. "The only thing I figure is that whoever ordered it had a lot of money because the harder the target is to kill, the more our guild would charge. You were the hardest target I'd ever had just to *reach*. And then, of course, I failed at my mission." She turned to smile at me. In the late evening shadow, her teeth were almost the only thing visible on her dark face. "Your mission was the only one I ever failed, but I'm glad I did."

"Because you formed an attachment to your target," I teased, using her own words from earlier.

"Exactly." Nyx relaxed again, gazing off into the distance. After a second, she sat up, as if remembering something. "Oh! Speaking of forming attachments, do you have the map to Whispermere that the messenger gave you?"

"Yeah." I reached down next to the log, grabbing my bag and pulling the folded map out. I was curious as to what Nyx had to tell me and handed it to her eagerly.

She unfolded it, turning it slightly so the light of the fire allowed her to read it. "Ah! I was right!" Nyx finally exclaimed, looking pleased with herself.

"About what?"

"Whispermere..." Nyx trailed a finger across the map to the northeast, where two large mountains were drawn, a path going up between the two. "...is here." Moving her finger to the left along the coastline of the Servis Ocean, she stopped at a small section where the messenger had drawn a couple tiny buildings. One word was written underneath which was currently unreadable to me from my distance. "Thornwell is here."

Thornwell. It sounded so familiar. "Thornwell..." I trailed off, tilting my head in confusion.

"That healer you knew in school before we met. The reason you fell face-first into puberty. The one who disappeared. You said he was from Thornwell, correct? The fishing village?"

My mind cleared. *Cerin.* "Yes," I said, understanding.

"We're taking the time to go out to Whispermere. Let's stop at Thornwell on the way and pick up his fine ass."

I couldn't help but chuckle at her crude enthusiasm. I finally admitted, "I don't know if he'll be there. I don't know if he's even alive. And if he is, he probably doesn't remember me."

Cerin Heliot would forever be a mystery to me. He was the one and only classmate I'd ever befriended, and our friendship was short-lived before he disappeared without a trace. One day, he wasn't in class. Thinking him merely to be ill, I tried not to worry, despite knowing he was skilled enough to heal himself if it was anything trivial. Days went by, and with no one else even acknowledging his absence, I'd gone to my professors about it and asked them for information. They told me a variety of things, all of them concerning. Some professors refused to admit they even knew who I spoke of, while others told me they had no idea what happened to him. One said he'd left the university, as if after a few years of very expensive schooling that was something a skilled mage would just *do*. I had even mentioned Cerin to my father, and after a steady and firm stream of dismissiveness from him, he'd blown up with anger at me. I eventually stopped asking and never heard from or of Cerin again.

"It couldn't hurt to try," Nyx said, bringing my thoughts back to the present. "Besides, Thornwell is one of the last villages before the mountains. It wouldn't hurt to get a last night of sleep in an inn before we have to camp in bad weather for weeks."

I nodded. "You're right." Nyx had never met Cerin. He'd come and gone before I met her, so the fact she mentioned him at all meant she had her mind on looking out for me. Nyx had always been angry with Silas for breaking up what we'd had. Nyx believed that if my life would be short, I might as well have as much fun as I could with it. And her idea of fun usually revolved around bedroom behaviors, so she was constantly thinking of setting me up with men.

"Speaking of beautiful men, that Theron's a piece of work, isn't he?"

"*Nyx*," I breathed, before a restrained laugh. "Please don't hit on our mercenary."

"Aww, why not?" She chuckled.

"He's going to be with us for a while," I reasoned patiently. "The last thing we need is hard feelings between everyone. Theron's human. Some humans actually *want* relationships."

"I'd be upfront with him," Nyx offered.

"*Nyx.*"

"All right, I'll keep my dirty paws off of him." She huffed, displeased.

"We'll find plenty of men out there for you. I'm sure there are plenty more attractive than Theron."

"I don't know, have you *seen* him?" she teased.

Silas and Theron returned to us a few conversations later, carrying with them a small doe. I knew Silas had already said his prayers over it in the woods. Theron butchered the animal. When he'd retrieved what was edible, Silas took over, gathering the remaining materials in the ways he knew how. Silas was an excellent materials maker; with bone and leather, he could make many things, from sheaths to pieces of armor and even small daggers made of bone. It was mesmerizing to watch him work.

When Theron finished cooking the venison over the campfire, Silas quickly cleaned up what materials he'd gathered and prepared to break for eating. The mercenary was a fantastic cook. The venison melted in my mouth.

"This is delicious, Theron," I commented. I wanted to open up the mercenary to conversation. If we were all going to be together for awhile, it would be best to get along.

"Thank you."

"Are you from Sera?" I asked him next from across the campfire.

Theron glanced up, his rough face seeming surprised that I directed my question at him. "No. I am from a village

82

called French, a couple of days west of Sera in the Hydrin Forest."

"I haven't heard of it," Silas commented curiously.

"That's because it no longer exists," the ranger replied, taking another bite of venison.

"What happened to it?" asked Nyx.

"It was a small community nestled in the most perfect of locales. In the forest, but near a variety of fruit trees, and a beautiful waterfall. There was an opening in the earth nearby where we found gemstone in the caves when I was a lad. It proved too tempting for the orcs." Theron took another bite of meat.

"They raided the village?" Silas asked.

Theron nodded. "Raided it and attempted to build their own stronghold right on top of the corpses of the people I knew."

"Attempted?" Nyx prodded.

He shrugged, as if unconcerned. "Well, I put a stop to that."

"Weren't you just a boy?" I asked for clarification.

"I was when they raided it. I trained for a few years. Went back on my sixteenth birthday and extinguished the fuckers. Burnt the stronghold, too, and then pissed on their shrine to Malgor." He spoke of the god of war.

My eyes widened, and I nodded, pleased with that image. "Sounds like a fun time."

The hints of a smile teased the edges of his lips. "That it was." Taking a moment to lick his fingers clean of venison juices, Theron then directed a question at me. "So, is it true what they say about you?"

"What do they say about me?" I retorted, more playfully than anything else.

"They say you defy the gods. That you have more power than any mortal." His deep brown eyes were on mine, searching, testing.

"I suppose, if it is possible to defy the gods simply by having an excess of power."

"You wield six elements, correct? Even the dreaded necromancy?" It was a question I wasn't used to hearing. Most people didn't like to acknowledge necromancy existed even in conversation. Theron seemed like the kind of guy who had worked on both sides of the law, so I didn't have a problem answering.

"I do," I admitted. "Though I only know one death spell, and the only reason I know it was because I was being tested. I was supposed to forget it, but I have a penchant for memorizing spells."

"What kind of spell was it?" he questioned curiously.

"The plague," I replied. I could still recite the spell in my head from memory. As a fourteen-year-old girl, I had been so excited to find I was as powerful as I was. Out of all the spells I learned back when they were testing me to ensure that I could wield all six elements, the necromancy spell was the one I'd wanted to memorize the most. It was the only one I would have trouble accessing ever again.

"So if you wanted to, you could kill any one of us right now with it? Just have our skin eaten alive?" Theron seemed to have a morbid fascination with this. Of course, most people did when they felt comfortable enough to talk about it.

"I'm not sure it would work on a human, to be honest. I used mine on a plant. They wouldn't allow me to use it on a person or animal." Since Theron still seemed intrigued, I went on, "When I used it, the plant started to wilt, then rot, then degrade. Eventually, it disintegrated into ash. It was really depressing to me."

"You felt bad for the plant?" Nyx teased. I could tell this admittance amused her.

"I did," I admitted.

"That is nothing to joke about," Silas spoke up, his eyes on Nyx. "Plants have consciousness just like other living beings."

"You eat them without prayer, *wood* elf," Nyx retorted.

Silas visibly gritted his teeth. *"Celdic* elf, thank you, and yes, because that is their purpose. They give us life, and we give them life. Your body will eventually rot into the ground and feed them, and they will offer no prayer to your corpse. It is a mutual agreement."

"How are animals any different?"

"Guys—*guys.* I believe we've heard this argument a few times before," I interjected, unwilling to hear two people I loved hash it out once again. Silas and Nyx couldn't be more different, and their arguments could often get heated.

"I don't yet know the connection between you three," Theron admitted, willing to be the one to lead us away from the moral argument.

"Silas is my bodyguard and friend. Nyx is a friend."

"Attempted assassin," she added with a smile. After a short retelling of the tale to Theron, he was caught up to speed.

"So if you are all friends, and this is a personal mission you're on, why did you hire me?" Theron asked.

85

"None of us have stretched our legs in quite a while," I admitted. "It's been a while since Silas or Nyx has been outside of Sera, and I've never been. We decided to hire help just in case, and since you're a ranger, you'll be particularly helpful to us. None of us have ever been to Whispermere."

"Nor have I," Theron admitted. "I can get you there, no worries, but I've never been there. I hope you know they're not particularly welcoming to strangers. The last thing you want to do is get there and be turned away."

"I'm aware. My presence was requested," I explained, though I offered little else. Theron appeared to understand my need to be vague. As much as I'd said so far, I wasn't sure I wanted to tell him everything yet.

"Good," Theron nodded, willing to drop the subject at my reluctance to say more. "As long as you know what you're getting into."

The group of us chatted more until the surrounding insects competed for attention, their chirps echoing against the thick trunks of the trees of the Seran Forest just behind us. We decided to take shifts sleeping since we had to camp outside. Nyx offered to stay up for the next six hours while Theron offered to get up early. In twelve, we would set off again. The small amount of sleep would work fine for Nyx, who could survive on little sleep and be just as energetic. I was a bit worried for Theron, but he waved away my concerns by saying he was used to this.

I was concerned I'd have trouble falling asleep under the stars. This would be my first time sleeping anywhere other than an inn or the university. In reality, once I was lying beneath the stars with Silas's warm body at my side, I found it incredibly peaceful. The melody of the insects was like a lullaby to my ears, and the stars and double moon gave soft glows which helpfully led me to my dreams.

On my first night away from home, I fell asleep easily and slept through the night.

Five

The next morning while Nyx was still sleeping, the rest of us packed most of our things and put out the campfire. Theron went off into the forest for a half hour or so, coming back with a bag full of gotton berries. They weren't known for being the sweetest berries in the world, but they made for an energizing breakfast.

During the last hour that we let Nyx sleep from her late shift, Theron and Silas pored over the map I had to Whispermere. Eventually, I wandered over to them to learn their plans.

"...it's a tiny village made of nothing more than huts," Theron was saying. "I doubt it."

Silas glanced up as I approached. "We're trying to figure out if we should head to Amere." He pointed to the map where a tiny village was drawn with its name beneath it. "We'll be passing there a little before evening so it would be ideal to stop and rest, but Theron's been there and says they don't have an inn."

"I haven't been there," Theron corrected. "I've passed it. There's literally nothing to stay for."

I shrugged. "It couldn't hurt to stop there and ask for shelter. Perhaps they have something they need help with that we can exchange."

"If that's the case, I doubt they have any gold. Shelter would be the only thing they *could* offer," Theron mused.

With that, we planned to stop at Amere that evening after a full day's walk. Even if they had no shelter, staying the night near the village would be better than in the middle of the wilderness.

The four of us set out as soon as we woke Nyx, our pace brisk with the energy of a night's sleep. With the valleys of Sera to our left and the forest to our right, we would eventually hit the village we were looking for on the edge of the Seran Forest. Today, we passed a few other travelers, some on horses and some on foot, and we offered greetings before continuing on our way.

Just as the sun was painting the sky a beautiful mirage of coral and mint green, smoke rose in the distance at the edge of the wood. A few minutes after that, and a tiny, ramshackle village came into view, nestled at the bottom of a small hill, the backs of its huts to the forest.

"Maybe we should just pass it," came a mumble from Theron's direction.

Amere was unimpressive overall. It was a ragtag group of houses, nothing more. The homes were rough stone with roofs of layered straw, giving away the fact that the village was a poor one. Fields of grain swayed softly in the breeze within the confines of short, hastily built stone walls that looked as if they hadn't ever kept anything out as intended. The gray smoke that rose into the early evening sky from the village came from a small outdoor fire, where a few people clad in dirty, frail clothes huddled to cook a meal.

I heard a moo and looked around to find a pasture of cows, most of them teetering on the edge of malnourished. Hearing the curious noises of their livestock, the villagers looked our way.

This was a stupid idea. The group looked as if they didn't have two gold coins between all of them. I felt particularly awkward about going up to such a group of poor people and asking them for shelter.

One of the group, an older woman, stood from a roughly made bench that sat beside the fire and wiped her hands casually on her pants. She wore a bonnet that kept her graying hair and most of her face out of the sun, and her skin held a map of wrinkles that directed toward sunspots that resulted from years of hard labor. She cautiously watched us approach.

"Hail, travelers," she greeted, glancing through all of us, her eyes lingering on Nyx. "Welcome to Amere. Where are you from?"

"Sera, originally," I replied. "You have a nice little village here."

The woman chuckled. "I appreciate your courtesy, though you are either lying or blind. We do what we can. Is there something we can do for you?"

I glanced back at my group. Everyone seemed content with at least asking. "Maybe, ma'am. We're mercenaries, and we're making our way east. We're looking for shelter and would trade a night's stay for work. Would any of you happen to need assistance with anything?"

The woman took in my statement with curiosity, before turning back toward the group. "Hank?"

My eyes followed her gaze to a plump, middle-aged man who looked perplexed. "Vilma, I ain't got nothing for them."

"Your livestock—"

"Listen, friends, here in Amere, we got problems, but no gold."

"We're not particularly worried about that," I replied. "We're just looking to stay the night."

The villagers didn't believe that statement. Perhaps no mercenaries had ever bargained with them before.

"What kinds of problems do you speak of?" Theron finally asked the man.

"I got livestock that goes missing. One cow a week, like clockwork. Didn't know if they was gettin' out or what, until last week, when I come out one mornin' and something ate one of my cows alive, right there in the pasture. Something's stealin' my cows, and I ain't got a clue as to what."

Theron looked off into the forest, thinking. "We're about a day's travel from Sera. It can't be much more than wolves or goblins. Considering they only take one a week, I don't think wolves are to blame."

Hank watched us for a moment, before reiterating, "I ain't got no gold."

"What do you have to offer?" I asked.

With a glance off toward his pasture, Hank twisted his lips, thinking. "I got cows."

I chuckled lightly.

"If you're considering helping us, I'm sure we could scrounge up some reward," the older woman interjected, a little desperately. "We owe a lot of money to Sera in taxes, and Hank's the only one here who raises livestock. His losses are making us all try to bridge the gap in profits, but grain doesn't sell for as much as beef."

"Ma'am...we're not looking to take your gold," I repeated, feeling like that wasn't getting through to them.

"Mercenaries never stop here. They figure we're poor, I suppose. You all are our only hope unless we all get our weapons and try to take care of it ourselves, and we're farmers, not fighters." The woman's voice held a tinge of desperation as if she figured we were about to turn and leave.

"I'll tell you what, ma'am," I started, "if you give us food and lodging for the night, we'll pull this problem of yours out by the roots."

"By the gods, you'd have yourself a place to stay whenever you're in town if you'd do that."

"...*and the loot*," Theron hissed from behind me.

"Oh, and if the creatures that are causing this ruckus happen to have any gold on them—"

"It's all yours," the woman replied, nodding with hope.

"You have yourself a deal, then."

The look of absolute relief on the woman's face filled me with relief to have finally bargained with them.

The old farmer led us out to his pasture, and he showed us the location where the cow was gutted. By this point, the corpse was gone, so we had to rely on the farmer's memory.

"Was it just killed, or was the meat torn from its body?" Theron asked, crouching to the ground and sifting through the grasses.

"A lot of the meat was gone. Not all of it," the farmer replied, watching Theron as he pulled something out of the grasses. It was a dark brown tuft of hair. Bringing it to his nose, the ranger looked up toward the woods.

"Goblins?" Silas asked, watching as the ranger stood and walked to the small stone wall separating the pasture from the nearby woods.

Theron shook his head distractedly. "Brownies."

"What's a brownie?" I asked.

"They're small woodland creatures. Usually peaceful," Theron explained, following a specific path to the woods from the small wall, stopping and crouching along the way. At the edge of the forest, he noted the matted grass between two particular trees. "Easily controlled, though. They worship these...totems. Somewhat like goblins, in a way. If a smarter creature gets ahold of the totems, brownies treat them like gods and do their bidding. Anytime I've ever heard of brownies getting into trouble, they're being controlled."

"How do we kill them?" Nyx asked, getting straight to the point.

"They're small and frail. Made of equal parts wood and flesh. So use weapons against flesh and avoid their mouths. They're poisonous." Glancing back at me, Theron added, "And obviously, for your sake, use fire."

I nodded, understanding. Because Theron was already tracking the creatures, I turned back to the farmer who still waited in his pasture.

"We'll be back when the job is done," I assured him.

The man nodded. "Please be careful."

Nyx looked nothing but excited as she followed Theron into the woods. "Let's bake us some brownies," she jested as she passed.

The four of us slowly made our way through the woods, allowing Theron time to track the creatures. Above us through a canopy of leaves, the evening sky darkened. I hoped we could finish the job by the time it got completely dark.

I found that I was nervous leading up to my first real battle. I had trained for years at the university for this, but this already felt much different than practice. Mages had to consider all the reactions their elements could have on environments and even their surrounding allies. When in controlled environments at the university, this was simple and even educational. Out in the real world, I wouldn't have anyone warning against my move if I were to misuse an element or not consider its repercussions.

Also, I had never yet killed anything or anyone with my magic. These brownie creatures sounded like victims themselves, beholden to another creature's will. Would I feel right in killing them?

Off in the woods, a short distance away, a slow, rhythmic beat met my ears, pulling me from my thoughts. Theron held one finger back, keeping us quiet and still. My heart picked up its pace, knowing now that we were closing in the culprits.

After a few moments, Theron continued, and we followed him, quiet and preparing for a fight. The closer we got, the louder the beat. It sounded like the drums musicians would sometimes bring to the tavern back in Sera, only now, we were in the middle of the woods, and the beat being played was much more tribal.

Past the trees ahead of us, an orange glow shone against the bark. Small, tiny high-pitched voices were chattering with glee, some to a melody, in a language unknown to me.

They're singing. My stomach churned. How could I kill such happy creatures?

Theron looked past the trunk of the tree before him, seeing the scene ahead. Raising my head up, I looked over the foliage and into the forest clearing beyond.

There was a small fire, and over it, roasting beef. Around the campfire in a small circle, tiny, short and fat creatures danced, almost as if they were worshiping the meat. The brownies were stocky and only two feet tall; half of that height seemed to be in their disproportionately large heads alone. There were eight of them around the fire and many more in the clearing beyond it. All around them, there were tiny makeshift huts and even small piles of wood that some creatures were using for burrows.

In the background directly across from us, larger greenish-gray humanoid creatures sat in chairs, one looking like a throne. I assumed these were goblins because I'd seen drawings. They were ugly creatures, with swollen, misshapen joints and rough, clumsy facial features. Their ears were large and pointy, even more so than elves, and many were pierced. Behind the goblin who sat on a throne was a shrine built out of bone and wood. On it sat a totem carved out of wood. Around it glowed a light blue magical aura.

Overall, there were dozens of brownies, and probably half a dozen goblins. We were outnumbered, but we were skilled, and the brownies were tiny creatures. It wouldn't take much to fell them. My mind sorted through the spells I'd learned, trying to figure out which one would be best. Using fire would be dangerous here; we were in a forest.

Luckily, I had access to all six elements.

Theron lowered his head and faced me. "Let's take most of them out from here and let the stragglers come to us."

In a whisper, I replied, "Let me make the first move."

Theron nodded, fine with that idea.

I moved forward and past him, standing up against the rough bark of the thick tree that separated us from the seemingly happy little community of thieving creatures beyond. I held both palms upward. Directing my attention to my left hand, I recited in my mind, *Creatius les fiers a nienda*. Even before the flame appeared, I was already reciting another spell for my right. Air magic soon swirled within its magical barrier.

I stepped out from the tree, alerting the creatures to my presence. The dancing ceased, and the goblin stopped beating on its drums. Rough screams of alarm echoed through the forest clearing. Directing my arms toward the sky above the population, I directed both elements together and forward. The resulting power blew the hair back from my face, both fire and air thrusting forward to combine and become one spell before me.

The evening sky above darkened further and crackled with energetic activity. Dark charcoal clouds rolled into a point above the clearing, forming a funnel that quickly swirled down to the earth below, accompanied by licking flames. As the roaring tornado reached the ground, it was already too late for the small creatures below. The flaming twister swirled and ripped through creatures and huts alike, its whirling winds deafening to my ears.

Nyx cursed and ran. Like her, I also felt fearful of my power. I had easily created a deadly storm that was just before us, killing the creatures below by setting them aflame and throwing broken bodies violently into dark tree bark with crunches and splashes of red. The tornado ripped through the small clearing and continued into the forest. The trees nearest to the twister caught fire before flaming branches broke and flew through the air like splintered shrapnel. The funnel swirled with a mixture of plant debris, bleeding bodies, and broken rubble.

"By the *gods,* put it out!" Theron screamed at me. "You'll burn down the entire fucking forest!"

Reaching toward the sky, I once again called upon the weather, reciting two identical water spells in both hands, doubling my efforts. I sent the magic upward, and the skies darkened further before rain meant to accompany a hurricane fell, pelting both corpses and trees with thick droplets. I dispelled the tornado next, and the storm funneled back into the atmosphere as if it had never been here at all.

Afterward, I was left breathing hard and assessing the damage I'd just inflicted upon creatures and the earth. With the rains still plastering my hair to my face and neck and adding weight to my armor, my eyes looked over the scene before me.

All the creatures were dead. Nyx, Silas, Theron—none of them had a chance to fight at all. My magic had killed everything, and if it hadn't been for my quick rain fix, it could have very well erased the forest from the map. The fiery twister charred the trees nearest the clearing, and the new rains glistened over blackened bark. The only color from the scene beyond was the blue aura of the totem which somehow made it through the attack unscathed.

With a quick murmur, I dispelled the rain, and all was silent but for the drips of water off pine needles. No one spoke for a long while. Nyx slowly approached us once again after having run for cover earlier. She still said nothing.

We all took a moment to survey the scene and think about what we'd just witnessed. No one said anything for a long while until finally, Theron walked past me to loot the huts and bodies before us.

"You could take over nations with that power," he mused, his tone awed and even somewhat reserved. Theron was clearly shaken. We all were.

Nyx stared at me as if she barely knew me.

"I'm sorry it scared you," I offered, my voice low.

"I guess I just never knew how powerful you really were," Nyx replied, her voice lacking energy. "I mean—I *knew*. There's only one like you. But..." she looked over the destruction and shook her head. She offered nothing else.

Nyx left then, moving to look through the wreckage with Theron before it was too dark to see anything. Silas walked up to me. I felt his hand at my back, slowly rubbing, trying to comfort.

"You need to leave some fighting for us," he commented. As usual, he was hard to read. His green eyes were on the results of my spells, but they offered me no insight into his thoughts.

"I will, next time," I promised, leaning toward him because it comforted me. Though we were both wet with the rain, I could still feel his warmth. "I didn't know I would start *and* finish the fight like that. Plus...I guess I got it out of my system, now."

"The eagerness for battle?"

"Yeah."

Silas nodded. "I'm glad." After a hesitation, he asked, "Do you feel...okay? Weaker?"

I swallowed hard. "No," I answered honestly. I was grateful for that.

"Good." Silas squeezed me into his side in a comforting move I was no longer used to from him. I missed it.

"Ah! We've got a hoarder," Theron announced, crouching as he came out of one of the goblin huts. "A whole chest full of gold in here," he clarified.

"Now, that's what I like to hear," Nyx replied jovially, walking over to see for herself. The energy in her voice made me feel better. It worried me that she might think less of me for my display.

We finished looting the small huts, and Silas went over to the trees I'd damaged, lying his hands upon them and whispering in Old Elvish. He offered them apologies and healing. Silas knew earth spells that could stimulate growth in plant-life, and I saw him use them on the trees. I felt guilty watching him do this; it was like he was cleaning up after me. Still, I was glad he knew how. Otherwise, I would leave damages in my wake with no reparations.

"They appreciate the rains you offered them," Silas said to me, just before we left to go back to Amere. "This forest is amid a drought."

His ability to communicate with plants never ceased to amaze me. It was an ability innate to the Celdic elves, but then again, Silas was the only one I'd ever known so thoroughly. He was my little window into a world I wouldn't have otherwise known existed.

"I'm glad I offered them more than destruction," I replied, a little relieved.

"You stopped it before it got out of hand. That's all that matters."

We offered the villagers of Amere the totem that had belonged to the brownies, both as proof we had found the culprits and as a gift that they could use in the future. The origins of the totem and its magic guard were mysteries. It was possible something drew the creatures to it, and that the villagers would someday find brownies on their doorstep willing to peacefully coexist with them and treat them like gods.

Other than gold, the loot from the creatures wasn't impressive. We took some goblin-made weapons which would go for a decent amount of gold at the next merchant we came across. The merchants in Sera sold goblin weapons to tourists who came from places where the creatures weren't common. They also made good first weapons for children, because they were often smaller and blunter than most. Gold-wise, we found two hundred coins which we split evenly.

By the time we left Amere the following morning, my share of the gold was left on the kitchen table of the family home they had given us as shelter for the night. Due to my place in Sera, I was privy to the financial information of the villages on the outskirts of the city, and I knew Amere was overcharged in taxes. They needed the money more than I did, especially given they had to build up their livestock again. I wasn't hurting for gold.

Amere would forever hold a special place in my heart. Though the goblins and brownies hadn't put up much of a fight, it was there that I realized just what I was capable of.

Six

Scrapes and knocks on stone created a pattern in the air as Theron set to work grinding down an herb with his mortar and pestle. The rest of us continued to eat, watching him.

The night sky twinkled overhead and was brighter than it would have been just weeks ago when only one moon hung over us. Now, a few weeks into our journey, the season of New Moon heated up and prepared to hand the reins over to the hot and dry season of High Star, so the second moon had made its appearance, as it did for a few weeks twice each year. Our planet of Arrayis only had two satellites; the first, visible year round, was Eran. It was quite small and not very bright despite its white and gray coloring. It appeared smooth save for long, mostly straight lines across its face as if one of the gods had reached up and scratched at it with uncut fingernails.

The second moon, Meir, appeared over Chairel twice a year and only for weeks at a time. It came to help the exchange of seasons from New Moon to High Star, and then from Red Moon to Dark Star. It was much larger than Eran, appearing almost like another planet. Some astronomers argued that it was another planet, but arguments had ensued over that for years. For now, we considered it another moon, and many in Chairel celebrated its appearance in festivals and events twice a year. Meir would first appear low on the horizon in the east, and for the first fortnight, makes its way to the top of our sky. Over the next fortnight, it would slowly make its way to the west horizon, before disappearing for half a year. Meir was a soft cream in color, though its surface also swayed toward reds and some browns in the imperfections of its land. The top half of the moon was dotted in craters of various sizes, but the bottom half was smooth. Those with clear enough vision even would claim to see waves on its surface, like it was a type of desert.

I stared at the celestial object for now. On the horizon, it seemed so bright and large, like it was ready to fall to our planet at any time. When I lived in Sera, Meir had only been slightly visible at select days of the year, as most of its course hid behind the Seran Peaks that ended in my home city. Our group had kept the Seran Forest to our right over our journey thus far since the edge of the woodland would lead us straight to the Cel Mountains where Whispermere was buried. Nothing but plains were to our left and had we walked over them, the Servis Ocean would eventually come into view. Over this land, Meir etched its path in the sky, boasting its full glory in a space that was usually unoccupied.

I found Meir beautiful. I also felt grateful for it because it was something that had always been just out of view. There truly were no limits to the benefits of freedom.

"We'll let this sit for an hour or so, and it will congeal." Theron's voice pulled me away from my thoughts for the moment. He had a wooden bowl in his hands, in which he'd combined the powder from the herb earlier with water and oils. The result was a milky green looking liquid. Theron spoke to Nyx as he said, "Then you can try it, see how it feels."

Nyx glanced over at me with a mischievous glimmer in her eye. I knew she was giving his words a double meaning, given her nature. I shook my head in humor at her.

"Thank you," she said to him. Theron made the lotion for her skin since the warmer weather was causing it to dry out quicker than usual. Nyx had already gone through most of the supply she'd brought with her. "Do you think there will be enough herbs like this the rest of the way to Whispermere?"

Theron shrugged. "In the forests? Yes. Once we get to the Cel Mountains? Not as much, but you won't have as many problems with your skin then. It gets pretty snowy and cold within a few hours of being on the mountain path. I can make you some extra lotions before we get there."

"I have a better idea," Nyx leaned forward. The campfire cast her face in light, though she was mostly hidden in her armor and hood to avoid dryness from its heat. "Teach me how to make it and how to spot these plants in the forest."

Theron nodded. "I can do that, too."

Silas and I both stayed quiet for the moment, eating. I hoped Nyx's idea was more about her learning something useful than getting closer to our mercenary, but I could say nothing more on the subject that I hadn't already. Nyx knew I didn't want her crossing the professional line with those in our group, but I couldn't keep her from becoming friends with anyone, and I wouldn't have wanted to. Silas and Theron had already developed a type of mutual understanding between them, and it was possible it had delved into friendship. I was happy about that. I wanted Silas to have more friends than just having me. If Theron liked being with us, it meant he would probably stay with us past Whispermere. He didn't talk much other than business, but he was useful to have around although we hadn't been in any trouble since fighting the goblins and brownies at Amere.

"Maybe now would be a good time to mention what we found today," Silas said, seemingly out of the blue. I looked over to find him staring at Theron, who nodded.

"Ah, yes." Theron's sharp brown eyes found mine. With no amount of emotion in his voice, he said, "We are being followed."

A sharp pain sliced through my stomach. The new knowledge sank into my skull, immediately making me paranoid. My eyes darted to my right as if they'd be able to see anything through the thick blackness of the forest. I was opening my mouth to reply when Nyx spoke first.

"Maybe your father sent his men, Kai."

I glared over at her. I knew she hadn't meant to admit such a thing in front of Theron, but her forgetfulness had gotten the best of her. Theron knew I was a Seran heir. He didn't know I was a Seran heir who was technically on the run.

Theron's facial expression didn't change. "These aren't soldiers who are following us."

"Then who *is?*" I asked for clarification.

"Orcs," Silas replied, looking slightly more concerned than Theron. "When Theron and I were hunting this morning, we ran across a human tracker. He had an orcish slave collar around his neck and was sleeping at the base of a tree within distant view of our camp, but didn't wake up in time. We woke him and attempted to get him to answer our questions, but he wouldn't."

"So...what happened to him?"

Theron shrugged. "I killed him. Some human slaves try to negotiate for freedom, but sometimes they have family members who are enslaved, too. Sometimes they are the only ones in their family who are slaves and refuse to give information for fear the orcs will find out and *then* find their families. There are many reasons. The only thing that matters now is that he followed us and relayed information back to other trackers. Orcs sometimes use this method of tracking until they're able to get an army to a location."

"An *army?*" My jaw went slack. "How many orcs do they think they need to send for four people?"

"I'm not sure. We found no evidence of any orcs yet, but they'll be coming." Theron reached into a satchel and pulled out a handful of nuts, which he held in a hand to snack on. "They might send a few, thinking they can overpower us. They may send more than a few if they have an inkling that you're as powerful as you are. Which they must know, or else I don't know that orcs would bother attacking us. None of us look rich, except for him—" Theron nodded at Silas, whose armor still had the emblem of Celdic royalty "—and we're not transporting much of anything, let alone goods that are expensive. Maybe they're just looking for a fight. Orcs love their war."

"Maybe they see that we're capable," Nyx suggested. "If they enslave humans, they could just be looking for more people to corral into their pens."

"That's one idea," Theron admitted, before eating another nut. Putting the rest back into his satchel, he leaned back on both forearms.

"You're not in the least bit worried about this?" I asked him, noting his relaxed body language.

The ranger returned my gaze thoughtfully. "I've dealt with orcs many times. Haven't lost yet. And besides, I've seen you fight. You shouldn't be worried, either. If anything, I've gone weeks without a fight, and I'm itching for the bastards to give me a reason."

"Surely, in the many years you've been a mercenary, you've seen people you like get killed?" I questioned. "Maybe even brutally?"

"Sure, I have," Theron agreed.

"I'm sure you've seen someone make a mistake that costs them their life, or even be ambushed by the enemy and killed before they can defend themselves...?" I observed the mercenary carefully. "Any of that could happen to us."

"It could. There's no use worrying about it now. Those kinds of things usually happen to the weak, so I wouldn't waste time thinking about it."

Theron was right. Worrying wouldn't do anything productive, let alone change the outcome of any potential fight. Perhaps it was my lack of experience that caused the anxiety to build in my gut. Maybe it was the fact that I'd never faced an orc but knew much about them due to the race's reputation. Orcs were responsible for the eradication of many a town, and they weren't known for being fair in the game of war. I'd once heard that one orc was worth the strength of three battle conditioned men, and I'd never wanted to test that saying out by facing the brutal race myself.

"I'd like to know why Nyx here seems to think it's a possibility that we have the Seran Army chasing after us," Theron went on after the silence had befallen us for some time. I exhaled through gritted teeth when he brought it up again. I figured he either hadn't heard us or hadn't much cared. "Unless you are not who you told me you were, I don't see why Sirius Sera would send an army after his own daughter."

The others were silent. I understood. This was my responsibility. The mercenary deserved to know what he was getting into with us. "How much do you know of Seran royalty?" I asked. It would be easier to explain if I understood how the common folk thought of us and what they knew of the lineage.

"I know that Sirius is the ruler of Sera and reports to Queen Edrys in Comercio. I know he has two heirs. Terran Sera and you."

"Terran and I are both heirs, but Terran is his only child," I replied.

Theron was listening, emotionless. "How does that work?"

"Sirius is not my biological father, but my adoptive father. I was dropped off at the Seran University as an infant, and he raised me as his own. I realized my powers at fourteen, and my father has tried to control me ever since."

"For his army?" Theron asked. Perhaps I was mistaken, but there seemed to be a smidgen of sympathy that crossed his features.

"Well...yes and no. Sirius wants me for his army, but I think he put off letting me use my powers because he knew that once I did, I wouldn't live for long. Maybe he was waiting for the right time to use me as a special weapon. In either case, I wasn't willing to let him use me as a tool. I disobeyed his orders to join the Fourth Order and left Sera without his permission or knowledge."

Theron hesitated a moment, contemplative. "You used your powers that day at Amere. Did that give you a death sentence?"

"It's always been a death sentence," I replied. "It is for any mage, but me more so than others. Some mages can wield one element and live almost a full life if they're smart about it.

Two elements, and you start to shave the years off your life. Six?" I shrugged. "You can see my issue."

"Then why use your powers at all?"

"I'd rather live a short life doing what I love than to live a long and unsatisfying one."

Theron nodded as if he agreed. More questions were in his features, but he remained quiet.

"You have questions," I stated.

"I do, but they are born out of ignorance," Theron admitted. "I have worked with mages before, but I have never understood them."

One corner of my mouth raised in amusement. "What's there to understand?"

"How magic works. Why it kills you. Why anyone would wield it since it does."

I considered my upcoming words. "Magic is essentially the manipulation of energy. To manipulate energy, you have to understand it and where it comes from. Bodies produce energy, movement makes energy. Weather—wind, lightning—makes energy. Mages can mentally call this energy into submission. That ability comes to people in a variety of ways—genetics have a lot to do with it. Some races are predisposed to magic, particularly different types. Most elves have magical abilities. Many humans. Few to no dwarves. Regardless, if someone has magical talent, their children are likely to have it as well.

"When mages call upon energy to use in spells, we pull it from reserves in an order we like to call the Kilgorian Law given the name of the magical scientist who founded it." Using my fingers, I counted down as I spoke the order. "Environment, weather, self. It will not pull reserves from the lives of plants, animals, or people because that is reserved for necromantic spells. Imagine going to a recent battlefield rife with the bodies of melee soldiers and getting into a fight as a mage. When you use spells, the energy is harvested according to the Kilgorian Law. In this scenario, the first energy used would be residual energy from the battle. The energy from the exertion of bodies that are now deceased. The type of energy that hangs in the air that most people can feel even if they are not mages. Next, it will attempt to pull energy from the weather. If there are winds or a storm, mages will pull energy from this until the weather dies down and ceases in the area. Then, it will pull energy from yourself—meaning, essentially, it drains your life, much like a necromancer would do in a leeching spell against someone else. It is not necromancy when self-inflicted, because you have permission to give your life energy to yourself. You are not taking from one and giving to another."

"And when you run out of reserves, you die?" Theron asked. I gave him credit for listening. He seemed legitimately intrigued by it all.

"You *can*. Mostly, mages know they are running out of reserves because they fatigue and retreat from battle, or they never let themselves get that desperate. Running out of reserves means that yes, you run out of life, but most mages pass out before they get that far."

"But mages have shorter lifespans than others," the ranger pointed out. "It seems like even the ones who are smart enough to conserve their energy still die younger."

I nodded. "They do. Allowing yourself to use *any* of your life energy at *any* point will cause that."

"Why?"

"The same reason why someone who never gets enough sleep will die younger, or why a poor diet can lead to sickness and early death, or why starving kills people. Depriving mortal bodies of energy weakens and ages them, whether or not you are a mage. Mages just do this as a living, so it happens more often and is much more severe because it is a deliberate act and takes more than if it were to happen naturally."

"Are there exceptions to that?" Theron questioned. "Perhaps elves aren't as affected by it because of their long lifespans?"

"We are still affected," Silas spoke up for the first time in a while. "It just doesn't seem like nearly as bad of a sacrifice as humans have to give. A full life for a Celd who does *not* practice magic can last anywhere from six hundred to one thousand years. For a Celd who practices magic, you're looking at four hundred to nine hundred years, depending on how often magic is used. It is rare to see any Celds die from magic use, or even die younger than eight hundred because we battle infrequently. Celdic mages visually age faster as well. A Celdic mage of two hundred might appear to be twice that."

"There are two other exceptions," I added once Silas was finished. "Out of the six elements, there are four *material* elements and two wild cards. They are all under the banner of elemental magic because we use them the same. The spell language is the same. Sometimes, you'll hear someone say *destruction magic* instead of elemental—it means the same thing and is sometimes called that because that is elemental magic's number one use: destruction, or use during battle. The material elements are fire, earth, water, and air. The wild cards are life and death.

"Life and death aren't material elements because they deal with transferring energy *alone* as its own element. The other four elements *use* energy to create or transform that element whether it is water or earth or otherwise. With life magic, you are using energy *itself* to transfer into a body and accelerate natural healing processes that would otherwise have been impossible without weeks of time. With death magic, you are, again, using energy *itself* to reanimate the dead."

"Life and death mages are exceptions to the rule, then?" Theron prodded.

"Yes—essentially. While these mages can still die from their magic use, they aren't affected near as much as other mages. This is because their elements combat the side effects that the magic use itself gives their bodies. Healers can reverse most damage done to their own bodies, except for the aging process itself. Necromancers can transfer life energy from other life into themselves in a spell known as *leeching*. Not only can that help to heal them, but it can also render them essentially immortal and is part of the reason they are so feared. Taking in that much life energy can slow down and even reverse the aging process, in some extreme cases, even for humans. This is why there are documented cases of human necromancers living to be two hundred, three hundred, and even four hundred years old by the time they are killed."

"Valerius the Undying," Nyx mused, speaking the name of the oldest human necromancer ever recorded. He had lived to be 457 years old by the time armies finally cornered him in his tower on an island in the northern Servis Ocean. Not wanting to face him, the combined armies from Chairel did the only thing that could ensure their safety while killing the target: they'd lit the tower on fire and hadn't left until Valerius's screams ceased.

"How do you think Valerius got away with it for as long as he did?" Theron asked.

"I know how he did it," I replied. "I read books and books on him at the Seran University. He had a good thing going with a family of krakens that roamed the Servis before he made his home on the island there. The krakens would sink merchant ships on the trade route between Chairel and Glacia within view of the island. They had free rein of the treasure aboard the vessels and would eat their fill of the sailors they could catch. The remaining seamen would do the only thing they could to survive by swimming to the shores of the closest island where Valerius fed upon their energies.

"There were so few survivors that Chairel did not know what was going on save for knowing that trade between them and Glacia was at a full stop, so they sent a navy out to investigate. Well, the same thing happened to them, and Valerius got even stronger and had enough weapons to equip any of the thousands of skeletons he'd been collecting on the island if he needed to use them. Chairel finally wizened up and sent scouts along with an army and found out a necromancer aided the krakens. Before long, a full-scale war broke out between a handful of sea creatures and a necromancer and the entire country's army. Two hundred years later, Valerius was finally dead."

Theron chuckled, surprising me. He looked immensely amused by the story rather than disturbed. "It took two hundred years for an entire *army* to take out one necromancer," he mused, shaking his head. "I can see why death magic is banned."

"Keep in mind that this necromancer had allies and strategy on his side," I pointed out. "Also...human armies take time to build. Valerius had thousands of skeletons at his disposal, all of which he could use multiple times if he had the energy for it. And considering the attacks came in waves, he always did."

"You know much about this necromancer," Theron mused, smiling over at me. It was the first time the mercenary had shown genuine admiration for me. I wasn't sure if he liked my knowledge on the subject or the fact that I liked knowing a lot about something that was so taboo.

"I know a lot about a lot of necromancers," I retorted with a hint of my own smile.

"Why? Your own father has necromancy outlawed."

"Yes, but its illegality does not make it less interesting. I don't agree that death magic *should* be illegal. Necromancy is likely the strongest element of them all. It intrigues me." I shrugged. "As do battle tactics and strategy in general. I read books on all of history's greatest war generals, regardless of their race or type of weapon. I study their methods, their tactics. It's interesting to see how the world was shaped and by who. Which decisions made victories, what mistakes ended in losses. If the losers of rebellions and wars had the power of necromancy on their side, it's probable the world would look much different than it does today."

Theron observed me. Our entire conversation seemed to warm him up to me. Perhaps he had once seen me as a green and inexperienced person of royalty. Technically, that's what I *was*. But he'd now seen me fight, heard my story of refusing to cave to my duty as an heir of Sera, and knew that I was knowledgeable of my craft. It seemed my open-mindedness of the banned and macabre also matched his. I was half his age, but he now knew I was both talented and motivated. It was enough to help him see me in a different light.

Finally, the ranger spoke again. "It would interest *me* to see you put all of that rebellious intrigue and battle talent of yours to the test."

I wasn't sure what Theron meant by that. He'd already seen me in battle. Unless he meant on a large-scale, like the war generals and wars I spoke so fondly of. But I would never have the opportunity to be like those historical figures I had always admired. The only army I ever had a chance to be a part of was the Seran Army, and I'd already squandered all opportunities of joining it.

I was afraid I'd have to disappoint Theron in that respect. There certainly would not be any large-scale battles or wars in my future.

Seven

It was so deep into the night even the insects slept. I watched the night sky, my mind on our little group's previous conversations. The others were asleep. Both Silas and Theron were silent. Nyx snored lightly beneath her tent. It was like this every night when it was my turn to keep watch; the assassin was somehow always the loudest sleeper.

I had described magic and its use to Theron in such great detail earlier that now it wouldn't leave my mind. I had been alone for long enough into my watch that my brain was creating new weird and ridiculous things to focus on. For example, I could wield six elements, which meant I could *also* use life and death. Would it be possible to prolong my inevitable early death, much like Valerius and other necromancers had?

Of course it would. I'd considered such things before. The only difference between Valerius and me was that I was unwilling to feed off of the energy of others. That was one reason necromancy was banned. Leeching energy was almost akin to cannibalism, was it not? And regardless, to learn and use death spells would be to sign my own death sentence.

Crack!

My head whipped to my right to follow the noise, my gold eyes staring into the abyss of the forest, beneath where the light of our campfire flickered off of the leaves. As my eyes adjusted to the darkness, shapes formed, differentiating themselves. For the most part, I only saw the vertical lines of tree trunks. Perhaps it was just a woodland animal like it had been so many times before. Perhaps it—

Then, the campfire flickered over the outside edges of the shadow, pushing it back into the forest by a couple of inches.

I saw the glimmer of silver on a sharpened point and immediately thrust my hand out. By the time my arm was straight, the spell was recited. With a *zwip*, a clear, flickering energy spread out in all directions from my palm, surrounding my body in an egg-shaped orb. A split second later, the arrow that had meant to kill me bounced harmlessly off the shield, landing in the brush some feet away.

"Company!" I exclaimed, letting the shield continue to take arrow hits while trying to decide what spell to recite next. I heard the others waking to help fight even as the uncertainty of our attackers still hung like a heavy curtain in the air.

I saw the silver glimmer again. This time, the arrow wasn't meant for me. Before I could decide on a different spell, I shielded Silas, defending him against the next projectile.

The elf already had his beautiful pearl-white bow in his hands, firing off arrows.

Arrows. Plural. I refocused on the forest. The would-be assassin was only the first attacker. Perhaps he had meant to kill me, the lookout, so that the others could be killed quietly; now that his plan had failed, the shadows of his friends grew in the forest until an entire group of orcs rampaged toward us.

I'd heard of orcs. I had seen paintings and drawings. Nothing could compare to seeing them in person. In pictures, one cannot see that orcs tower above most men at seven to sometimes eight feet tall, or that their muscles bulge much too far in husks of dark green and gray skin, thick veins threatening to pump their raging blood straight into the air. Drawings cannot recreate the seething hatred that exudes from the blood-red or black eyes of the creatures. Their heavy charging footsteps caused the ground to tremble, even the flames of our campfire shaking in intimidation. Each orc held a weapon stained in the blood from previous battles while more swung heavily from belts at their waists. There were no orc archers; the archers in the woods were all human or goblin slaves. Orcs were clearly partial to melee weapons, particularly of the ax, mace, and club varieties. Most of their axes had either holes in the blades or hooked at the end, ensuring maximum pain and trauma when creating a wound or exiting it.

Orcs were simply another race. So despite how intimidating they were, they were mortal and could die by battle. I had all the elements at my disposal, but this close to the forest, I didn't want to use fire and recreate the risky battle at Amere. I needed to remember that woods caught fire much too quickly, and that like the orcs, my friends could also die by flame.

Nyx locked her attention onto the first orc to make it to our camp and engaged him in melee. She was much quicker than him, dodging around most of his weapon swipes that meant to crush bone or break skin and muscle. At the same time, she sliced and diced through him with her blades, and he barely noticed.

There was another orc engaged with Theron who was prickled from Silas's arrows. It was only when one arrow went through an eye that he fell.

I decided then to support my allies rather than attempt to kill the orcs through full force. There were probably fifteen orcs, with three slaves left shooting arrows from the edge of the forest. We had only killed one orc and two slaves thus far. I needed to buy my friends time.

Creatius la agua a friz. Water lapped up against the magical barrier above both my palms before a crackling, sizzling noise popped in the air as the water hardened and froze, the sharp designs of ice clinging to the barriers. A faint coolness cast over my hands, the ice I held so frozen that the temperature leaked through the safety of the magic shield.

I hurried over to Nyx. Her foe noticed me and sidestepped Nyx to focus on me instead. Perhaps he tired of getting nowhere fighting her. I thrust my arm toward his legs, and the ice encapsulated them, crawling up his legs with a crackle until he roared in frustration and became stiff, stuck to the ground in one place. It wasn't but a few seconds after that when Nyx gouged out the orc's throat, and hot blood gushed from his severed jugular, running in deep red streaks over the bright whitish-blue of the ice as it convinced it to melt. The dead orc's eyes showed rage even in death.

The orcs surrounded Theron. He held his own and had even felled two of them thus far. Silas still loosed arrows from near the campfire and added another orc to his kill count while I helped Nyx. It was Theron who needed the most aid, as he attracted the most attention by engaging the enemy in melee where they were most comfortable.

With my remaining ice spell, I froze two of the orcs who were focused on Theron. Because I had split the energy between two targets, the spell didn't entirely freeze them to the ground, but it made them stiff and slow to react, which was enough for Theron to finish them off.

I heard a growl. One orc redirected his attention at me, sick of my meddling. He swiped his ax toward my stomach, but I jumped back to avoid it...just barely.

I'm not trained for this. I could hold my own in a fight. I could *not* go up against an orc physically and win. The orc knew this; most mages were trained to support and complement melee fighters in battle. He wasn't interested in fighting fair. He was interested in killing me.

The ax was swiped again, and this time when I dodged, I didn't dodge far enough. The sharp, filthy blade missed my stomach but ended up slicing across both of my arms which were held before me defensively. The pain was immense and biting, and I tried to re-focus myself over my own whimpers as blood ran down my arms. The orc grinned, pleased to see he made progress. Yet another one of Silas's arrows pierced the orc's back as the elf tried to protect me. It was yet another arrow that was ignored in the orc's rage.

The orc went for another swipe. He knew he'd forced me to the defensive; I was getting clumsier and had to spend most of my time defending rather than thinking of an attack.

Focus. You didn't leave Sera just to die here. This time, when the ax completed its arc toward my gut, I shielded myself while backing up. The shield absorbed most of the ax's momentum, but it flickered with the force.

I left the shield up. My energy reserves ran low. It was a dry, calm night. My spells so far had taken power from the exertion of the warm bodies surrounding me, and in the distance, I could see our campfire wavering as my magic siphoned the energy from its heat. There were still orcs fighting my friends, and I would need to heal myself after the fight. I needed to save all the energy I could...

...or recycle it.

The shield shuddered as the ax once more attempted to break it. Within its protective barrier, I lifted a hand toward the sky.

Generat la bolta!

A low rumbling vibrated from the skies above me. Thick, dark clouds accumulated in a thick blanket that blocked out the stars and part of Meir, stealing some light the large moon had cast over the land. The orc before me realized I'd cast a spell, but he wouldn't let that slow him down. As the sky prepared its attack, I quickly whispered another spell command. A new ward spread out from my left hand, its energy clear with a tint of blue, meant to protect me from magic energy. As the sky opened up above me, I knew I would need it.

Sss...CRACK!

The lightning bolt was so bright and had such purpose it threw me back, and I tumbled over the ground some feet away. I watched through dazed eyes as the orc jerked around in place, the lightning channeling electricity through him from the sky. Within seconds, his deep green skin sizzled, and the brutal energy scarred his upper arms in such a way that looked like the branches of a fir tree.

The brute's eyes rolled back in his head before they smoked, wisps rising from his sockets. Then, the bolt retracted into the sky, and the orc collapsed, dead.

I hurried to stand, the stench of charred flesh heavy in my nostrils. The lightning bolt was powerful and took a lot of energy; but as planned, the spell left the energy rife in the air, prepared to be reused. Now, another orc was dead, and I was no worse for wear—save for the deep gashes in my arms.

I ran back toward the campsite where my friends were still fighting the remaining enemies. In my defensive maneuvers, I had led the now fried orc quite far away from where we'd begun. As I approached everyone, I let myself note the situation.

Nyx had an arrow sticking out of her upper arm. She knew better than to remove it and cause unnecessary blood loss. She fought an orc who was missing an arm, and it must have been amputated recently because the limb was limp on the ground nearby.

Silas was untouched. He'd remained on the outskirts of the battle, letting his arrows puncture the softest of places, killing orcs and fatiguing others.

Theron had taken the brunt of the damage and was fatigued from his efforts. Blood dripped from a wound in his upper thigh, and his right eye was closed. He had missed entirely dodging a hit with a blunt weapon just above his eyebrow, and the blood overwhelmed his eye. When he grunted, I could see red between his teeth, from where blood had seeped through his lips. I didn't allow myself to be overly concerned; head wounds bled far more than most, so I doubted the injury was as severe as it looked.

By the time I arrived, there were only three orcs left with one focused on Nyx and the other two on Theron.

"Givara la mana," I breathed, dodging the two orcs with Theron, and directing the energy toward the ranger. Theron became distracted for a moment and glanced up at me before he realized what I'd done. No longer as fatigued, he took on his remaining foes with much more gusto, and they were dead within the minute. By the time I turned to help Nyx, her opponent was already dead and lying on the ground, blood still leaking from his stump of an arm.

The four of us just stood there and breathed hard for a few moments. The thick clouds from my previous spell dissipated, allowing the moonlight to highlight the scene of the battle. The stench of clotting blood and body odor from the orcs was overwhelming, as was the smell of burning flesh. With a glance toward our campfire, I noticed that one of the deceased orcs had fallen into it, and the fire made short work of the flesh of his back.

"Ah. Well," Theron finally spoke up, before wiping some blood from his face with a forearm, "that was refreshing."

Nyx laughed heartily, the edges of her voice laced in fatigue that did not affect her spirit. "I knew I liked you for a reason."

"Just one?" I teased.

Nyx glanced over at me, her black eyes catching on the blood running off the tips of my fingers and to the ground. "Kai, take care of your arms."

"Both you and Theron have wounds," I replied, nodding toward her arrow. "Let me help you both first."

Theron shook his head, wiping his swords off on an orc corpse nearby to get the majority of the blood off of them, before sheathing them on his hip. "The healer is healed first, lest the healer be rendered unable to heal."

I wasn't sure if that was a phrase or Theron's own words. In either case, it made sense to me.

"Fine," I agreed, sitting down on the log near the campfire like I had when the battle had started. Putting my right hand to my left arm's wound, I murmured, "Promotus le imun." Though I felt the heat on the wound, it did not close. But it wasn't supposed to. I remembered how filthy the orc's ax had been. Before closing the wounds, I needed to boost my immunity to infection. After the heat from the spell settled into my arm, tingling through my bloodstream past the wound, I used the next spell. "Givara le life." Holding my palm just an inch above the wound, the energy transferred to it. More tingling, then itching. I watched as new, fleshy pink muscle built in the cut, slowly connecting itself to either edge of the injured tissue. I'd never had a wound this bad, and it itched more than anything I'd ever experienced as my body repaired itself at an intensely accelerated speed. Once the muscle repaired, my skin followed, the two broken halves of it slowly mending together.

Healing my wounds had all my attention, so I was a little startled when I heard Silas's voice just beside me. "How are you feeling?"

"Tired," I admitted, watching my second cut slowly heal itself.

"From a lack of sleep, or otherwise?" I knew from this second question that he genuinely tried to figure out how the battle had affected my mortality. At this point, I supposed I should have just expected him to ask.

"A lack of sleep combined with the thrill of battle, I think," I replied, watching my healing wound push a rush of blood out of its edge. The blood had a tiny piece of botanical debris in it that must have gotten there when I'd fallen to the ground. It always amazed me how the body could detect such things and proceed to help itself heal, with or without the spell.

"I am sorry I couldn't protect you." Silas was usually good at keeping emotion out of his voice, but there was legitimate sorrow that exuded from him this time. Perhaps he thought he would really lose me.

I wanted to tell him it was not his job to protect me, but it *was*. It always had been. Of course, that job was bestowed upon him by my father, *not* me.

"Silas, it is not your job anymore to protect me. For as long as my father is out of my life, his actions should not affect us." Finished with my healing, I stared up at him.

"Regardless of your father's actions, I am here to protect you." He said it as a statement, not a question.

"You may be here for that, but I'm telling you now you don't have to stay for it." I glanced away to stand. "I want you to be here because you want to be, not because you feel obligated."

"I haven't felt obligated for years," Silas replied, his voice soft.

I hesitated from walking over to where Nyx and Theron were chatting. They needed healing, but Silas was oddly personal at the moment. I looked back at him, uncertain as to what, exactly, his deep green eyes portrayed.

"I have a lot on my mind. It wouldn't be wise to distract me with conflicting statements that make me wonder what the last year has really been for you." I called him out for confusing me. It was almost as if Silas opened himself up to something more with me again. As much as I would have loved that, I didn't want to be jerked around.

"My apologies, Kai. It wasn't meant to be conflicting." Silas hesitated. It was a rare moment when he sounded as uncertain as he did now. "I, too, have a lot on my mind. I'm not used to failing you like I did tonight, and you were seriously hurt as a result. It calls a lot of things into question for me."

I looked away toward the friends I had yet to heal and swallowed hard. I hated rejection, and I'd already experienced heartbreak by Silas just the year before. For him to seem to be warming up to me just to wave away my concerns hurt all over again.

Silas spoke when he realized I wasn't going to. "Theron told me today you have plans to visit Thornwell, and that is why we are making our diversion from the forest tomorrow."

It was true. Nyx's idea to visit the small fishing village and search for Cerin had planted itself into my plans. Because the town sat on the northern edge of Chairel beside the Servis Ocean, we would need to take a slight detour to visit it. There was a distance of plains between the ocean and the Seran Forest, which we'd been following on our trip to the Cel Mountains. Everyone knew of these plans except for Silas, at least until today. I hadn't told him simply because of the reason we were going.

"Yes. It is one of the last villages marked on the map before the mountains," I replied vaguely.

"There are villages too small to be on any map," Silas pointed out. "They do not draw Amere on most maps, and we had shelter there."

"I realize that."

"You are hiding something from me."

"I am not," I said, realizing that could be seen as a lie. "Ask me anything you wish, and I will tell you the truth."

"Why are we going to Thornwell?"

Despite how I'd said I would tell him the truth, it was still hard for me to respond. "There's an old classmate of mine that I would like to find. He is from Thornwell."

"Cerin Heliot, the healer," Silas said, almost as if he answered a question. I was shocked that he remembered me telling him the story, let alone that he remembered his name. I had only mentioned Cerin to him once, and it had been many years ago. "Do you think he will join us?"

125

"I don't even know if he's alive, but he was the closest thing I had to a friend until I met Nyx."

Silas nodded. Just before I left to heal the others, he said, "Then we will go to Thornwell and find him."

Eight

The aroma of salt and fish hit our noses over a day away from Thornwell and only became stronger as our journey continued. The plains on the way to the village were beautiful. Long, green and yellow grasses waved rhythmically in patterns over rolling, small hills, creating a constant hum as a backdrop to our conversations. Up ahead, toward the Servis Ocean, the sky grew gray and cloudy. When we were still half a day's travel from our destination, the first of the storms came.

"What is it about the ocean that makes the gods so angry?" Theron mused, hints of annoyance in his voice. We were amid the plains, and the sun hid bashfully behind the thick storm clouds. We were all tired and looking to rest for the night, but we had no shelter save for our tents.

Needless to say, it was a miserable night, spent cold and soaked under tents that did little to keep the pelting rains off of us. I woke up in the morning feeling as if I'd barely slept. Within an hour or two of resuming our journey, the rains ceased like a mockery.

"This Cerin better be *really* easy on the eyes," Nyx teased me, just as the first sounds of the ocean met our ears. Out of all of us, Nyx was the least miserable. The heavy rains and lack of direct sunlight had been more comfortable for her than the previous hot and dry weather.

"He better be *here*. If he is, *then* we'll worry about his appearance," I replied in jest. In reality, that was my primary concern. I doubted we would find Cerin here. I had good intuition and I wasn't anxious about seeing him again, which meant I probably wouldn't. Regardless, I wanted to find out what had happened to him all those years ago, if his family or neighbors knew anything at all. It would at least ease my mind about the university's secrecy when it came to one of their most promising students.

Rising smoke in the sky was the first bit of Thornwell we saw over the last hill before the ocean. Then, the small village revealed itself. It was far bigger than Amere, and much better built. Cabins made out of stone and thick wood dotted the beach and the plains immediately by it. The village had a few different docks, some attached to buildings that sat above the ocean on pilings. Boats were tied to the docks in various places; most were small fishing boats, though an impressively sized merchant ship swayed beside a large trade building, its wood creaking and sails rippling in the wind.

The people here looked quite poor, though self-sustaining. A man in commoner's clothing chopped wood beside one cabin, a wagon full of logs beside him. A corral nearby held a few pigs and chickens.

There were men, women, and children moving about the small village, working or fishing or transporting. It seemed as though everyone was a cog in a single machine, and to watch it all was intriguing. While Thornwell reported to and paid taxes to Sera, it was so far removed from its mother city that the civilian hierarchy was non-existent. In Sera, there were apparent differences in the classes of its people. Here, everyone worked together.

They soon noted our presence. A middle-aged human man was the first to approach us. He had been amid descaling fresh fish at an outdoor butcher's table in an open shack but came to see us with nothing more than a wipe of his bloody hands on his apron and a smile on his face.

"Hail, strangers," he greeted, eyeing us with curiosity. He didn't seem to much care about Nyx, though he did take a second glance at her. Most people had tremendous fear or hatred of the Alderi. Perhaps he was smart enough to realize she was with us and not a threat, given two humans and a Celd trusted her.

After we all greeted the man, he asked, "Here to trade?"

"Trade, shelter, and information are what we seek," I replied. The man focused his attention on me, figuring me for the group's leader.

"Well, you can trade with anyone here, but if you go up to the trading hub on the dock—" he pointed at the biggest building on pilings beside the large merchant ship "—Tiana there can direct you to where to go and take any supplies or goods you have and give you coin. Our inn is the two-story building poking its head up over those cabins there." He nodded toward his right. "It doesn't look like much, but it's the last inn you'll see for quite a ways in either direction, and it's quite popular with the merchants and sailors. As for information, what is it you're looking for?"

"I'm looking for a man who used to live here about ten years ago or so."

"Ten years, you say?" the man asked, before nodding back toward the inn. "I just moved here a couple of years ago, myself. I would go to the inn and ask for Red. If she didn't know him, she might know who you can go to." He hesitated. "Not a criminal, is he?"

I smiled. "I would hope not. Just a former friend and classmate."

He nodded. "Aye. I hope you find him, then."

We said our thanks and goodbyes to the man, who went back to descaling his fish. I turned to our small group, where everyone seemed unwilling to split up.

Nyx looked at Theron and Silas. "Why don't you two take our loot to the trade hub? Kai and I can get started at the inn. Check the place out."

Theron glanced down at his satchels. Both he and Silas carried the loot, while Nyx and I were in charge of the tents and other supplies. "Sounds like a plan." Though Silas looked a little reluctant to leave my side, he said nothing, and the two men went to follow our plan.

Nyx glanced at me. "I figured you wouldn't be as willing to talk about Cerin with the innkeeper if Silas was glaring over your shoulder."

I nodded. "Yeah. Thanks."

We walked toward the inn, our supplies heavy on our shoulders. It would be bliss to have a warm meal and bed for the night and somewhere to put our stuff. Thornwell was a little less than half of the way from Sera to Whispermere, so knowing this would be one of the last inns on the way there was daunting.

"You told Silas why we're here, I'm assuming?" Nyx inquired. "He didn't seem too shocked to hear you tell that fisherman about it."

"Theron told him we were coming here. Silas asked me why on the night of the attack." I watched as a little boy walked by us, a fishing pole and a bucket full of bait in his hands.

"And he wasn't angry?"

"Didn't seem to be. He remembered Cerin's name, though, which was a surprise. It was years ago that I told him the story about his disappearance and the university waving me off about it."

"He remembers because he's not stupid," Nyx commented. "You were a juvenile when you knew Cerin, right? There's only one reason why a girl that age wants to *befriend* a boy. Silas is probably jealous because he knows you had a thing for the guy."

I huffed. "Silas doesn't have the right to be jealous. We're not together, so it's none of his business."

Nyx nodded. *"Right.* So let's find this healer and get you laid."

"Nyx."

She only giggled.

The inn was much larger on the inside than the outside would have one believe. The front door was on the far right-side of the building, leaving the entire floor open to the left as soon as we walked in. For a village that wasn't very large, it was a nicely sized inn equipped with a small stage for musicians or performers. Small tables dotted the floor save for a dance area next to the stage, and the bar was directly ahead, as long as the building itself except for a stairway to the right of it that led up to the rooms. Clean mugs hung from pegs above the bar, and they lined alcohols of various types up on three shelves behind the innkeeper.

As for the innkeeper, I saw why the man called her Red. Her hair was as red as mine, and this was notable because it was rare in humans. It wasn't the orange-red like Bjorn had, it was the deep red that many leaves would become in the middle of Red Moon. Because of how deep the color was, I instantly wondered if she could wield fire. With a glance at her hands, I noticed she didn't wear rings. Most mages did since spells were more accurate and powerful when transmitted through metal, though the lack of jewelry didn't discount the notion.

Red was an extremely obese woman, but I had the inkling that she could act as her own guard, so there were probably muscles beneath the bulk of her weight. She smiled when we approached the bar, exuding the same friendliness as our greeter outside; however, I had the feeling she could be mean when the situation called for it.

"Welcome, ladies. Looking for a room? Exotic ales?" She took a step to the side, waving toward the shelves of alcohol behind her. I could practically hear Nyx salivating.

"Uggh, both," my friend groaned, plopping heavily onto a bar stool.

Both Red and I chuckled. Before we could be barraged with a sales pitch, I spoke up, "I'm looking for someone. I was told you might be able to help me out."

Red's thick, unruly eyebrows raised. "Oh? What's their name?"

"Cerin Heliot."

Red's green eyes flashed with recognition and alarm. A pang hit me in the gut. *She knows him.* She hesitated before she asked, "What brought you here to look for him?"

"Cerin was a classmate of mine at the Seran University. He up and disappeared one day about six years ago. I knew he was born and raised here, so I thought he might have returned."

Red reached beneath the counter, pulling out a wash rag. She wiped down the bar which was already clean. "How well did you know his family?"

I swallowed hard. I wasn't sure why this was relevant. "I didn't."

Red sighed, before looking up at me. "Look, you seem like the honest type. I'd like to return the favor, but I need you to promise me you're not gonna cause a scene in my bar."

"Why would I do that? I'm just looking for information."

"Because the information I have for you might not make you happy."

"I don't care if it makes me happy or not. I want answers." I paused. "I won't cause a scene in your bar, I promise."

Red stared at me for a few seconds before exhaling. "Okay—I knew the Heliots, ever since Lucius was a teenager."

"Lucius is...?"

"Cerin's father," she answered, before putting her attention into her wash rag once again. "Lucius went into the same line of work as *his* father and became a trader, transporting goods from here to Glacia." She spoke of the country that was also a continent of its own, north of the Servis Ocean. It was a frozen land and the home of the Icilic elves, sometimes referred to as *snow elves,* which had the oldest lineage on all of Arrayis. I had never seen one. Icilic elves were extreme isolationists and a proud and arrogant race.

"Well, you know how the story goes," Red continued. "Lucius crossed the line of professionalism and fell in love with the daughter of a very prestigious Icilic merchant. Icilic elves don't approve of diluting their blood, so when she inevitably got pregnant, she ran off with him and came back here. Sweet woman. Twice Lucius's age, but looked eighteen the entire time I knew her."

"Who was she?" I asked.

"Her name was Celena I'lluminah." Red raised her eyebrows. "Try saying that ten times fast."

I chuckled softly. "She's Cerin's mother?"

"Yes." Red said this like she wasn't sure why it surprised me.

I looked to Nyx. "I would have had no idea Cerin was a half-breed. He had human ears."

"The kid was pale, though," Red commented. *That* was certainly true enough. Cerin's pale appearance had been yet another reason the other students made fun of him. His skin had been closer to pure white than the cream color of most of the mages at the university.

"Icilic elves are pale?" I questioned.

Red nodded. "Outrageously so. They have this glow to them at night like many creatures of the ocean. When Icilic traders come here on their ships, which is rare anymore, you can see the veins under their skin if you get close enough to them. They're pretty elves, for sure." Red hesitated. "Pretentious and atrocious bastards, the lot of them."

"So Cerin was born here?" I asked, eager to get back to the story.

"Yes. Born and raised. Lucius quit his job as a trader and became a fisherman to be close to them both. Celena taught her boys everything she knew about fishing. If them Icilics know anything, they know how to fish. Most of everything we know about the Icilic, we learned from Celena. They don't like to talk to races outside of their own.

"Anyway, to get on with it, Celena and Lucius sent Cerin to Sera when he was eleven. Icilic elves are highly magical, and given he had their blood, they knew he would make it far with magic. About two years later, we were attacked."

I frowned. "By who?"

"A group of Icilic. It was so out of the blue that we had no time to prepare. They hadn't stopped trading with us or anything. Some of their trading vessels came to our shores one day and attacked with little rhyme or reason. The story was that one of their traders had relayed the information back to Glacia about Celena living here with a human husband and a mutt of a child, and they didn't take kindly to that. Killed a good number of people on our docks before Celena came out to offer herself up if they'd stop their attack. Thankfully, Cerin was in Sera, or else they would have killed him for being an impurity in the bloodline."

"Offer herself up for *what?* What did she think they'd do, forget their grudge?" I knew this was going nowhere good, and it frustrated me. To have tragedy befall what was a happy family because of some elven racism enraged me.

"I don't know what she thought, dear. I wasn't in her head. Celena just saw people dying and thought it was because of her. So she went with them as Lucius was held back and screamed after her."

Red exhaled slowly and stopped wiping at the bar. It looked like it would upset her to continue. I prodded, "And then?"

"And then we waited. Lucius knew she would come back to him if she could. It was a full season before an Icilic trade ship arrived with a package addressed to him."

My stomach felt like it was drowning in its own acid. "What was in it?"

"Two things, actually. Celena's decomposing head, and her arm with a ring Lucius had given her still attached."

"I have to be honest," Nyx spoke up, "I've never seen one of these elves, but if I ever do, I'm pretty sure I'd be stabbing first and asking questions later."

I felt nauseated knowing Cerin's parents had gone through so much, and then, by association, him as well. "How can the oldest race of elves also be the most savage?" I pondered aloud, my voice lacking energy.

"You're asking someone who doesn't have the answer," Red replied. "As you can probably understand, Lucius went a little crazy. He became an alcoholic overnight. His neighbors told me they could hear him screaming from his cabin. He'd come here and drink all day and night until I'd kick him out. He'd ramble drunkenly about getting a war party together and going to Glacia to kill every Icilic he could, but he was never sober or motivated enough to try to follow up on it. Sometimes he'd go into rampages. Sometimes he'd cry. It wasn't a problem until he picked fights with my patrons.

"So one night, he was sitting at the bar, and I had this lute player up on the stage working for tips. Well, Celena played the lute, so that didn't sit well with Lucius. He got up from the bar, shambled on over to that stage, and knocked the musician straight to the floor. I was already halfway to him since it wasn't like him to get up from his bar stool without some prodding. He fought me for a little bit until finally, after one good punch to the head, he went down." Red hesitated. I stared at her, waiting for her to continue. She didn't seem to want to.

"You took him home?"

"No, he was gone. All it took was one good punch to the head." The bartender's voice was thick with remorse.

"You *killed* him?" My chest felt heavy. This was too much tragedy for one family.

"I didn't mean to. But sometimes, that's all it takes." Red watched me through teary eyes like she waited for me to cause a scene.

But I didn't. Because I believed her. I knew she felt for the family; I could see it in her eyes. She had merely been protecting her bar and her patrons.

"It wasn't long after that when we received a message from Sera. I remember that day because it was the first and only time I'd seen a griffon."

"They sent the Twelve?" I asked. The Twelve was a small arm of the Seran Army, which included twelve of the most experienced battle veterans from across Chairel, each of them with their own griffon mount. It was the only armed unit I knew of that utilized griffons as the beasts were notoriously hard to train and equip.

"They did. Can't remember their names. One asked if we'd heard from Cerin Heliot yet, and we told him we hadn't heard from him in many years. He went on to tell us that if Cerin ever came to Thornwell, we should send an immediate message to Sera. If we were to ever harbor him, our village would become an enemy of Sera and everyone with knowledge of him would be imprisoned or killed."

A sharp pain sliced across my stomach at the severity of that statement. "*Why?*" I asked desperately.

Red simply replied, "He wouldn't tell us."

"Did Cerin ever come?"

Red watched me carefully. "No."

"You're lying," I retorted, testing her. "I am on the run from Sera, myself."

"Why would you tell me that?" she asked me, concern etching itself through her skin.

"Because you won't tell me the truth with the fear it will reach Sera, and it won't. I have no plans to return."

Red's eyes moved over to Nyx, who had been quiet for awhile. My friend lifted two dark hands.

"I know the discomfort of the Seran dungeons," Nyx said. "I have no love for Sera."

Red looked conflicted. She must have decided we were as trustworthy as I had deemed her to be. "Yes, Cerin came. Once, about six years ago. The loss of his parents was devastating to him, and he kept his reasons for leaving the university from us. He was only fifteen and was a mess. He'd traveled alone for the better part of two seasons to get home, just to learn all of that. And then, he found his childhood home was sold since his father's death, so he asked me for a place to stay. Cerin had no money, but he offered to trade me a night's rest for any of his belongings."

"Did you?" I questioned.

"No." Red paused, looking downright depressed by this point. "I told Cerin he wasn't welcome here. I told him what the messenger told us because no one else had the guts to tell the kid that. I told him I could lose everything I own and my life if Sera were to find out I'd even spoken to him." The innkeeper paused, inhaled slowly, and went on, "Poor kid was a broken mess. Begged me for help. I told him all I could do was give him a loaf of bread and send him on his way. I promised him that I wouldn't ever report his visit here to Sera, but I couldn't promise that someone else wouldn't."

"That was the last you saw of him?" My heart broke for my former friend. I wish I had known any of this was going on at the time. Though knowing about it wouldn't have made it easier to do anything for him.

"No…he asked me where we buried his father. So I told him about the small tombstone we'd had fashioned for Lucius up on the hill, and he left. The last time I saw Cerin, he was standing over his father's grave. I'll never forget that, because he had such long, black hair like both of his parents, and it was waving in the wind." Red paused for a moment. "It stormed heavily that night. I remember having trouble falling asleep, hoping he was safe."

Silence settled over us in the bar. Even Nyx was quiet and thoughtful. After a few minutes, the innkeeper said, "I haven't heard from him or of him since. I hope he's okay. Can't imagine where he would have gone, given this was his only home. Was hoping maybe he'd figured out how to get through whatever trouble he'd gotten himself into in Sera, but given you came here from there, that's unlikely."

I turned around on my bar stool, glancing out the window. "Where did you say Lucius's grave was?"

Red pointed to the right, where there was nothing but more bar. Outside, though, there was a crest of a small hill. "We put him up on the hill where he and Celena would picnic in better times. Lucius made his wife a spyglass that she would look through up there. Swore up and down she could see Glacia if the skies were just right."

"Thank you," I said, before standing. Turning to Nyx, I added, "I'll be back."

I walked alone out to the grave, finding it only after some intense searching in the long grasses. The gravestone was a simple cube of smoothed stone with Lucius's full name etched through the polish, and the years of his birth and death. It was a nice gesture from a village that had been the life and death of the man.

The wind blew past me, coaxing my red hair to ride along its current. I looked to the ocean, where the water waved in trepidation for another oncoming storm. I could see why Cerin's parents found this to be a beautiful and peaceful spot. I tried to find Glacia somewhere along the farthest reaches of the ocean that my eyes could see, but I could not.

My eyes found the gravestone again. I tried to imagine what was going through my former classmate's mind as he stood here, broken and alone. Where would he have gone? Would he have survived? Along the horizon from which we'd walked from not long before, I could see just the slightest image of the forest we'd left behind. Far to the left were the peaks of the Cel Mountains. If I were him, I would have sought the shelter of the forest.

I ambled back toward the inn. Perhaps I would never find the answers I sought, and maybe I would never see Cerin again. Seeking answers had only created more questions. Perhaps finding out the secrets to my parentage in Whispermere would allow me to be at peace with leaving one mystery in my life behind.

Nine

    The table before me was of average size, but it was so stuffed with extravagant foods that my little girl mind looked upon it as a feast. Roasted pheasant, desserts made of exotic and rare desert fruits from Nahara, all manner of meats cooked in ways I'd never tasted before.

    Father had entertained Naharan diplomats just hours ago, and what was left of the feast was given to Terran and me to pick over. As a child, times like these were almost as fun as entire event festivals held in the merchant district. Food was my only vice.

    As I chewed through a mouthful of pork, I looked over the table at Terran. I found him to be so admirable. He was fourteen. Fourteen! As a seven-year-old myself, that was so old. Terran was now at the age where girls in his classes swooned over him, but he didn't seem to notice. Yet, anyway. Despite father's grunts over the length of his hair, Terran kept it shoulder length. Now, it was held back in a ponytail as he ate. Over the past few years, Terran's face had sharpened. He had the high cheekbones usually reserved for the models that the expensive clothing merchants hired to show off their clothes to leering tourists.

    I was glad he kept his hair long. I had always thought men were more attractive with longer hair, and my brother was no exception. His hair glimmered in the nearby candlelight, the shine a golden hue over seas of dark chocolate. Then, my mind moved back to my father's disapproval of its length. I realized that had it been me who asked, father wouldn't have relented. But because it was Terran, he'd allowed him to make up his own mind.

I frowned over my next bite of food. I didn't know why that still hurt me so bad. It was the way it always was. Father would refer to me as his daughter, but he didn't feel it. He often reminded me of the sacrifices he made to raise me to where I wondered why he'd decided to if it would be so much trouble.

"Brother," I blurted before I could stop myself. Terran glanced up at me, the bright green of his eyes much darker in this light.

"Hmm?" he murmured through a mouthful of pie.

"What was mother like?"

Terran's eyebrows betrayed his amusement at my question, and he smiled. After he finished chewing and swallowed, he asked, "Mother? Is that what you've taken to calling her? You two never met."

I felt embarrassed, then. I just assumed that father's wife would have been my mother. She'd died before I had even been born.

"You can call her mother, you know," Terran went on when I hadn't responded to him. I had been too hurt; perhaps he sensed that. "She would have been, had she been alive to see you."

"Do you think she would have liked me?"

"Of course she would have liked you. Mother liked everyone."

"Just like father hates everyone."

Terran chuckled. "Precisely." He took another bite. Chewed, swallowed. "Did you know that mother was pregnant with a girl?"

"The second time?" I asked stupidly.

"Yes, silly. The first time, she had me. The second time she was pregnant, she wanted a girl so bad. She prayed every night to the gods for a girl. Then, she hired an illusionist to finally tell her when she was far enough along. And he told her she was having a girl. Everyone was so happy. I think even father was, in his own way. Then, of course, you know the rest of the story."

I did. Mother had immense complications in labor. She was a dual caster, and before marrying father was one of the Seran Army's top elite soldiers. Magic use had taken an enormous toll on her, aging her past her years. The pregnancy ended in death for her and the baby.

"As for what she was like..." Terran trailed off, pushing the last bite of pie around his plate, distracted. "She was strong. And smart. Really, really smart. I could ask her anything and she would either have the answer or would know where to go to get it. If she wasn't training the mages or working, she was reading. She was like a kid in that way. You know how some kids actually like to learn?"

I nodded. I knew exactly how that felt. I thirsted for knowledge.

"Well, then you become an adult, and you stop caring. At least, that's what it seems like. Not mother. She was always learning about something new. Annoying father by talking his ear off about her latest obsession. She read me a bedtime story one night when I was about your age. And when she got done, she told me, 'Terran, never stop learning. If I have one regret in life, it was that I didn't take advantage of my years in the army to learn everything I could about the places I went.' In a way, I think she might've regretted marrying father because it tied her down. But don't tell him I said that."

"She sounds a lot like me," I said, unable to keep the hopefulness out of my voice. There was no bringing her back, but I wished to make some sort of connection with her, anyway. The only father I'd ever known loathed me. I could hope for a mother who loved instead.

"You are a lot like her," Terran agreed with a smile. He was so mature for his age, able to talk about his deceased mother without a tear. Perhaps he just had too many good memories of her and could not find his sadness. "Sometimes I think my memories serve me incorrectly, sister. Sometimes I think the baby was born that day, and that she's sitting right across from me."

Terran stood up from his chair just to lean across the table and ruffle my hair. It was a loving gesture, but as a child, I wrinkled my nose and acted annoyed.

I could not get the idea of parents who loved me out of my head after finishing my meal, so I headed through the castle to outside. I didn't hear fighting, so I figured melee training was finished for the day.

I found Bjorn sharpening a sword at the grindstone just outside of the armory. His cheeks were red from a day in the full sun. His hulking frame looked too large for his tiny seat. People of his size normally scared me, but his familiar form was nothing but comfort.

Dad. The word really only made sense with Bjorn. As a child, I didn't yet have the confidence to ask him if I could call him that.

Bjorn looked up, saw me standing outside the gate and watching him. He must have been fatigued after a day of training. Still, he greeted me with a beaming smile.

"There's my girl!"

A cheesy, child-like grin spread across my face, and I squeezed between the wood planks of the heavy gate, hurrying to him. Bjorn dropped the sword he'd been working at beside the grindstone and opened his thick arms just before I jumped into them.

"Ohhh, boy!" Bjorn feigned falling back before catching himself. "Uggh, girl, you're going to kill me one of these days. What are you, two hundred pounds?"

I gasped. "I'm fifty-seven pounds, not two hundred!"

"Fifty-seven...two hundred..." Bjorn trailed off as I pulled back from him. I felt his sweat from a long day's work on my own skin. "Not too far off though, are ya?"

"Bjorn!" I groaned, embarrassed.

He laughed. "I'm just teasing ya, girl." He watched me with suspicious eyes. "You've got something on your mind."

I nodded, too shy to admit it verbally.

"What's going on in that lil' head of yours?" he asked curiously.

"Do you think mother would have loved me?"

His hazel eyes widened. "Are you kidding? She would have adored you! Who doesn't love you?"

"Father," I replied, a sharp pain in my gut accompanying the word.

"Ohhh, come now. Your father loves you. He's just a grumpy old man." Bjorn reached over, rubbing my forearm

145

affectionately. *"He's a smart man when it comes to politics and magic, love, but he is socially and emotionally stupid."*

I frowned. *"What do you mean?"*

"He's not good at showing love or letting you know he cares."

I blinked up at Bjorn bashfully. *"Do you love me?"*

"You know I love you. Very much." *He grabbed me around my waist with an arm, pulling me toward him for a quick peck on the cheek.* *"Do you love me?"*

"Mm..." *I looked away.* *"Maybe."*

Bjorn scoffed playfully and started tickling my sides. "Maybe? *Now, that's not fair at all. I think I got the raw end of the deal!"*

Giggles overcame me.

*

"I hope that smile means it's a man you're dreaming about." Nyx's voice mused from beside my ear.

I opened my eyes and looked over at her. "It was, but it was Bjorn."

Nyx made a disgusted face, and I laughed. "I mean, if that's what you're into," she teased with a wiggle of the eyebrows.

"Get your mind out of the gutter. I was just reminiscing about him and Terran. I miss them both."

"As I'm sure they miss you," she replied, before laying back, staring at the peak of our tent. "Just don't be getting so homesick that you want to go back to Sera."

"To live?"

"Uggh...you asking me for clarification means you're thinking about it."

"No," I retorted. "I don't want to live in Sera. What if we were to visit again someday? Would you go with me?"

"If I could spend the entire time in the tavern getting drunk? Maybe," Nyx answered. "You know...you better think long and hard about doing that if you wanted to. Your father's treachery has few limits."

I frowned. There was much to be desired when it came to my relationship with my father, but Nyx abhorred him. Still, I didn't find her to exaggerate with her words. It was hard to admit I didn't know what he was capable of. For all I knew, the Seran Army could have been looking for me, much like I'd been told they'd searched for Cerin.

"What do you think our plans will be after making it to Whispermere?" Nyx pondered.

"I don't know. I guess that depends on my mother's plans for me."

"Your *mother,*" Nyx murmured, before a huff.

"What?"

"I just think it's weird that you called her that."

"Why? She birthed me. That's what she is."

Nyx shrugged, her shoulder bumping into mine. "In that same sense, Queen Achlys is my mother, but I couldn't stand the bitch." Disgust lined her voice.

"She's the one who—"

"Yes," she retorted quickly. "She personally picked out the ten males each year for the Reaping." Nyx spoke of an annual event held in her underground home city of Quellden, where the female Alderi celebrated their coming-of-age by sexually dominating a handful of males. While most cultures considered the genders to be equal, the Alderi were a race where only females could be in power, and males were thrown into slavery.

"It made me sick," Nyx continued, after a moment. "She picked Jemia'h as one of the males, thinking she was gifting me something. I grew up with the kid. I considered him a friend, as much as I was berated for it. And there he was, being repeatedly raped by my peers, and all I could do was watch."

I stayed quiet, waiting for her to continue. Nyx had told me about the Reaping, that she sometimes nastily referred to as the *Raping*, because in her words, "Well, that's what it *was*." Never before had she been this detailed. Perhaps all this talk about parentage brought those bad memories of hers to the surface.

"So, I did the only thing I could think of to do, and I stood there. Let all the other girls go before me. Achlys thought I was just waiting for everyone else to finish so I could be the center of attention because she was demented like that and thought I was, too. There I was, the only one left, and those poor ten juveniles on the floor in chains, all watching me to see who I would victimize. And my *mother* is standing outside of the arena, reminding me that she picked Jemia'h for just such an occasion like I was fucking *blind* and didn't see him laying there shaking.

"I turned to her and said I felt sick. She told me maybe a little sex would make me feel better. I thought about telling her I didn't want to have sex in front of my mother, but many of the girls there were my blood. I ended up saying I didn't want to do it. I didn't tell her that I found sex horrific if the men weren't into it because I knew such heresy could get me killed. So I found a safer way to say it and told her I wanted to *take* sex from men on my own time. That's when she insisted, and all the other girls started their ceaseless chatter."

It was an intensely uncomfortable story to hear. I couldn't imagine growing up in such a culture. Now that Nyx spoke about her own mother, I felt like any issues with mine should be non-existent.

"In the end, I finally decided to fake my way through it. Out of the ten guys there, Jemia'h was the only one I knew. I knew he liked me, and I thought he was attractive. In a fucked up way, I thought maybe it wouldn't be so bad because we did like each other. But..." she trailed off, her voice breaking at a point. "It's not like he consented. I knew he found me attractive. He didn't walk up to me on his own free will and tell me he wanted me, you know?"

"Yeah," I murmured. After a few moments, when Nyx said nothing else, I asked, "Did you end up sleeping with him?"

"Well...eventually. I just straddled him for so long that the audience got bored, and Achlys was grumbling a bunch of different words, many of them some rendition of *disappointment*. I said something stupid to Jemia'h...something like, 'I really do like you,' which sounded so childish, but he seemed to appreciate it. He said he liked me, too, and then awkwardly told me to go ahead and do what I needed to. So..." she hesitated. "I did. Then I apologized. I kissed him on the cheek because I cared for him. The audience found that to be a show of weakness, so I lost most of my high regard and any friends I'd managed to make, and Jemia'h was thrown into the crawler pit for fear he weakened the women."

I stiffened. I wasn't sure what the *crawler pit* was, but it sounded awful. Whatever it had contained clearly killed Jemia'h.

"So...yeah. You can share blood with someone and not be family," Nyx finally continued, completing the circle of conversation. "Don't forget, Kai...you're an adult. Whatever your mother has *planned* for you doesn't matter. I mean, if it sounds good, by all means, go for it. But it took you long enough to escape your failure of a father. I don't want to see you run to a mother who has convenient reasons for missing out on the first twenty-one years of your life just to become enslaved in *her* plans for you. Make your own."

I nodded slowly as if Nyx could see it; we both had our eyes on the roof of our tent. The morning sun tried hard to shine through the canvas but only poked light through the tiny holes in the crisscrossed pattern of the fabric.

"Like you," I said after a moment.

"Hmm?" She must've been lost in thought.

"You made your own plans and escaped the underground. And now you live a relatively normal life."

Nyx chuckled. "Relatively normal," she repeated, finding it amusing. "Is that a compliment or an insult?"

"A compliment, coming from me. To you, probably an insult."

She huffed in amusement.

"Seriously, Nyx...thanks for telling me about that. The *whole* story."

There was a short silence. Then, "I've always been afraid to. I was considered weak underground for the way I handled things, but to a human like you, I always worried you'd think I didn't do *enough*. I've fought with self-hatred over the years for the way I handled it. Wondered what I could have done differently. I've even wondered if I'd just gone through with it right away if Jemia'h would still be alive. He'd be traumatized, but alive. But then I think...could I have lived with myself? It would have been me who assaulted him, which might have been worse because it wasn't me who ended up killing him." She paused before a long, frustrated exhale. "I don't know. I could go back and forth with myself all day over that. I just appreciate you listening."

"I appreciate you telling me. And as promiscuous as you are, it's nice to know you have limits and boundaries."

"I can't imagine anything worse than being intimate with someone who isn't into it. That's what makes it so fun, you know? Being wanted. Being attracted to someone and finding out that they like you, too."

"And then moving on to the next," I teased.

Nyx chuckled again. "Well, that's the *best* part. You don't know what you're missing."

Ten

20th *of High Star, 417*

A fortnight passed since we had left Thornwell. The forest to our right became thicker, and the Cel Mountains ahead loomed ever larger. We were still a while from the base of the mountain range. When we reached that point, we would head into the forest, where the path leading up into the mountains would be a few days travel to our left.

Meir had long ago completed its semi-annual trek across the sky, so the nights became darker and the bright blue skies of the days missed its presence as well. We were now deep into the heat of High Star; the detour to Thornwell had cost us a few days of travel. If we had any further delays, it was possible we wouldn't make it to Whispermere until early Red Moon. If that were the case I would arrive in Whispermere a full year after my mother had written her letter requesting me to visit.

Travel had been relatively calm concerning trouble from wildlife or enemies since our little run-in with the orcs back before Thornwell. It didn't mean the trek was easy. The days were hot, particularly while stinking and baking in leather armor, and water was scarce this far from the ocean. We would run across a small stream now and then, and I'd even created rain a few times for relief, but full on bathing was out of the question without a more substantial body of water. Theron had spoken about the existence of hot springs in the Cel Mountains, which was news to me. Right now, in the heat, the idea of a hot spring sounded awful. Once we were freezing in the mountains, however, it would be a lifesaver.

It was mid-day, and the sun was relentless upon the earth below. Because we followed the forest anyway, we'd decided long ago to walk just within the line of the trees, allowing the shadow to give us relief. The group of us were quiet, amid pleasant silence.

That was when we heard it.

It was an ongoing crackling coming from to our right, deeper in the forest but getting closer. It reminded me of when mages would wield chain lightning, letting the bolts strike out directly from their palms...only this was different. It was magic, yes. But it wasn't air magic.

Theron was in front of the group, as had been his place since the beginning of our journey. Since he was the only one of us who'd been to the Cel Mountains, it seemed only natural. But now, he stopped in his tracks, and we eased up behind him.

The mercenary turned and made a gesture to lower ourselves to the ground. We did so, squatting amongst the brush without a word.

Seconds later, footsteps—lots of footsteps—followed, clomping down in the forest, overriding the crackling. Then, a roar. My heart raced at its familiarity.

Orcs.

As the sounds got louder and closer, more became audible. Orcish war horns, the harsh warning echoing off the nearby thick tree trunks. More massive footsteps, though just one set, that sounded much larger than even the orcs. Then, the clash of metal, followed by the skidding of it as one blade sliced down the length of another.

By the gods. How many are there? As the noises came closer, my eyes darted through the thick foliage, looking for the sources. A moment later, a flash of black passed through the forest ahead, followed by a small army of orcs.

There was one man. Hidden beneath a black cloak, he wasn't equipped to handle the entire orc army that was after him. He held a scythe in his right hand that appeared forged for battle rather than agriculture, for the weapon's handle was half-length and not a polearm, giving the man the ability to wield it single-handedly. He quickly backed away from the orcs, nearly tripping over the mess of foliage beneath him, but he didn't fall. It was almost as if he knew this forest inside and out.

Before him were masses of orcs. At least three times the amount we'd fought weeks before. Surely, all these orcs weren't just after him. I figured the man was part of a larger group—army, even—and was the last one standing.

The man finally broke through the edge of the forest up ahead and to our left, clunky black boots backing over the smoother ground. The orcs charging after him were still in the woods, rampaging over fallen trees and bushes. Somewhere farther in the forest, a frightening, deep roar shattered through the trees, shaking me to my core and running a chill down my spine. Whatever it was, I couldn't see it yet.

I felt such sympathy for that lone man, then. My friends and I were ill-equipped to help him. Theron was smart in simply waiting out the man's death. It didn't mean I would like watching him die.

Then, standing a small distance away from the edge of the forest, the man did something unexpected. He put the scythe on his belt, the long curved blade arced down behind him to avoid accidents. With his hands free, he splayed both arms toward the ground, his palms parallel to the earth. Beneath each hand, dark energy formed in swirling balls.

My exhales blew out shallowly from my nostrils. The energy was so dark; it wasn't just *black*, but it was like an abyss. I was a mage of the six elements. I found it absurd that I didn't recognize it.

"Earth magic?" Nyx murmured just behind my ear.

I shook my head, distracted. There was no way. Was there?

Then, the mage released the energy to the ground. The black, abundant energy spread like dense fog over patches of dirt and grass before separating into vein-like tendrils, slithering across the land in dozens of directions, before further splitting, and splitting again. Seconds after he'd released the spell, there were hundreds of tendrils, crawling over the land in all directions like they had free will.

Concerned, my eyes followed the cirri that came closest to our hiding place, though the magic stopped a few meters ahead of us, the blackness sinking into the ground as if the spell fizzled out.

And maybe it had. The orcs prepared to break out into the open field, and so far, nothing had come of the spell. But then...

The earth trembled. It started as just a vibration, and then it deepened all the way to where it felt like an earthquake would split the ground beneath us. Some orcs tripped up in the forest, falling clumsily to the ground as they lost their footing. One of my hands held onto the bark of the tree beside me for balance.

The mysterious man stood in the same place he'd been in, his head tilted down beneath his black hood. His right hand reached for his scythe, pulling it off his belt as the ground near his boots broke.

Crack! Dirt erupted from the broken earth, before a single, bony hand rose from the ground, followed by a forearm, then a humerus. Dark energy connected the bones in the place of muscle and tendon. The arm bent at its elbow, the hand falling to the ground to help push the rest of the skeleton out of the earth.

It was only when I felt light-headed that I realized I'd stopped breathing. Before us, in dozens of places in the field and along the outer edge of the forest, the dead were rising. Skeletons of humans, orcs, and animals alike rose from their slumber to heed a necromancer's call. Partially decomposed corpses gathered around their master, leaking a sludge of brownish-yellow fluids as they shambled into place. One particularly bloated zombie was missing its entire right leg, but was still determined to heed the request and crawled slowly toward the man in black, leaving a trail of decomposition from the stump at its hip.

My eyes were glued to the sight. This was the type of thing I'd been fascinated with reading about my entire life. Here necromancy was, just before me. Somehow even more intriguing and gruesome than I could have ever imagined. In seconds, one man had raised an army willing to fight blindly against all the odds against an ordinarily unstoppable force.

The necromancer reached behind him, pulling a long, orcish sword from his belt, possibly looted from an earlier enemy. Moving his head to his left and away from us, he held the blade out to the nearby skeleton of an orc. As if the orc could read its master's thoughts, the skeleton reached out, taking the sword and readying itself for battle.

Then, the horde of orcs broke through the border of the forest, spreading out over the field like a green plague. The sickly hisses and gurgles of the undead rose as a collective battle cry to meet the roars of the orcs as the two small armies collided.

The necromancer fought among his minions, clashing his scythe with orcish metal, switching from one-handed to two-handed as he utilized magic and melee. All around him, the dead fought with limitless energy and no fear. Though the dead were plentiful, they weren't nearly as strong as the heavily muscled orcs. The skeletons could shatter in an explosion of bones with one heavy strike of a club, and it happened numerous times, leaving the ground scattered with bones from various bodies. A few orcs were deceased, fresh blood staining the grasses below. The undead, however, were much fewer in number. Those that had lasted this long would loot weapons off of the dead orcs, equipping themselves with better weapons as they became available as if they had the brains to plan.

The *clang* of metal called my attention back to the necromancer himself as he held his own against a hulking beast of an orc with a two-handed ax. The hooded figure switched from using his scythe with both hands to just the right hand before he thrust his left arm out. The crackling noise from earlier popped and sizzled in the air as a fog of black energy siphoned through the air from the orc to the man.

He's leeching. It was a sight to behold. The man had raised an army, fought alongside it, and now regenerated the energy he'd lost with the enemy's own life. As the energy rapidly

157

seeped from the orc's chest, the brute became slower, clumsier. Finally, with no wound on his body from an enemy weapon, the orc fell, dead, its life harvested from its very soul.

More orcs fell, and even more undead. It was now the necromancer and just a handful of undead against a dozen or so orcs, though more enemies piled out of the forest. The shambling footsteps from earlier shook the ground until a giant monstrosity of a creature exited the woods and let out a deafening roar.

I stared at the creature, stiff from shock. The word *ogre* came to mind, but I wasn't sure why. Perhaps I had seen a drawing of the creature. Either way, it was one of the ugliest things I'd ever seen. Its head rivaled the trees at the edge of the forest, so the creature was at least thirty feet high. Its skin was also green, though it was a lighter, milkier color than its smaller orc allies. It was muscular and fat all at once, its eyes spread far apart on either side of its massive head and uneven in both shape and size. It suffered from such a hunchback that the ribbing of its spine stuck through the skin of its upper back, the bone brown with exposure. It wielded a club that was simply three meters of a tree trunk, the bark still attached. Thick leather straps over its shoulders and around its waist led to a backpack of sorts built out of wood where it carried war supplies and extra weapons. It also wore a pathetic excuse for a waist cloth, the short pieces of fur and leather not doing enough to hide the creature's dangling genitalia.

The necromancer barely moved as the ogre roared again, so loud and brutally that it shook the trees nearby and sprayed the creature's brownish saliva in multiple directions. Without flinching, the man lowered both arms toward the ground. The same black energy from earlier formed and released in tendrils, though this time, they stayed above ground, attracted to the fresh corpses. The bodies of the orcs rose again. Living orcs nearby were either enraged or afraid at witnessing brother and kin rise against them, and their battle cries became desperate and angry.

The rattling of bones called my attention back to the ground, where black tendrils dragged the bones of the original army back together over the distances that they'd been separated. All the skeletons that had their pieces scattered were put back together and rose for a second battle. The decomposed zombies, some of which had been splattered in multiple chunks of flesh and acid, spliced back together via the dark magic.

Just like that, the undead army was not only put back together again, it was doubled, and the intimidating act of using their own against them worked in the necromancer's favor. Orcs were distracted by having to fight their own and made mistakes that quickly got them killed. The ogre, however, remained unfazed. He shambled forward, swiping his trunk-sized club across his path, scattering a handful of the dead, exploding boils of zombies and scattering bones. The giant's attention was on the man, and his undead minions understood this. As they slaughtered orc after orc, the dead moved in to protect their master, rushing the ogre in such a way that any creature with a brain would know was suicide. Skeletons hacked away at the ogre's shins with orc weapons, and even the zombie with no leg from earlier had a hold on the giant's foot, gnawing with gusto at his heel.

The ogre paid no mind to this. With his eye on the collection of undead before him, he raised his club for another swipe. Then, the necromancer pulled another surprise out of his hat.

He thrust his hands toward the group of undead, just as the club was in its downward arc toward scattering them all. One by one, a glowing, clearish-white orb surrounded each of them before the impact of the club. This time, the club hit but was met with such resistance that it might as well have hit a stone wall. The skeletons and zombies stumbled back a few feet from the impact but were otherwise unharmed and continued to fight.

He's shielding them. I was outrageously confused. That was impossible. Wasn't it? Shielding was a life spell. The necromancer had clearly used death magic, and now he used the element of life.

In all my studies at the Seran University, I'd never heard of such a thing. Life and death were the rarest elements. It was unusual enough for someone to have access to one, and I'd never heard of a mage who could wield both. Of course, I supposed that even if they could, they wouldn't. Given that necromancy was banned, if a healer could also use death magic, he or she may never know it.

Either way, now that I knew this mage was a dual caster capable of both life and death magic, I was both intrigued and terrified. He just may as well have been unstoppable. Now, I almost felt sorry for the ogre. It had no chance.

The necromancer ensured he kept his minions shielded with an outstretched left hand, before holding his right out toward the ogre and leeching from its life. The creature swiped at the undead again and again with its club but became frustrated as it got nowhere. For each swipe was mostly negated by the shields, and its own life energy was being used against it, being sucked away from its body just to fuel its enemy's defense.

The minutes dragged on as the giant refused to give into its fate, despite becoming fatigued. By this point, the fight had lasted the better part of an hour, and one would have never have figured it given the energy of the man clad in black. The necromancer hadn't lost a thing. He'd regained everything he had lost through the smart use of his magic.

He would be an amazing ally. Despite knowing I shouldn't feel such a way given the law of the land, I did. And as the ogre swayed, light-headed and weakened, I stood up in the forest, my legs screaming with aches from maintaining the same crouched position for so long.

"Silas," I said, watching the fight before me come to a close. "Loose an arrow."

Silas stood up just in front of me. "At which one?"

The question amused me. I understood why he'd asked it. "The giant."

Silas took a step toward the edge of the forest so his arrow would be free of any obstruction. He pulled an arrow from his quiver, raised his bow, and nocked his ammunition. Eyeing the ogre in the field ahead, he tilted the bow upward.

The arrow flew, barely making a sound as it arced toward the giant. Silas's aim was true; the arrow pierced the skin between two vertebrae of the ogre's spinal cord, paralyzing him. The giant stiffened and began to fall. The necromancer and his army scattered around the corpse's trajectory. When the ogre hit the ground, the earth shook and dirt clouded upward from the edges of its body, coating the nearby skeletons in brown dust.

The necromancer stared at the ogre's back and noted the pearl-white arrow that stuck out from it. He glanced toward us, his face cast in shadow. A wisp of pure black hair waved out of the bottom of his hood. The minions still nearby turned their attention to us, but they made no move to attack. None of them made any movement at all.

I walked forward on aching legs, emerging from the forest to show myself and try to establish trust. I heard the others behind me warning me and cursing me in hushed tones, but I paid no mind. I took a chance on this man not being as insane as some of the necromancers of legend. I was all too aware that despite being unable to see his face, he could see me. He knew what I looked like. If he didn't kill me here, he could find or follow me, and I wouldn't have been able to pick him out of a crowd.

But it was a chance I felt I needed to take, regardless.

I walked slowly toward him, stopping a few meters away. Skeletons standing around the mage watched me curiously from empty eye sockets, their chests rising and falling with low *creaks* as if their bodies still needed air.

Most interesting, though, was the man. Even at this short distance, I could not see his face, just his chin and the top of his neck. He was pale. As a necromancer, I wouldn't have expected anything else. His black cloak hung over light leather armor of the same color. His armored leggings had all manner of sheaths and belts, straps and silver buckles. Blood dripped slowly from the sharp edge of his scythe. His black boots were thick and worn. Silver rings adorned each of his fingers, some of them etched with arcanic symbols. One was shaped like a skull, which I found fitting.

"Leave me at peace, and no harm will come to you." His voice was low, with a natural rough edge few men had. The sound of it traveled pleasurably down my spine on a shiver.

"I promise you, I mean you no harm. I witnessed the—"

"Serans mean me *nothing* but harm. Just admit you are here for the bounty your father put upon my head and be done with it."

My heart stopped before it tripped over itself to beat doubly as hard to make up for lost time. I wore nothing that would let strangers know I was Seran, let alone an heir of royalty. Slowly, over a few seconds that crawled through molasses, my brain caught up to my gut.

Black hair. Pale skin. Wields life. Knows who I am. Lives just a fortnight away from his home.

"Cerin," I said. It was a statement of bewilderment and relief, all rolled up into one word of confusion.

"You could be an actress, Kai. You sound surprised." He tilted his head, slightly. I glimpsed a full lower lip before it was hidden again in his hood's shadow.

"I am surprised. I'm shocked, actually." I hesitated before my eyes widened with realization. "By the gods, it all makes sense now." Cerin said nothing, and he didn't move. Finally, I added, "You must have practiced necromancy at the university. They caught you, didn't they?"

A huff of dry amusement echoed out from his hood. "I have no time for your act. Get it out of your head that you're going to capture me, or prepare to die. I have no plans to return to Sera."

"Neither do I," I replied. I heard the others approach me from the forest. Perhaps they figured this would all go quickly downhill at Cerin's threatening words. I couldn't pretend they didn't hurt me.

"Like hell," Cerin retorted. "They welcome you there."

"They used to welcome me there before I refused my duty and escaped. Don't pretend you understand who I am today, Cerin, when you haven't seen me in years." It was risky to get an attitude with such a dangerous man, but I was more than able to handle myself if things were to come to blows. I hoped that wouldn't happen. I wasn't sure how I expected things to go if I were to see Cerin again, but it certainly hadn't been anything like this.

"You're right. I don't know who you are, and you don't know who I am." There was a hesitation. Cerin's skeletons watched me with just as much curiosity as they had moments ago. "Humor me, then. Why are you here, if not for my bounty?"

"Not for you. I'm headed to Whispermere. I have reason to believe I have biological family there."

Cerin was silent a moment. He had been one of the few to know I wasn't Sirius's daughter by blood because I'd confided in him years ago. I also realized that admitting this clued Theron in to our true purpose. "I have been to Whispermere," Cerin finally said. "If you have family there, you may not like what you find."

A thick ache seized my gut. "You were there? Why?"

"I move around," Cerin replied vaguely. "I was there. They wouldn't let me in, but they didn't banish me like most. They allowed me to trade with them outside the gate and sent me on my way." A pause. "It's neither here nor there. The fact remains that you are on this personal mission, and yet you stopped to speak to me. Why?"

"Because I just witnessed one man single-handedly demolish an army of orcs and come out of it no worse for wear," I replied as if it were obvious. "I like to surround myself with capable people. I wanted to ask you to join us."

"Kai, you must be jesting," Silas interjected, stepping forward to grab my arm. "Former friend or not, he is a necromancer. You would doom us all."

"You forget that I am a necromancer as well," I retorted.

"In name *only*," Silas replied. "You do not practice."

"As I'm sure Cerin wouldn't if he would ever be discovered," I reasoned. "And besides, I am already on the run from my father. It is not like I'm still on the good side of the law."

"You are on the run from him because you disobeyed his orders and fled recruitment to his army. A much lesser charge than harboring a necromancer!" Silas argued, exasperated.

"I told you weeks ago, Silas, that you were no longer under my father's rule. If you disagree with my decisions, feel free to cut your ties with me and go." I stared at my former lover, defiant. His green eyes softened before he looked away, hurt and defeated.

"Do what you must," he murmured, his voice conflicted. I felt the pain on his tone and instantly regretted my sharp tone and words. Now was not the time to talk with him about that, however.

I turned back to Cerin, who had listened to our whole argument with interest and in silence. He turned his head to face me directly. Finally, the angle allowed the sunlight to reach his face, albeit barely. Piercing silver eyes met my gaze for the first time in years. There was a curiosity in them despite their distance. I swallowed hard at seeing him fully again after all this time. It was Cerin, all right. Six years older and carrying plenty of tragedy.

"Join us," I said. It was a plea, but my tone did not betray this.

"What do you offer?" he asked.

"A cut of the money we make, all loot we acquire. Work. Adventure. Friendship." The last word slipped its way out. It sounded so pathetic once it was in the air between us, but I couldn't take it back. And I did mean it.

One side of Cerin's mouth raised in an amused smile. "You must think I am so quick to trust."

"No, I can see you're not. That hurts me, given our past." I watched as an emotion flashed through his eyes, before he blinked, getting rid of it. I went on, "I do accept it, though. I will earn your trust. In the meantime, if you ever suspect anything in the slightest, you are free to leave."

Cerin watched me for a moment. His eyes then flicked over to my ragtag group of companions before he lifted a hand at his side, waving it quickly through the air. Just like that, all the skeletons and corpses nearby collapsed, dispelled.

"Very well," he agreed.

Eleven

Camping for the first time with Cerin would be awkward. The man clearly didn't like to speak more than what was necessary, and he also was suspicious of our true intentions. I hoped that the fact we were traveling in the exact opposite direction of Sera would put his mind at ease.

As a child, Cerin had been shy, but he had also been sweet and humble. Time and mysterious tragic circumstances had changed him. After offering to stop by his home to grab any necessities before he joined us, he told me he carried anything he couldn't live without on him and had no home. It didn't surprise me, given he was likely hunted by everyone who knew of his skills. Cerin wasn't aware that we'd visited Thornwell so he couldn't have known that telling me that would sadden me like it did.

Nyx pulled me aside that night as we set up the tents. There was a fire in her eyes I hadn't seen in quite some time.

"You have impeccable taste," she mused with a smile.

"I don't need you to tell me that," I replied, to which she chuckled joyously.

"I'm so happy we found him, Kai. First him, then meeting your birth mother in Whispermere...have anything else you wish to cross off your bucket list?"

"Yes...for both those things to actually go well," I admitted, before glancing over to where Cerin sat, poking at the campfire with a stick. He offered to fish for us, but we camped so far out from the nearest stream that the other two men offered to go out and hunt instead. My stomach ached when I thought of Silas. Out of all of us, he probably was having the worst time accepting the new member of our group.

"The first thing did. The second, we'll just have to wait and see."

"Seeing Cerin didn't go well at all," I argued.

"Are you kidding? He's here, isn't he?" Nyx paused. "And I know a look of attraction when I see it, friend. That man there was paralyzed when he saw you again, I can tell you that." When I said nothing, she added, "Considering what he's been through, it's amazing he agreed to come at all."

I agreed with that, at least internally. There had been a few desperate moments earlier on the battlefield where I thought I'd found someone I had once lost, only to realize he wasn't the same. I told myself that even if we never became friends again, at least I had Cerin as an ally for the time being.

Theron and Silas returned with a small doe and quickly set to preparing it for dinner. Silas took the bone and hide and prepared it for use like he always did. Tonight, though, he was withdrawn and didn't seem to want to participate in the conversation with the rest of us.

"Forgive me for overhearing," Theron began, while roasting slabs of the meat over our campfire, "you have family in Whispermere?"

Cerin glanced up at me in my peripheral vision. We hadn't yet fully introduced him to the others he'd never met. It may have been a surprise to learn that not everyone knew the reasons for which I was traveling.

"Allegedly," I replied, my eyes watching the waves of flame dance in the air. "I received a letter from a woman claiming to be my mother. She knew things about me that I didn't think anyone outside of Sera knew. She requested for me to come see her in Whispermere."

"It's a curiosity that she didn't come herself," Theron commented.

"Yes..." I trailed off. There were so many things about the letter and its circumstances that didn't make sense to me.

"The messenger claimed they built the city for her mother," Nyx spoke up beside me.

"Whispermere is very old," Theron pointed out. "And Kai is human. Something about that stinks to me."

"Maybe you're a half-breed like Cerin," Nyx suggested.

I gritted my teeth. Nyx and her big mouth again had offered up information that Cerin didn't know. To tell him we'd stopped in Thornwell was to give him a reason to suspect us since I'd claimed I wasn't after him.

The necromancer's silver eyes were giving me an even stare when I finally dared to look. "You know more about me than I remember telling you," Cerin said, low.

Nyx cursed under her breath when she realized her mistake. My mind rushed to think of the right words. "We took a short detour to Thornwell on our journey," I admitted.

"What does Thornwell have to offer you on your way to Whispermere?" came his response, calculated and cold.

"I thought maybe I would find you living there," I replied. "You were my only friend from the university, and I never knew what happened to you. This was my first time away from Sera, and we were passing it."

"Did you find the answers you sought?" Cerin's rough voice formed it as a statement, not a question. He seemed annoyed that I'd found any information at all. I couldn't blame him; everything I had learned of him there was very personal.

"No, not all of them," I answered honestly. "I do know about your parentage."

Cerin kept his fixed stare but seemed unwilling to broach particular subjects as he said, "It is rare for a half-breed to have human shaped ears like I do. It is a recessive trait. Improbable. Not impossible."

"You learn something new every day," Theron mused, his statement distracting me from Cerin's glare. "So perhaps your mother is an elf."

"Wouldn't that be a wonderful development?" Nyx piped up beside me. If I were part elf, it was possible my life wouldn't be nearly as short as I once imagined. I didn't want to allow myself to think this yet, however, lest I be disappointed.

Nyx, Theron, and I continued to speculate about my mother, while both Silas and Cerin remained silent. Theron was unusually talkative about the subject. Perhaps it merely interested him, or perhaps his problem-solving abilities as a ranger and tracker were happy to have something to feast upon. Theron didn't seem to care that I had withheld this information from him. He was probably used to it, given the mercenary's line of work, though I hoped that having everything open between us meant we could become friends. We'd been together for the better part of two seasons, and I found him hard to get to know.

The five of us ate dinner and prepared to go to bed. It was my turn to stay up for the first shift watch, though I caught Silas as he prepared to go into his tent.

"Wait," I pleaded, my hand on his arm. He stopped and glanced back. All the hurt from the day was still at the forefront of his stare.

"What is it?"

"I wanted to apologize for being so blunt with you today," I replied. "I didn't say what I needed to in the nicest of ways. It's true that you are no longer under my father's rule, and I do not place you under mine. You *can* leave if you wish, but I'd much prefer that you stay." I watched Silas as the words registered in his mind, before he exhaled through flared nostrils and broke eye contact.

"There was once a time when you took my opinion under consideration," he said quietly.

"I still *do,* Silas. Taking it under consideration does not mean we will agree."

"Your decision today affects us all," Silas protested, conflicted. "You have gone from a law-abiding citizen of Sera to willfully breaking the law. As soon as we are found out—and we will be—you become an enemy of Chairel. *I* become an enemy of Chairel. And I have my family to think about." He met my gaze again, his jaw set so stiffly the tension creased his cheeks.

I understood his position. People of royalty, like the two of us, had to consider the consequences our actions had on our family's reputation. The difference between Silas and I was that I simply didn't care. It would be my father's decision to come after me, and any conflicts from there that reflected upon his name would be his own doing.

"You can leave, and you haven't yet. What would you have done if my father sent his army? When they would inevitably attack us, would you have fled?"

Silas sighed after a moment. "No, I don't think I would have. I'm conflicted, Kai. I have followed you for five years. I care for you. But I do not care for our circumstances."

My heart ached with sadness. I hated that my decisions had affected him in such a way. For the first time in a while, Silas wasn't happy here with me, and I didn't know what the future held for us.

I left Silas to his tent and turned toward the campfire. To my surprise, Cerin still sat beside it, though he'd turned toward the night sky, watching it in silence. I knew that by now, Theron and Nyx were probably asleep.

I tentatively walked over to the seat beside him and sat down. If Cerin noticed, he said nothing. I wanted to talk to him, but it was hard to break silence with a man partial to it. Thus, the two of us sat in silence until I was sure even Silas was asleep. Then, I finally got the nerve to speak.

"It is my watch tonight," I said. When Cerin didn't reply, I added, "You are free to sleep."

"I am fine where I sit," he responded, barely after the words left my lips.

"I understand you don't trust me, but you will not make it long or far without sleep."

"I don't know how much of the battle you saw, but I absorbed the better portion of an entire ogre's life force. I will not need sleep for a day or two." Cerin said this without looking over at me, and with no extra emotion to his voice. He must have been used to this.

"Forgive me. I should have figured, given the way necromancy works, but...I have yet to experience an abundance of energy reserves. I can only replenish."

"As it should be," he replied simply. I allowed myself to look over at him then. Cerin had pulled off his cloak once everyone had settled for the night, so his face and hair were free.

The pale white moonlight gave his skin a slight glow, indicative of his mother's Icilic blood. His pitch black hair laid softly on his shoulders, which seemed slightly smaller now that his cloak was off.

I had often thought over the years since Cerin vanished how my memories of him could have made him more beautiful than was the reality. Now that I was with him again, I found my nostalgia trustworthy. He truly was the most uniquely attractive man I had ever seen. It didn't hurt that he was also immensely talented and had an air of mystery to him, or that his rough voice scratched the right itch every time he spoke.

"You can wield all six elements, can you not?" Cerin asked me then, breaking my leer.

"Yes." He'd known that already, but I was just happy he'd said something without first being spoken to. It was a step forward.

"How do you know, if they wouldn't teach you death?"

"They did. Just one spell and I was supposed to forget it. It was the plague."

"And you were successful with it like all the others."

"Yes."

"You really are an anomaly," he murmured.

An ache of longing settled in my gut. It meant a lot coming from him; he'd said much the same years ago after the discovery. "As are you, wielding both life and death."

"Yes, but there are few like me. There are none like you."

"Would you teach me your spells?" I pleaded since we were on the subject.

For the first time, Cerin looked over, surprised. "Knowing them would doom you to my fate," he protested.

"Being here with you dooms me regardless," I replied. "I might as well equip myself with as much knowledge as I can get."

Cerin blinked a few times, deep in thought. Then, he looked back toward the skies. "I'll teach you when the time is right." He clearly didn't trust me. As if to further prove it was about trust, he asked me, "Is your Alderi friend an assassin?"

"Ex-assassin, yes," I admitted. "How did you know?"

"I have killed many like her," Cerin replied bluntly.

I thought for a moment about his past, according to what I was told back in Thornwell. "The Icilic have worked with the Alderi to kill you?"

There was a short silence. "How much did you learn of me in Thornwell?"

"Everything they knew," I replied, to be open with him.

Cerin stiffened beside me. "Then I suppose I have nothing to add."

"You can add to it whenever you'd like." When he did not reply I said, "I am *so* sorry for what has happened to you."

Cerin said nothing for a long while, so neither did I. I had nearly given up on the idea of continuing conversation with him when he spoke again. "How did the Alderi escape the underground?"

It reminded me that Cerin had yet to really learn about his new companions, so I decided now was as good of a time as any. "She was tasked to assassinate me within the same year that you left Sera. She decided not to do it, we got to talking, and

I saved her life from my father's wrath." I hesitated. "Her name is Nyx, and she is my greatest friend."

"You must have a habit of befriending outcasts."

"I don't try to on purpose. They're usually the most interesting people." I paused for a moment. "Silas is the Celd. My father arranged for him to be a bodyguard for me after the attempted assassination. He is an heir to the royal Galan family of Celendar."

"And you two are together," Cerin added as if I'd forgotten it.

"No," I replied, surprised at his statement.

"Oh—forgive me. Perhaps I sensed something that wasn't there." It was the first time in years that I'd seen Cerin embarrassed.

"We tried our hand at it for a time," I admitted. "Silas couldn't get past the difference in our lifespans. I don't expect I'll live very long." I laughed softly and awkwardly. "He will." Cerin said nothing, so I continued, "And Theron is the human. He is a mercenary we hired back in Sera to take us to Whispermere since the rest of us don't know the way outside of looking at a map. He's been immensely useful and I'm hoping he will stay with us past our destination."

Cerin pondered this new information. At last, he said, "I will teach you the spells I know."

"Is the time already right?" I asked with a small laugh. His proclamation to teach me so quickly after not seeming to want to came as a surprise. I wondered what I said that had caused the change.

"Necromancy is the only magic that prolongs your lifespan," he argued. "The sooner you learn, the better."

Ah. Cerin's reasoning made sense, of course. I remembered confiding in him about my lifespan as a child, and he'd seemed concerned even then. His offer was selfless considering that he had no reason to trust me not to use the spells against him. Only one thing gave me pause.

"I will need to come to terms with stealing the life force of others first," I murmured.

"I'm surprised you asked me to join you if you are against that."

"I don't know if I'm against it or not. It just seems...cannibalistic."

"There is no moral difference between killing a man with a sword or killing a man with magic, even if it is death magic that is feeding you. As long as you are not leeching off of innocents you wouldn't otherwise be fighting, I don't see the problem."

As usual, Cerin made sense. He'd clearly thought this through many times. Perhaps there was still humility within that hard shell of his.

"Let me earn your trust, Cerin. *Then* teach me the spells."

He exhaled slowly beside me. "You place a lot of value in trust."

"Yes, and especially with you. You have little reason to trust anyone." My words were met with silence. I decided to risk a question. "What happened in Sera?"

It took Cerin so long to answer me that I started thinking he ignored the question. "As you know, I was a shy kid with no friends and many enemies, so I spent most of my time in the library. I ran across an old text that had been donated to the university, but not yet processed. Someone filled the first and last one hundred pages with generic nonsense. The middle section was a study of necromancy and listed many spells."

"Clever way to hide it," I mused.

"Clever enough to where I found it before the library could catch it," Cerin agreed. "I taught myself as many of the spells as I could before I had to leave that night because I wasn't certain I'd ever see the book again. And I didn't, on subsequent visits. At one point, there was a rat that died in my closet. So for the first time, I tried a spell on its corpse, and it worked. I was ecstatic because I'd taught myself a spell and used it correctly before we'd even learned our elements at school."

"You learned death magic before life?" I asked, surprised.

"Yes...which is why I was so, so relieved when I learned life as well." Cerin hesitated. "As embarrassing as it is to admit, I was lonely enough that I kept that rat's corpse in my dorm to revive repeatedly. It was almost like having a pet. After learning life magic, I practiced shielding him. Before long, it decomposed into a skeleton. Little did I know that two snitches spied on me from through the keyhole. They fetched an adult who burst my door in and caught me sitting there with an undead rat. I knew I might as well have signed my own death sentence, so I fled. Left most of my things and just fled. I didn't know how my parents would react, but Thornwell was the only place I could think of to go. I was a kid—kids always turn to their parents when they need help."

Cerin fell silent. I didn't speak for fear of interrupting his words or thoughts. I knew that considering where this story ended up, it would be hard for him to tell me. I felt grateful he was trusting me with this information as it was.

"Your father sent his men after me," Cerin finally admitted. "A dozen or so mages, and three of the Twelve, later on." An exhale blew through his lips. "I killed them all."

A sharp, painful ripple waved through my body at that, and a dull ache throbbed at my temples. I remembered when my father had been distressed over their losses, particularly of the three Twelve veterans. I had attended their ceremonies as royalty of Sera were expected to do. I had seen Bjorn in tears over losing men he'd once trained. Men that the necromancer sitting beside me had killed.

Cerin waited for me to say something, anything. He had to have known that I knew the severity of his crimes, that I'd known the men he had killed. But I couldn't say anything at all for the moment.

"I pleaded with them not to attack me and to let me be, as I did with you," he finally said, his voice having lost its energy. "I told them I didn't want to kill them. They barely let me speak before they attacked."

"It was self-defense," I said weakly. I did fully believe that. In my opinion, neither side had been completely wrong, but one attacked before the other. I believed Cerin when he said this, for it is what he had done with me. Still, it was little wonder that my father and the rest of Sera had gone to such great lengths to find and kill him. Now that he was here with me, any would-be assassins would come after the rest of us as well. Befriending Cerin while he was a necromancer was a crime by itself. Given his past with Sera, he was likely one of my father's most-wanted criminals, which would make my newfound connection with him even worse. Even so, I didn't agree with necromancy's illegality, and I'd never been one to blindly follow flawed laws.

"It was self-defense at the time. But I'm glad to hear you say it." After a lengthy exhale, Cerin continued, "Anyway, I did make it to Thornwell, feeling like a disappointment, a failure, and a murderer all in one. I found nothing but a gravestone and a village that wanted nothing to do with me. I spent the next six years killing everyone who hunted me and becoming exactly the type of necromancer all those Seran history books warn about because I had no other choice." He stood and continued in an awkward self-reflective ramble, "Forgive me if I don't wish to relive it at the moment." He looked off toward the tent we'd prepared for him. "Perhaps I am tired, after all."

"Oh..." Cerin's sudden departure caught me off guard, and my eyes followed his retreating form. It upset me that he was leaving. I felt we were slowly finding common ground as he opened up to me, but perhaps he'd just needed to get it off his chest. "Good night."

Cerin glanced back toward me at the face of his tent, looking regretful. "Good night, Kai. Thank you for your company."

Just like that, he was away from sight and in his tent, leaving me alone with only the night sky and plenty of time to question our conversation and its repercussions.

Twelve

The Cel Mountains were so grand in scope they put the Seran Peaks to shame. The weather became cooler the closer to the path we traveled; now that the sign for Cel Pass sat before us, it was like the season changed to Red Moon overnight.

Nyx finally felt comfortable enough to keep her hood down and stopped wearing long sleeve shirts beneath her armor since she no longer needed to cover her skin. Both her and Cerin were more comfortable in the cooler weather given their blood.

The dirt pathway before us was a simple one that rose along the side of the mountain. Whoever built it had quite the job, for large rocks were cut through to make room for the path. Far above us where the air was foggy with snowfall, I could see just the hint of shaky wooden and rope bridges crossing over the gaps between peaks. The journey from here on out would be more perilous.

"Was this path made for Whispermere?" I asked, my question directed to Theron and Cerin.

"It's possible they created it for that, but it leads to many places," Theron replied, looking above us at the cold gray rock of the nearby mountains. "Cel Pass is the only way to get from western to eastern Chairel if you don't want to go far to the north or south. It splits in multiple places along the way. The dwarven city of Brognel lies to the northern end of the mountains. It is a beautiful city; half above ground in the peaks, half below. The Mirren River leads directly from the coast of the Servis to the north to underground where the lower half of the city was built around it. It is entirely self-sustaining and sends out trade carts to Comercio only sparingly."

"You have been there," I commented, noting the detail in his description.

"Yes. It is the reason I was out here at all. Brognel sent requests out to all of Chairel about a decade ago, offering crazy sums of gold for defensive jobs. Dwarves pay extraordinarily well, given they are the ones who mine the gold."

"My father always complained about dwarves for just that reason," I said, watching the snowfall far above. It was amazing that I could see it snowing, but the view was from so far below that the precipitation didn't reach the ground here. I always found snow beautiful. I was sure traveling in it would change that perspective. "He said their constant influx of gold depleted its value and put Sera's economy at risk."

"I am sure that is true," Theron acknowledged. "But when you need skilled mercenaries and your city is so isolated, you need to offer them enough gold to make the trip and the job worth it, and so they did."

"What sort of trouble did they come across that required such a request?" Nyx asked curiously.

Theron watched her carefully as he replied, "Their miners broke through to the tunnels of the Alderi."

"As I thought," Nyx commented.

"The two don't like each other, I gather?" I asked.

"They abhor one another," Nyx replied. "The Alderi believe the underground belongs to them, and that dwarves are infringing on their territory. We're built for the underground, while the dwarves are an above ground race, so they taught us it is our right and our natural habitat, while they are the aggressors."

181

"But you don't believe that," I commented. Nyx had nothing but love for the dwarves. They were such partiers that I was sure she had both befriended and bedded quite a few while they were tourists in Sera.

"The underground is gigantic, and the only parts the dwarves are interested in are the areas ripe with gemstone. The Alderi can go suck on dwarven cock."

Her statement humored and shocked the lot of us. It was the first time her despisal of her culture had shone through to Theron or Cerin, so it caught the two off guard.

"I have a feeling you know a bit about what that is like," I teased her.

Nyx grinned. "The dwarves are almost as hungry for sex as the Alderi, friend. If they didn't despise each other, we would be overrun with a new race of half-breeds. If I could bear children, the majority of the illegitimate bastards would have dwarven blood."

That Nyx was rendered barren was both a blessing and a curse. That option had been forever taken from her as a child. Most Alderi females were sterilized forcefully; only Queen Achlys and a select few of her most prized heirs could breed with the males. They selected male breeders for both their looks and their strength; they deemed all others unworthy. It was a wonder that the Alderi could continue to exist under such a culture of incest. Nonetheless, as an heir to the queen but far from the first in line, Nyx was sterilized as a young teen. However, she had never once lamented this fact. Nyx valued her freedom and her wild ways, and I doubted she would ever lose sleep over the absence of children in her life.

"Are there any places in the mountains we can stay to get out of this weather?" Silas asked, bringing our attention back to the journey ahead.

"Caves and the like," Theron replied. "Brognel and any mountain settlements I know of are too far off the path."

"Perhaps we should begin our trek, then," Silas said, impatient with the talk at the bottom of the mountain. "The sooner we're off, the sooner we can look for shelter."

Theron raised his eyebrows at me. He was as surprised as I was at the Celd's impatience. "Shall we?"

We began our trek up the path, leaving the Seran Forest behind us. The change of scenery would be nice; we'd traveled through grasslands and forests for nearly half a year, though that proved to be much more comfortable than the uphill climb now. The path was over hard ground and rock, causing backaches much sooner than walking over softer ground.

Over the next few days, the path became steeper and colder, and looking toward the ground at the bottom of the mountain range only served to instill fear in my gut. The Seran Forest seemed laughably small from here, the trees that once towered above our heads now appearing as dots along the landscape. All it would take was one tumble, and one of us could be dead. I found it hard to believe that I had blood relation this far up in the mountains. The weather was bitter and uncomfortable for me here, and now that we had stayed in it for many days and nights, there was a chill persistent in my bones that no amount of campfires could cure. Surely, if it were this hard for me to journey through it, it would be even harder for those related to me to live.

We finally reached the highest path of the first mountain where the snow was thickest and heaviest. The day had dragged, and we were fatigued. Just off the trail was the blackness of a hole cut into the rock of the mountainside, the snow-covered rubble still sitting on the ground beside it.

"That was not here the last time I came through," Theron commented, his voice raised so he could be heard over the biting winds. He motioned toward the cave.

"Let's check it out," I suggested. "We could have our shelter for the night."

The others quickly agreed. The night before, we'd had no shelter save for our tents that we'd had to resort to setting up on the side of the path. My body felt stiff with how cold I was and had been for days. At this point, even Nyx and Cerin were desperate for warmth.

Theron led us into the cave. As soon as the shadow of the rock walls fell over me, it felt almost warm. It wasn't, but the lack of wind and snow deceived our bodies into thinking it was. The entrance to the cave was long, winding, and dark; whoever had built this hadn't meant to create a cave as a shelter, but a path to a destination.

From within the stone walls, the wind outside sounded like nothing more than a low whistle. The farther we traveled, the lower it became. At a certain point, Theron turned, asking us if we wanted to stop and turn around. We decided to keep going.

Finally, after feeling as if we'd been walking for the better part of an hour, we saw natural light ahead of us from through the rock. I wondered if we had entered the cave on one side of the mountain just to walk through to the other. It was clear once we got close enough to the light, however, that that wasn't the case.

Theron was the first to escape the rock tunnel into a large cavern. There were a few inches of snow on the center of the floor ahead, just below where the mountain broke open to the sky above. The cavern had to have been thousands of feet across, and the ceilings were at least one hundred to two hundred feet high. Because it was so open and had direct access to the outside, it was much cooler here than it had been through the tunnels.

"Well, we came all this way to rest just to find it's still cold," Theron said, sounding apologetic.

"It's better than the outside, at any rate," Nyx replied. "It actually feels pretty good in here. To me, anyway."

"There is more to this place," I said, pointing to the other side of the cavern where it appeared black. From this distance, I couldn't see the contents of the room the opening led to. Given that all other sides of the cavern shone with the natural light bouncing off of cold or moist rock, I knew the darkness meant the absence of a wall.

"Let's go over there, then," Nyx suggested, walking across the cavern. "We don't want the humans to freeze to death."

Merely trekking across the cavern took a while. It was gigantic, and one would have had no idea it existed if not for the tunnel entrance. It was a curiosity how someone knew it was here in order to build the tunnel. I wondered if we would come across someone here. Maybe some people had made a home in these caverns, safe from the biting chill of the outdoors. Perhaps this was a quick detour someone had made through the mountain, and the cavern had just been here to find.

We finally made it to the opening in the cavern wall, where it molded into a large hallway of sorts, with sides that were one hundred feet apart, and a ceiling that was similarly sized, though stalactites dotted the otherwise smooth rock in various places. The hallway sloped downward so slightly that I didn't notice until I kicked something and heard it roll away from me at gravity's mercy.

It was dark in this hallway, so much so that I couldn't quite see what it was that I'd kicked. Theron fashioned a torch that he swooped down toward the ground where the orange firelight flickered over a human skeleton.

"I thought that sounded like bone," Nyx mused. Glancing up at Theron, she asked, "How fucked are we?"

The ranger looked down the path where it did nothing but slope downward even farther. "Perhaps they were waiting out a storm and starved," Theron suggested.

"How stupid would someone have to be to allow themselves to starve? I'd weather the cold to get food," Nyx argued.

"You don't know how many of them there were. Clearly enough to dig out a tunnel into this place," Theron replied. "Maybe someone left to get food. This person stayed." Theron started to walk again, leaving the skeleton behind. Without much more thought, we followed him.

Up ahead, there was a slight orange glow at what appeared to be the end of the hallway, at long last. It looked like it opened up into another room, but at least this room had a fire. Wherever there was warmth, we would be able to camp comfortably. And it was about time, too. I was tired before entering this cave, but I felt worse now.

We walked farther and farther, ever closer to the orange glow. As soon as we were level enough with the next room to see into it, we were all taken aback.

There was gold. Millions of coins in piles half the size of a grown human lined the walls on either side of us. Further in, the collections grew, becoming even larger than us, the gold pieces scattering out around the piles on the bottom. None of us said anything for the moment, speechless. Even as royalty, I'd seen nothing close to this amount of gold at any point in my life. There were dozens of piles, all that had to have had thousands upon thousands of gold each.

Perhaps out of morbid curiosity, we kept walking. This was—oddly enough—the only room in the cavern that was well-lit. Sconces lined the walls between the piles of gold, each holding a nicely sized flame. I walked toward one, eyeing it closely. Whoever had put these lights here knew advanced alchemy or something similar. The fire burned brightly, but it also had done so for quite some time. The flames licked outward from cloth doused in a black, thick sludge. Whatever it was, it provided long-term light or heating.

The room opened even farther as we passed pile after pile of gold, and that's when even more gold added itself to the mix in the form of furniture. Chests, statues, and even pure gold frames with the artwork still attached stacked up between coin piles or leaning against them.

"Secret dwarven stash?" I wondered aloud, seeking answers.

"We are days away from Brognel at the quickest route," Theron replied. "I would highly doubt it."

Our findings became even odder when shiny things of all types appeared. There were weapons, many broken. Wagon wheels made of steel. Slabs of aluminum tile, as if for roofing. Even mirrors, most of them cracked and decrepit.

"Am I the only one who finds this weird?" Nyx asked.

"No," Theron agreed, walking past another large gold pile, where the room opened even farther. "It's definitely—"

The ranger stopped. I ran into his back, making him stumble forward a bit. The rest of the group stopped where they stood just behind me. Only Theron and I could see beyond the wall of the room, as the others were still behind it. And what I did see made my blood run cold.

Ahead, in the open room, were more of what we passed. Gold piles and shiny objects littered the cavern before us, in no particular pattern. The hallway leading here was organized compared to this, where shiny loot was merely tossed with no planning. What didn't look similar were the piles of skeletons, or the partially decomposed bodies of scavengers of all races that littered the room. Some corpses were partially buried in gold or loot. All around the cavern were the markings of plenty of battles. Stalagmites and cavern walls alike were scarred with sword strikes that missed their targets. Hundreds of arrows littered the ground in a variety of places, some arrowheads brown with old blood. Most frightening of all was the sweeping, bluish-white stains on the walls that cut across rock and treasure alike. Much of what was stained was cracked as well, proving that strong water magic in the form of ice had been used here, time and time again. Unfortunately, I was sure I knew the culprit.

One huge reptilian white eye watched Theron and me without a blink from the floor of the cave. The scales surrounding the eye shimmered silver and appeared blue depending on the light. All I could see from here was its head as massive piles of loot hid its body from view. Its head alone had to have been five feet long, and three of that was just its jaws, with long, sharp teeth that extended past its scaly lips. Two long, dark grayish-blue ribbed horns extended past its neck and out of view at the back of its skull.

This was my first time coming across such a creature, but just by its head, I knew what it was given the art of legends and fables. We were dealing with either a wyvern or a dragon.

I froze in place, my eyes stuck on the creature. I still leaned into Theron from where I'd run into him because I was too afraid to move backward off of him. I felt his heart beating fast even through his armor. Theron never said whether he'd ever run across a creature this size, nor if he had ever beaten one. I knew for a fact that three of us in the group hadn't. I wasn't sure how to deal with such flying beasts.

It was only when Nyx spoke that anything changed. "...Guys?"

The reptilian head lifted, and expelled a snort through its nostrils in puffs of mist, the noise sounding both inconvenienced and angry. The soft clicking of scales fanning out against each other in movement echoed off the rocky walls as it hefted its weight off of the ground on which it had been slumbering.

Theron unsheathed his swords. Even as I backed up off of him, I said, "You wish to fight it?"

Glancing back toward the uphill climb behind us, he asked, "Do you wish to outrun it?" He had a point. We had no hope of outrunning a creature of this size with the amount of walking we'd done to get here.

I supposed we would fight.

"What are we up against?" It was Cerin who asked, though Silas also looked concerned, his strung bow already in his hands. From their positions, they still could not see it, though the vibrations of its footsteps meant that would soon change.

"Dragon," I answered. I noted Cerin's exasperated look. He looked fatigued. We all were. And now here we were, having to fight a dragon in its territory.

The creature chose that moment to walk past the wall, revealing itself in all its glory. In another situation, I would have found it to be a magnificent being. Standing upright on two thick, muscular legs with claws sharp and curled from overgrowth, it measured twenty feet tall. Given that its tail was long and curved in a half-circle behind it, it was at least thirty feet long. Its silver-blue scales glimmered in the nearby firelight, and it spread its wings, curling its neck forward to roar. The result was a high-pitched, crackling scream like some mix of a bird of prey and something downright demonic, and it shook the walls and burned my eardrums. The creature meant to intimidate with the display of its size and its roar.

It succeeded.

"Wyvern," Cerin stated behind me. I glanced back to see him releasing necromantic energy from both palms. Black tendrils slithered past my boots, making a sizzling noise as they went.

"What?" I asked breathlessly.

"Two legs," he said shortly, grabbing his scythe and running ahead.

Silas was already shooting his arrows. The first few bounced harmlessly off of the wyvern's thick scales, so he focused on the soft spots of the creature. Between scales, through the wings. Nyx, Theron, and Cerin surrounded the beast, engaging it with melee weapons. From around the corner ahead, dozens of skeletons and zombies came running and shambling to heed Cerin's call, their hands all equipped with what weapons were closest. Almost humorously, some undead had chosen the broken weapons strewn across the floor and attempted to damage the wyvern with nothing but steel handles or half of a sword.

At least they were trying their best.

Creatius les fiers a nienda. Fire energy materialized over one palm. *Sheel a mana.* Life energy appeared over the other.

I hurried to the three friends engaged in melee. The wyvern was angriest with Nyx, who had stabbed it in the lower stomach where its scales were weakest. So I directed my spells together toward her, allowing the two elements to mix before reaching her.

Zwip. Sssss. A magical shield encapsulated her, flames licking out from its energy. The wyvern hissed, fire reflecting off of its white eyes with a glare. I figured that the wyvern could use ice magic given the evidence of it throughout its lair. I wanted to protect the others as much as I could from that.

The wyvern lifted its head. At first, I thought it was to dodge Nyx's fire shield, but then I heard the rumbling. The scales on his throat rippled upward, and it curled its neck downward, stretching its jaws to the limits. As the ripple reached its head, the rumbling deepened before a barrage of pure ice shards shattered out of the wyvern's mouth.

Nyx somersaulted to the side to dodge the hit. Even still, the ending seconds of the spell hit its target, dimming the fire shield and weakening it. Nyx didn't let it faze her. As soon as she landed her dodge, she ducked back into melee range, striking in a flurry of moves so quick, her daggers were nothing more than blurs of silver.

Cerin hacked away just beneath the wyvern's wing over and over again with his scythe, and all while leeching energy from the creature with his left hand. He'd nicked a spot in the wyvern's hide where its scales broke from repeated trauma, flecks of the silver-blue falling off to the floor below. The wyvern turned its head and snapped at him, proving Cerin's methods were working. Repeating my first two spells, I gave Cerin a fire shield.

My energy reserves were running low. Cerin and I pulled from the same sources. The exertion, the heat of the fire in the sconces. The necromancer received an abundance of energy by leeching from the wyvern, but his spells would not utilize those reserves until all else had run out. So he essentially took power from the environment just to recycle it into a form I couldn't use. I needed access to that energy and knew Cerin could give it to me as long as he knew the life spell. But to ask him now amid battle would be to both inconvenience him when he fought so well and to ask him to trust me with energy he worked hard to get.

So I didn't ask. And I did all that I thought of to do, which was to use what little precious energy I had to distractedly give Theron the same fire shield as he fought behind the creature's wing. The wyvern spat ice at a handful of Cerin's skeletons, and they all collapsed to the ground in a pile of mismatched bones. Perhaps the creature learned that using ice against my fire shields was moot.

Then, Silas did both a wonderful and terrible thing. He fired an arrow when the wyvern slowed its tantrum for a millisecond, and it pierced one large, white eye. The creature screeched, jerking the back half of its body to the side during a panic. Along with the body, it swiped its tail across the floor as fast and sharp as a whip. I heard a *crack*, then a gut-wrenching scream, and then Theron was thrown against a nearby gold pile.

Next, came the blood. Lots and lots of blood.

I dodged the wyvern's next jerk of panic and hurried to Theron's side. He was screaming, and the wyvern was screaming, and it all combined in my head to create an awful backdrop to my thoughts. Two tanned hands held at his thigh. Blood pooled around his legs. I was uncertain what had been injured until I realized that the two bright buckles on his armor were actually both of his tibiae, bright white and broken cleanly through both body and armor.

I was too shocked to speak. Tears of pain rolled down Theron's face, and his ordinarily calm eyes sharpened with panic. I tried to focus on my healer's training back at the Seran University. They required any who knew life magic to go through it. It dealt with anatomy, and wound treatment, and what to do in emergency situations like this.

I needed access to his legs, and I needed them free of their armor. The bone was stuck through even the leather, however. To pull his pants down past his ankles would be to risk further agitating the wound and the bones.

I glanced up toward Theron's sides. One of his swords was just some feet away. The other must have dropped closer to the wyvern. I grabbed the sword near him, trying my best to ignore the battle raging on behind me. I peeled the armor off the skin below his knee just enough so I could begin cutting it off with his own sword. I removed the armor from both of his knees down, being careful not to snag the leather on his broken bone.

Next, I held up one piece of loose armor toward Theron's face. "Bite this," I said in a rush, watching as he immediately followed my directions and did so.

One leg at a time. One at a time. Theron already had both legs lying as flat as they could be. Putting both hands on his left leg, I took a breath and twisted, snapping the broken bone back into alignment. The leather between Theron's teeth muffled his screams, but it didn't stop me from nearly urinating then and there from hearing his pain and fearing further hurting him.

Putting both palms to his wound, I said the spell to boost his immunity. The last thing I needed was to put him back together just for him to die of infection later.

Finally, I began to heal him. Because the wound was so deep, I laid my hands flat over his skin so I could feel the spell working and ensure the bone did not reform incorrectly. Heat escaped my palms, sinking deep into his wound and going to work. I closed my eyes to focus, trying to ignore the clash of metal and scale that continued to ring out from behind me.

Eventually, I felt the slight tug beneath my palms as the bone reconnected, the marrow slowly building between the broken halves. I swayed over Theron's leg, feeling light-headed. This was a deep wound, and it was taking all the energy I had to heal him. For the first time, I gave a spell permission to drain my life, keeping my hands close to the mercenary's skin.

If it weren't for me, Theron wouldn't be in the middle of the Cel Mountains and he wouldn't have gone this far into a cave that I had suggested. He had no personal quest for which he was here. I did, and he was here for me. Failing him was not an option.

I frowned as I felt another wave of intense fatigue, but I kept my eyes closed in focus and continued to heal him anyway. The wound reconnected nerves and tissue beneath my palms. Theron's screams faded, but he continued to breathe hard, his exhales echoing in the air between us.

I swayed over him again. A dull throbbing pumped through my head, heating me as if I had a fever.

Failing him is not an option.

Everything went black.

Thirteen

Someone finger combed my hair, almost maternally. But I didn't have a mother who would do that, so I just laid still, letting it happen because it felt nice. I was dreaming again, but that was fine. I would take pleasurable dreams if I could not have the reality.

"How does it feel?" Cerin.

"Better," came the reply on Theron's voice. "I'm afraid to stand up. It broke the bones through. I can't really believe I'm fully healed."

"Shock is normal from both the break and the cure. Just lay there a moment." I heard movement. Then, one hand came to my forehead, another lying on my abdomen from through armor. There was a rush of heat, and a tingling sensation spread through my body, washing the fatigue from my bones. "She's breathing," Cerin continued after a moment. "Her organs are all working. She's just sleeping."

Perhaps I *wasn't* dreaming.

I opened my eyes, slowly recognizing my environment from when I'd left it consciously. Theron sat as he had, though his legs were healed. A pool of blood below him thickened with time, a reminder of how severe his wounds had been. Above me, Nyx's face came into view, and I realized she held my head on her lap and brushed my hair. Her face registered immense relief once my eyes met hers.

"Morning, sleepyhead," she greeted as if to downplay her worry.

Cerin was beside my hip, watching me closely. He only ensured my eyes were clear and that I was of mind, but it still gladdened me to have the attention of such a man. Silas stood at my feet, arms crossed over his chest.

The corpse of the ice wyvern was amid its loot. Its throat was gashed out, and that appeared to be the final blow. Blood pooled below, though ice had frozen bits of it on the bottom flap of the wound. It seemed the creature was shooting ice when Nyx finished it.

"How do you feel?" I turned my attention back to Cerin after he asked. His forehead furrowed with concern.

"I'm...here. How is Theron?" It was a stupid question. I knew how he was; I could see both of his legs in alignment. I'd asked it just to make myself feel better since I had been unable to finish healing him.

"I am alive, Kai," Theron answered. His eagle-like eyes were sharp and on mine despite the fatigue of his recent trauma. I was so happy to see them clear again. "Thanks to both you and Cerin."

"I'm sorry I couldn't—" My voice broke with emotion, and I stopped speaking to swallow.

"The only thing you should feel sorry for is over-exerting yourself," Silas spoke up. "You could have died."

I ignored that concern for now and focused on Theron's right leg, the one I hadn't been able to heal. "Did you boost his immunity to infection before closing the wound?" I asked Cerin.

Cerin grimaced. "I don't know the spell."

Theron held a hand out to stop me before I panicked. "I have potions on me that should keep away infection. Do not concern yourself."

I finally sat up from Nyx's lap, my eyes darting around at the hoard of gold. "Are we staying here tonight?"

"That's the plan," Nyx replied, massaging her leg where I'd been laying. It must have fallen asleep with the pressure. "The sooner, the better. I'm exhausted."

Cerin and I volunteered to keep first watch for the night since he had leeched energy from the wyvern and had recently refreshed me. We wandered around the wyvern's hoard, searching through piles to see what we could find, keeping our friends within view.

"I wonder why all this is here," I pondered aloud, picking up what appeared to be an expensive dwarven battleax. I tossed it aside when it turned out to be dull, like a ceremonial weapon.

"Dragons like shiny things," Cerin replied, rummaging through his own pile.

"Don't we all?" I teased. Cerin laughed low and I was happy he appeared to be enjoying himself. "I thought this was a wyvern," I added, remembering his earlier words.

"Agh, I'm one for semantics, forgive me," he replied. "It *is* a wyvern, but it is also a dragon. Wyverns are types of dragons. They have two legs rather than four, and are much weaker and smaller."

"I'd hate to run across a dragon, then."

"Yes. Me as well." I assumed he never had.

"How do you think this wyvern got all this gold in here?" I asked, motioning toward the piles. "I get that it probably flew around and picked up whatever shiny things caught its eye, but these piles of gold are taller than us. That's a lot of weight for a flying creature, not to mention it would need something to carry it with."

"The gold is an offering," Cerin replied, motioning toward the sconces along the wall. "You can tell people have taken care of this place. There must be a village nearby that does it."

"Why?"

"I've heard that some view dragons as gods, or that they offer gold for protection."

"Does that work? The wyvern didn't seem one for talking," I mused.

"I don't know if it does or not. I've never met anyone from one of these villages, myself."

"Forgive me. My questions must tire you," I offered, given his short answer.

"They don't. I simply find it interesting that an heir to Sera is so green to the world and its ways." I wasn't sure if that was an insult or not.

"All I know of the world is from what I've read in books," I replied. "You may remember my favorite subject is warfare. Other details never concerned me until now. This venture to Whispermere is the first time I've traveled outside of Sera. Terran is the true heir; not me. Father never included me in on his political discussions like he did my brother."

Cerin was silent for a few moments, processing my words. "You call him father, but you don't believe it."

I stopped rummaging through the loot for a moment, my eyes sticking to the gold pieces before me. "I don't. And neither does he."

"I see why you traveled so far just to meet your mother," he commented, a note of sympathy to his voice.

Warm air blew through my nostrils as I exhaled. "It's pathetic of me to drag all of you through this long and difficult journey in some quest to meet her. I am an adult. I have no need of parents." I'd allowed a little too much of my own self-reflection out into the open, and I squinted my eyes shut in embarrassment. It was easy to talk to Cerin, just like it had been years ago. Maybe too easy. I admitted far too much around him because he would know just what to say, or simply listen when I needed someone to.

"This journey is far from pathetic," Cerin finally replied. I didn't hear him rummaging through the loot anymore. "You are not dragging anyone. We are all here on our own free will." He hesitated. "I've lost both parents, Kai, but at least I *had* them. I can only sympathize with your need to discover where you came from. I just hope you like what you find."

"That is the second time you've mentioned that, like Whispermere is some shithole of a place."

"Whispermere is beautiful from what I saw of it. But its problems run deep." Cerin hesitated. "I don't wish to say more. We will reach it soon, and I want you to form your own judgments."

I sighed, frustrated. Everyone I had ever spoken to of the place was so secretive. Unable to focus on sorting through loot, I turned and sat down at the bottom of a gold pile to take a break. Cerin walked over spilled coins, but he was behind a collection of them so I could not see him. Reaching up, I pulled my long hair slowly out of its hair tie, not needing it out of my way while I rested. My long, bright red locks fell around my face, billowing out with new freedom. I let my head fall backward with a *clink* against the coins.

I opened my eyes a moment later to find Cerin staring at me, holding a golden urn beside a nearby pile. As soon as my eyes met his, he blinked and looked away, putting the urn on the ground.

"I will come back to help you in a minute. I'm a little overwhelmed," I explained, keeping a straight face. Really, I wanted to smile. Nyx was right. The attraction between Cerin and I was mutual.

"No, you're fine," Cerin replied in a rush, though he stopped after a moment and met my gaze again. "I will teach you my spells."

Even as I replied, Cerin walked over to sit beside me. "I thought we agreed to wait on that until you trusted me."

Cerin sat down on the ground just two feet away, leaving enough distance so that his move wasn't awkward. He was a smidgen of black on a backdrop of gold. "We did, and it nearly cost you your life. Had you leeched energy from the wyvern, you wouldn't have passed out."

He was right, of course. But his explanation also meant he still didn't trust me, which was frustrating. "Then allow me to teach you what healing spells I know that you don't."

Cerin nodded. "All right. An exchange, then. A trade." Thinking of it this way seemed to make him feel better.

"A trade that I come out of looking better than you," I mused, given the number of spells we'd be exchanging.

"No, you are getting the raw end of the deal, learning magic that you can't use except for circumstances in which there will be no witnesses."

"There won't be any witnesses to any of our battles," I teased. Cerin huffed in amusement, having not expected my light-hearted jest in such a situation.

"I suppose not," he agreed.

Cerin taught me what necromantic spells he knew, including informing me of what words in the spell language meant in ours. Many of the words he taught me—*corpa, enflic*—were ones not used in any other schools of magic. By knowing how these words were translated, there was always a chance that I could someday create my own spells without learning them from outside sources.

Cerin also taught me the details of necromancy I would have never thought about. For example, while combining two elements could sometimes create a nearly unstoppable magical force, much like my fiery tornado in the woods near Amere, mixing fire and death was not always a good combination. Using *corpa te risa a multipla* to raise corpses in an area of effect attack along with *creatius les fiers a nienda*, which normally would attach fire to another element, would not result in an army of fiery undead that could inflict fire damage. Instead, it would result in an army of flaming undead, but the fire would only char bone and melt the decomposition off of my own zombies.

There were also differences in how spells were cast. Raising only one corpse required thrusting the energy in its direction, much like many spells focused on just one other person, whether that person was an enemy and being hit with an element, or an ally and being hit with a support spell. It also required a visible corpse as the weaker necromancy spell didn't infiltrate the ground. The higher powered area of effect necromantic spell was cast as if the earth itself was the target, much like I had seen Cerin use it many times. This spell did not require visible targets since the energy would absorb into the dirt and seek its own.

Finally, Cerin taught me much about the behavior of the dead once it was reanimated. The dead would use anything at its disposal as a weapon. He described instances where he'd risen woodland animals, just for the skeletons of deer to ram their enemies, or small rodents to chew through skin. Humanoid enemies would seek out weapons, resorting to sticks or even long bones of fallen skeletons if no metal weapons were available. The dead would always seek to protect the necromancer, focusing on the closest enemy causing the most damage. Once they had that enemy surrounded, they would spread out, attacking others as they saw them. The necromancer's thoughts affected the dead, Cerin told me, meaning that thinking someone was your enemy when they were not would still cause the dead to attack them. Paying extra attention to an enemy or weapon would cause the dead to attack the enemy or equip the weapon.

I asked Cerin if the dead could be healed, and he told me they could not because their cells were dead and could not rebuild. The only life spells that would work on the undead were shields because they worked on any object. One could, technically, shield a piece of furniture before taking a hammer to it, and the shield would protect the wood until it had taken enough damage. Most mages would never use their magic so frivolously, but it was a possibility and helped explain how one spell from the life element would work on the dead, while others did not.

It had been a few hours since Cerin and I had first sat down, and he was just now getting around to teaching me how to leech. He put his arm out toward my chest like he would use the spell, just to show me the correct method.

"You want to take the energy from the person's—or beast's—core," Cerin explained. "If you were to leech from the head, there's a possibility the target would become confused, but the leeching process overall would take much longer. Leeching from the core pulls energy from the midsection, and by virtue of anatomy, everything leads there. That's where most of the major organs are, so all veins and arteries connect here. While you are taking energy, the body itself is helping to resupply you by pumping more blood to where you are taking it."

"So you were standing behind the wyvern's wing for a reason," I said, understanding.

"Yes. You could leech from a wyvern's chest or side, but I was also trying to break my way in through its rib cage with my scythe," he admitted. "It's the closest way to the heart. Or hearts, if you're dealing with a much larger dragon."

"The larger the creature, the longer to leech?" I asked, because it seemed to be true for Cerin thus far.

"Usually, but not always. The longest it ever took me to leech the life out of a creature, it was a vampire. And vampires are tall, intimidating creatures, but they aren't even half the size of the ogre I fought back in the Seran Forest."

"What are vampires?" I feared it was another stupid question. I'd heard the word before, but never more than that.

"Soulless creatures who subsist on blood from other creatures alone," he replied. "Pray you never cross one."

"I would if gods existed to pray to," I mused.

"Ah," said Cerin, "another nonbeliever."

"Which gods do you subscribe to?"

"None. I am the same as you. I said *pray* as more of a figure of speech. Because if you come across a vampire, you will wish you had a god to pray to."

I watched him, intrigued. "How did you make it out alive?"

"Very carefully," Cerin said, before a dry laugh. "Thankfully, I know death magic. Vampires and necromancers are similar in the aspect that they absorb life. If you can absorb it right back out of them, they can fall. Which brings me to another thing about leeching—you cannot leech from the dead. If we ever come across an enemy necromancer, don't attempt leeching from anyone but the mage."

"Can't get blood out of a stone," I mused.

"Exactly. Now..." Cerin readjusted where he sat just before me. He'd changed his position earlier so he could show me how to leech. His legs were on either side of mine, silver buckles begging for attention by shining brightly over black leather. "Before you try the spell, there's one last thing you should know. Have you ever gotten high?"

A smirk spread over my face. "Is this conversation still about leeching?"

A rare smile appeared over Cerin's full lips. "It is, I promise."

"No, I have not been high. Been drunk a good too many times, but never high. You?"

"Not once. Rempka does not grow in the forest."

"You could have gotten it beforehand. At the university, or in Thornwell," I pointed out.

"Yes, at the university, where I had no friends," Cerin teased, before sobering. "When you leech, it affects your mind. You feel this intense euphoria...no, that's not the word." He hesitated, looking off to the side as he tried to find his words. "It's this overwhelming feeling of power. You are full of energy, and it *feels* good. You may want that feeling more often. You have to learn to control it, lest it start to control you." He paused, looking over me carefully. "The first time is the hardest."

This all felt oddly intimate to talk about with him. "How did you get through it?"

"I used it against your father's men the first time. Wanted that feeling so badly again afterward that I went hunting for animals to leech off of in the forest." Cerin clearly wasn't proud of admitting this, breaking eye contact with me. "Not long after that, I made it to Thornwell. Learning what I did there broke that powerful feeling pretty quickly. I've been much more careful ever since." He raised his eyes back to mine. "It gets easier the more you get used to it, but I want you to try the spell on me just in case."

I frowned. "You want me to leech from *you?*"

"Yes," Cerin replied as if he didn't see the problem. "Better here in a controlled environment than out in battle."

"I could hurt you," I protested.

"If you meant to, yes," he admitted. "But I still have an abundance of energy in my system from the wyvern. It is safer to try it now than on any other night. I will stop you if you start getting out of hand."

Cerin watched me with expectation. I found nothing but kindness in his silver eyes. I wondered if he trusted me.

Surely, he wouldn't offer his energy for a spell of mine if he didn't?

"Very well," I finally agreed, exhaling slowly and hoping some of my anxiety would float out along with the breath.

"Okay. Now, remember what I told you," Cerin said, putting his hand out toward my chest like he'd shown me earlier. "The spell is *absort la mana del life.*" Black energy swirled over his palm beside my chest before he dispelled it harmlessly.

"Absorb energy from life," I murmured, recognizing the language. I put my hand out toward the center of his chest, took a deep breath, and repeated the spell for myself. When I felt it accumulating in my palm, I directed it toward Cerin. A funnel of black energy started to siphon his life to me.

My arm shook with the abundance of energy. I stared at it, watching my veins become more pronounced from the pressure. As soon as I felt the tingle of power run through my shoulder and to my chest, I knew what Cerin had been talking about.

It was like my whole body was a trembling mess of power. By the gods, I *had* such power and was raring to use it. I watched with gusto as necromantic energy swept away Cerin's life, knowing that if I kept going, I had the power to kill him without making another move. My brain trembled against my skull, laughing with glee as if it had just found something it hadn't known it had been looking for. My vision sharpened. Everything—from Cerin's gorgeous face to each individual gold piece in the surrounding piles—was more precise, the colors sharper and robust. It felt like I could count each coin around me in seconds if I wanted to. My hearing, by contrast, had dulled. Because Cerin was yelling at me, and I couldn't hear him.

No—I *could* hear him. He was just telling me to stop, so I ignored him. Cerin grabbed at my arm, trying to pull it away from his chest, but I overpowered him.

More. More. More. I watched that black funnel, obsessed with it, barely caring that Cerin fought for his life.

Then, I was brutally torn away from my seat, and the funnel broke because of our new distance. Slowly, my senses came back to me. I could hear my heart beating in my head, and felt confused by that. Everything the extra energy had given me —the sharper senses, the overactive brain—was still there. But now that I wasn't absorbing energy, my mind was clear enough to have control once again.

"What in the *hell* were you doing?" Silas yelled at me. It shocked me to hear him speak to me like that at all. I glanced back, seeing that it had taken both him *and* Theron to pull me off of Cerin.

Cerin. I found him lying on the ground where he'd been sitting. He breathed shallowly with a hand on his chest as if reaching for some type of pain.

"Let me heal him," I pleaded, lurching toward him.

"Not until you tell us what's going on," Theron replied, sounding much calmer than Silas.

"He taught me how to leech, and he wanted me to try it on him, and I went overboard, and I almost killed him." It was a ramble, words tripping over themselves and merging together. "Please let me heal him."

The two men finally let me go, and I collapsed beside Cerin. His eyes were closed, and his long black hair fanned out around his head from where he'd fallen. For the first time, my eyes picked up on a freckle on his neck just beneath his jawline. I wasn't sure why I focused on that. Perhaps because it was something new to know about him.

I put one palm on his forehead, and the other on his stomach, much like he had done earlier for me. "Givara la mana," I whispered, giving him back the energy I'd stolen from him. Over the seconds that followed, I could feel the difference. The sharpness of everything dulled until my ordinary senses seemed like a handicap, but still, I gave.

Then, Cerin stirred. His silver eyes opened and immediately latched onto mine. "You are too powerful," he blurted desperately.

My heart ached painfully at hearing that. "I'm so sorry, Cerin. I was not myself."

"No..." he trailed off and sat up, causing my hands to fall away from him. "I meant...your power. It's *immense*. You leeched everything from me in a fraction the time it would take me, *and* I had excess." He looked toward Theron and Silas as if just noticing them standing there.

"It was foolish to try this while the rest of us were sleeping," Theron stated. I assumed he spoke to Cerin since I didn't face him.

"It was foolish to teach her this at *all*," Silas added bitterly.

Cerin's eyes widened at the Celd. "Kai could have *died* today. If she had known this spell, she might not have run out of energy at all."

"And now she knows it, *necromancer*, and it will bring us nothing but ill," Silas spat.

I breathed carefully through my nostrils, uncomfortable with the hostile air between everyone. I turned to face Silas and said, "If you are to blame anyone, Silas, blame me. Cerin can't teach me something I have no wish to learn."

"I will blame who I wish," Silas replied. I had never seen him this angry. It creased his normally smooth features. "You have lost your *head,* Kai. Let us hope you still have enough sense within you to find it."

My nostrils flared with anger, but I said nothing. It was clear Silas and I had completely opposite views on the matter of necromancy, and nothing I could say would change him. I watched my former lover walk back to where Nyx still slept, having not heard the commotion. I looked at Theron, who appeared pensive.

"What say you?" I asked him, anger prevalent in my voice though it wasn't directed at him. "Are you disgusted to be among necromancers?"

Theron met my gaze. "If it weren't for two particular necromancers, I would be dead," he replied evenly. "I have no love for bureaucrats or the laws they make up so carelessly. There are clearly many productive uses for the magic."

"You aren't just saying what we want to hear?" I prodded.

"I do not form opinions by coin, but by experience," he replied.

I turned my head from him with a nod. "Thank you for your support, Theron. I apologize for waking you."

"It's not a problem, Kai. But if I may be so bold, perhaps you should wait until the morning to learn any more spells?"

I chuckled. "No worries. I think we're done for the night."

Theron headed back toward the camp, leaving Cerin and me alone once more. After I could hear no rustling from the camp's direction, I finally spoke.

"I cannot express how sorry I am, Cerin."

Cerin shook his head, dismissing it. "You couldn't help it. I was prepared for it to be hard for you. I apologize for underestimating you."

I said nothing, my mind on Silas. I couldn't help but feel that even our bond of friendship was on shaky ground.

"It appears my joining you has caused contention," Cerin went on as if he'd read my mind. "And for that, I apologize."

"My decisions are causing contention. Not you," I replied, my tone low and ashamed. "Silas agreed with me on nearly everything in Sera when we both lived under my father's laws. I am thinking the two of us are more different than I could have ever imagined."

Cerin nodded. Even now, after I'd nearly killed him, he listened to what I had to say. "Do you regret leaving Sera, then?"

I let my eyes scan over his face, the light from nearby sconces flickering over his handsome features. From this view, the shadows over him were many, cast over his white skin from the sharp angles of his defined face. His black hair brushed softly against his elongated neck, free from the confines of the cloak he usually wore. A ripple of attraction waved through me before I answered him.

"No."

Fourteen

49th *of High Star, 417*

"Whispermere," Theron stated, coming to the crest of the path before us, where it opened up to become flat. "At long last."

My heart pounded in anticipation as if it hadn't been working hard enough through the uphill climb. The trek had been painfully vertical since we'd taken the path to Whispermere from a split the day before. The constant blizzards from days past calmed. I wasn't sure what I would see when I reached where Theron stood, but when the peak of a mountain came into view, with an open cavern of sorts tunneling through it, I found only disappointment.

"It is a cave," I said, my voice deflated.

"No," Cerin replied, his voice thick with labor as he came up to stand beside me. "The cave is the entrance."

We continued forward, approaching the cave with caution. The peak of the mountain stretched into the sky to our left and before us. To our right, the mid-day sun glistened off the fog of the clouds that dotted the skies as far as the eye could see. It was little wonder why the blizzards had stopped. We had traveled above them. The land was not visible from here. Perhaps it would have been, had the sky been clearer. But no, as far as we were concerned, we were walking on a piece of floating mountain.

Once we'd come over the crest of the path, the temperature warmed, as if we had somehow broken through the freezing weather to enter the sun's own territory. It was still chilly, but within the direct rays of the sun at this height, it tricked the mind into believing otherwise.

The temperature cooled again when we entered the shadow of the cave. Once we were inside the rock's embrace, it became evident that it was more of a tunnel than a cave. I could see straight through it to the other side, where a rope bridge led from the tunnel to the next mountain peak over. Long ago, during our first few days in the mountains, we'd had to cross many bridges like that. Now, at this height, just the idea terrified me all over again.

Even before the rope bridge, however, there was a gate. Built into the rock of the tunnel itself, it encompassed the entire opening. It was made out of metal bars to allow vision through to either side, but it was solid gold. I assumed someone had painted the gate, for gold was far too soft a metal to be trusted for such a structure.

At the center of this gate stood two guards, one on our side of the gate, the other waiting just inside. Both were men dressed similarly to the messenger from Whispermere half of a year ago, their skin golden-hued. The men did not look up as we approached, casting their eyes down to the rock floor beneath their feet. It made me remember that even the messenger avoided eye contact back in Sera. The two guards before us couldn't have known who I was, and yet they avoided my eyes. I found that odd.

The men also did not speak as we stopped before them. I finally greeted them first. "Hello," I began. "I am Kai Sera. My mother requested my presence."

The guard on our side of the gate nodded. "Yes, Miss Sera. Thank you for coming. You must come in alone. Your companions may wait at the gate."

I watched the man, suspicious of his words and unable to intimidate him via eye contact. "My friends will enter with me, or I will turn around and leave the same way I came."

The guard stiffened before he turned to the other from through the gate. They spoke with rushed whispers before the guard closest to Whispermere hurried away across the rope bridge. On the other side, there were golden structures and the tops of plants, but little else could be seen aside from the next mountain peak.

"Forgive us, Miss Sera. We must request permission."

"Very well." I turned toward the others. We were all taken aback by the workings of this place.

We waited for some minutes for the other man to return. All the while, we did not speak, but I let my eyes rest on the next mountain peak over. Somewhere, over there, was the woman who had birthed me. What was she like? Would she be proud of all I had accomplished? I had fantasized over the past weeks of our reunion. Perhaps we would embrace, and she would tell me the story of how we were forced to part. Maybe we would have much in common. Perhaps I would find that some of my hobbies or interests or mannerisms had come from her when I would never otherwise have known. I wondered if she had my hair or my rare eyes; after all, I'd never seen such metallic golden eyes other than my own. And what of my father? What would she tell me about him?

"You may enter." The guard's words broke me out of my thoughts. I hadn't noticed that the other one had come back.

"Thank you." The guards before us did not answer but pushed open the massive gate with a heavy *creak*. We walked through, my friends leading the way. I didn't want to risk them closing the gate behind me to separate us, though I hoped such a thought didn't cross their minds.

They also painted the rope bridge crossing the gap between the two mountain peaks gold. I wondered about the obsession with gold here but couldn't focus on my questions as I took the first step on the bridge.

Up this high, the air was still, so the bridge did not move by any means other than those who stepped upon it. Even still, it was frightening to begin the trek over the long bridge, as it trembled beneath our weight. A direct stare downward showed nothing but clouds beneath us, too thick to allow any view of the ground or the mountains below. Perhaps that was for the best. I doubted I wanted to see how far we would fall with one false move.

I didn't look up at Whispermere until I was back on the solid rock. On this mountain, it appeared as if the builders of Whispermere had carved half of the mountain peak itself out of existence, leaving the rock flat as a floor under our feet. The carvers had even left a barrier of rock standing about three feet high along the edges to prevent accidents. Up ahead, they had carved the mountain peak in half, the side facing us vertically flat, leaving the village below in direct view of the sun.

As for the village, it was entirely out in the open. Tables, chairs, and gardens alike were all in full view of the sun. There were no walls with which to shade or separate them. The village still had its designated areas, but it was mostly due to the set up of furniture or hedge bushes that one could tell where one area started and ended.

I wondered how so much plant life could exist when the village was higher than the clouds that could give them rain.

Finally, I saw my answer, in the form of a man who was retrieving water via a pulley on the side of the mountain. That was an awful lot of effort to go through just to live here. It gave me the impression that the people here were in hiding.

As for Whispermere's people, they were all the same golden hue. I also noticed that there was a distinct difference between the men and women here. All the men were amid physical labor, and none of them held their eyes level with the others. The women, however, were all in states of leisure. Some drank and laughed at cafe tables, or relaxed in the gardens. All of them were capable of eye contact. I tried to find one man or woman in the opposite position, and I could not.

From past the village where the other half of the peak rose above us, they carved another tunnel into the lower rock. Given its relative darkness to the first tunnel we had left behind, I supposed this one did not lead all the way through.

One man hurried over to us and nodded toward me. I wasn't sure how they could tell which one I was, given they could only see our feet.

"Miss Sera, please follow me. You are hungry from your journey, yes?"

"Yes," I admitted, glancing back toward the others. We had been eating nothing but berries and dried meat Theron had prepared in the Seran Forest since ascending the mountain.

The man led us through the village. The women observed us from all directions, chatting amongst themselves. The scent of flowers hung pleasantly in the air, the lack of winds keeping the smell strong.

We followed our guide into the man-made cave. Once our eyes adjusted to the darkness, I realized there was much more to the cave than it appeared from outside. Inside the mountain was a mansion of sorts, with rooms and hallways and furniture. Men hustled to and from various places with their own objectives. Expensive looking art adorned the walls, and all the furniture was handmade and trimmed in gold. Golden floor lamps lit the rooms, the firelight flickering across stone walls.

We were led down a staircase carved out of stone, into yet another floor of rooms. Ahead was a long table with enough seats to entertain a group four times our size. The tablecloth was, like most other things, white and bordered in gold, and felt to be made of pure silk. Candelabras adorned the table in three places, and arrangements of fresh flowers sat in pots between them.

"Please, sit," our guide urged, motioning toward the table. "Do you wish to sit with your servants?"

"My...servants?" I glanced toward the guide, confused. He simply motioned toward the others. "These are not my servants. They are my friends, and they are to go wherever I do."

"Forgive me, Miss Sera. Sometimes the differences between Whispermere and the rest of the world escape me."

We sat at the table, and the man left with promises that a feast was being prepared for us. Nyx and Cerin sat on either side of me, while Silas and Theron sat opposite us. To my right, the rest of the table stretched out, empty.

"I wonder if your mother will meet us here," Nyx pondered, breaking the silence when no one else would.

"I don't know," I replied. "Whoever runs this place seems to control all of this; hopefully my mother knows I am even here."

"If it's true they built Whispermere for your mother, perhaps she is the one who set this up," Theron suggested.

I was uncertain whether I wanted to entertain that possibility. If my mother was the leader here, I wasn't sure that was a good thing. That would mean I had left one royal family just to become entangled with another. By the looks of Whispermere, it was magnificent, but I had issues with the way it was run.

If we hadn't believed them when they'd told us a feast was being prepared, we believed them once they carried it out. Ten men, each carrying a tray stuffed with food, filed out of the nearby doorway. My stomach grumbled as my eyes feasted upon the food before it could. They served meats, vegetables, fruits, and cheeses, prepared exorbitantly with fresh herbs that I was sure did not grow within a reasonable traveling distance from here.

One man left the room and returned with a bottle of wine, which he promptly poured for each of us. Another set plates and silverware before us, all made of solid gold.

"Excuse me," I spoke to the worker nearest me, as he put Nyx's plate on the table.

"Yes, Miss Sera?"

"Will my mother be joining us?"

"Not for dinner, no. We will take you to her after your meal."

I tried not to be disappointed by that. I was overeager to meet her, and I had to imagine she felt the same about me. We had come so far, and it had taken so much time to get here that she was probably just getting prepared. She'd had so little time since we'd first arrived at the gates.

"How do they get such varieties of food all the way up here?" Theron pondered, examining his forkful of roast beef.

"I don't care how they do it," Nyx replied, continuing to stuff her face and gulp her wine. She wasn't one to drink wine, but she'd been without alcohol since Thornwell, so she drank it like fresh water in the desert. "It's delicious."

The food *was* delicious. I sampled a little bit of everything. Pork chops marinated in a maple glaze, cooked with bright green, roasted brussels sprouts. Grilled fish in lemon spruced up with bright green herbs. Roasted asparagus with a sweet balsamic vinegar glaze. Pies made with berries I'd never seen before, juices of various colors spilling out onto the plate.

We ate until we were gluttonous embarrassments, and even when we finished, the table was plentiful with food. Nyx and I leaned back in our chairs, fatigued with eating. Nyx glanced past me to Cerin, whose wine glass was still full.

"You going to drink that?" she asked.

"No, go ahead," he replied, passing it to her.

"Thanks, bud." Nyx downed the drink within a breath. When she still looked thirsty, I offered her the rest of mine, since I'd only drank half. She took it gratefully.

All the men who served us earlier filed into the room again to clean up after us.

"Who made all that food?" Nyx asked bluntly.

"We did, Miss," the closest man replied, bowing toward her. "Was it to your—"

"It was fucking delicious," my friend replied, before a pleasured sigh.

The man looked shocked at her response, but he bowed again anyway. "Thank you, Miss."

One worker walked over to me, bowing down beside my ear. "Your mother will see you now, Miss Sera," he said.

My heart picked up its pace. "My friends are coming with me," I informed him, remembering the exchange earlier at the gate.

"Yes, she allows this." *Allows*. What interesting word usage.

The five of us stood up, and we followed the man through the doorway we'd entered earlier and back up the steps. When we reached the floor leveled with the outside, he continued to lead us up past more stories until he finally stopped. At the top of the stairs was a thick wooden door. White with gold trim, like everything else.

I glanced around the wall of the stairwell, finding even more steps. "There are many floors here," I commented, trying to get my mind off of meeting my mother for the first time.

"Yes," the man replied, before knocking on the door twice. Footsteps padded toward us from the other side. "Floors continue to the top of the mountain. Whispermere has fifty in all. Fifteen above the bridge, thirty-five below."

"...wow." That new information made me realize that everything outdoors was not the actual village of Whispermere, but just a ridiculously large patio.

I heard a lock sliding out of place, and I focused on the door, my heart raging in my ears. It before us, and a young woman, her skin gold like the rest, answered the door. She nodded toward me.

"Come," she said simply. The man who led us here had already disappeared down the steps from where we'd come. I hadn't seen him leave.

I followed the woman through the door. This was a large room, with higher ceilings than the other floors, and a deep red rug stretched from the door to the other side. Unlike the other stories, this floor had no hallways, no extra rooms. The level *was* the room.

My eyes caught on what appeared to be a throne, sitting against the other wall at the end of the red-carpeted path. Upon it was a woman. My heart beat even harder, feeling as if it was tripping over itself.

The walk toward her was impossibly slow. The closer we walked, the more I saw of her, and the more I realized this could not possibly be my mother.

She dressed in an immaculate golden gown, the V-neck of it barely containing her large breasts, which were apparently a source of pride for her as she puffed her chest outward like the only rooster of a coop. The fabric cut diagonally across her legs, showing more of her right leg than her left, which she had crossed. A golden band with a rainbow of gemstones across the front covered a strip of her hair, which was as black as night, like Cerin's; her eyes were metallic gold, unlike anyone else I'd ever seen—save for myself. Her skin was the same almond cream as my own, but was free from imperfection, unlike mine, which had freckles speckled across my forearms. Her toenails were painted gold and showed themselves beneath the golden strap of a pair of heels that defied the laws of physics with their height.

The woman and I had our similarities, but she was so far removed from how I viewed myself that I refused to believe she was my mother. I knew for a fact, however, that this woman was the ruler of Whispermere. She was sitting on a throne, after all, and she was the only one whose skin wasn't painted. But she could not be my mother. She appeared to only be in her early thirties.

Our guide left us just a few meters from the woman in the throne. If I were to prove to this woman that I came from royalty, the time was now.

"I am Kai Sera," I greeted her, my voice clear and confident. "I am looking for my mother."

The woman smiled, her eyes moving from me to each of my companions, before coming back to me. The smile was not one of happiness, but amusement. "And you have found her."

An ache lodged in my gut. "Have I?"

"Why yes," the woman replied, before chuckling. The gold-painted fingernails of her right hand drummed along the armrest of her throne. "My dear."

Questions and confusion overwhelmed me, and what made it worse was that this woman seemed to delight in it. "You are too young to be my mother," I protested, desperate for answers.

"Am I?" She laughed heartily like this was the most amusement she'd had in a while.

"You are not elven," I said, staring at her human ears.

"No, I am not. But you, daughter, *are* a half-breed."

This information only served to further confuse me. I stood there for awhile, silent, my mind sorting through possibilities at incredible rates. The woman before me looked human. She admitted she wasn't elven. She was too tall and thin to be dwarven. She was not some beastman race that I had only heard stories of.

"I will tell you my name, child, so that we may hurry this along," she said, uncrossing her legs just to switch to her other hip and recross them. "I am Nanya."

Nyx gasped softly behind me. It made me realize just where I'd heard the name before.

"You are named after the goddess of lust," I said, my words nothing but desperate rambles. "I don't understand—"

"Oh, dear *child,*" Nanya replied, rolling her eyes with impatience. "I did not expect you to be so daft." She sighed and sat up straighter, the eyes that perfectly matched mine looking over me. "Kai, you are a god."

Fifteen

Nanya's words echoed in my mind over and over while refusing to fade in strength. The room spun around me. I was getting all the answers I ever sought, and I hated them more than I could have ever imagined.

My mother watched me process this information, but no one said a word. The only person in our group I knew to believe in the gods at all was Silas. Nyx had often jokingly thanked Nanya for the successful sexual experiences in her life, but I figured that was due to an association with her as a child, as the Alderi worshiped the goddess.

I heard my friends awkwardly shift behind me and knew the silence became overbearing. None of them spoke out of respect for me. Nanya, however, expected an answer, and by the looks of it, it annoyed her that I hadn't immediately celebrated.

I finally replied to her, and the word echoed loudly against the chamber's walls. *"Bull*shit."

Nanya's perfectly groomed eyebrows rose. *"Excuse* me?"

"I don't believe in the gods," I said, our golden eyes locked and growing in hostility.

Nanya laughed heartily, though her eyes were wide with disbelief. "You do not? I am sitting here in front of you. Tell me, are you both dumb *and* blind?"

"You look as human as anyone else. If you are a god, what are your powers?" I prodded.

Nanya looked offended. "I have no need to prove my powers to you."

"Then I suppose I have no need to believe what you say. Perhaps you are not a god, but a scam artist."

"You are testing my patience, *child.*" The last word was barely more than a hiss. "I can make any mortal fall in love with me, for so long as they are not romantically attached."

I raised one eyebrow. "Can you?"

"Yes." Nanya scanned her eyes over our group. "And I can sense that only one of you is untied from romance."

One of us? I thought over our group, mainly of Theron and Nyx. Either Nanya was incorrect, or we had secrets amongst ourselves.

"I am unimpressed, Nanya," I replied. "You have a power that benefits only you. My friend Silas, here, can understand plant-life. Does that make him a god? Theron can brew potions that can heal or poison the body. Does that make him a god? Nyx can see clearly in the dark. Does that make her a god? Cerin can raise the dead. Does that make him a god?"

Nanya's nostrils flared. "They are not gods, for I do not know them."

"And you know *all* the gods?"

"Many, yes. They have existed for hundreds or even thousands of years. We are discouraged from breeding. It is why you were taken to Sera."

For once, my anger subsided during our conversation, paving the way once more for curiosity and desperation. "Why do I exist?"

"Because I had sex with a man who was more powerful than I knew," Nanya replied. "I did not think I could breed with mortals. He appeared mortal. *Human*, even." The word *human* dripped with disgust. "I don't know what he was. All I knew was that I was pregnant and it wasn't supposed to happen. I have bedded thousands of men and have never been pregnant."

"Perhaps he had golden eyes," I said. "Perhaps he was one of your breed."

"*Breed*? You would mock the gods?"

"I do not mock them," I replied evenly. "I simply call them out for what I see them as. Just another race. There is nothing that makes you special from any other."

Nanya's jaw stiffened. "If you want any more answers from me, I suggest you respect my position."

"I will respect it as I respect anyone else's," I retorted.

My mother and I stared at each other for a long while, before she finally broke, looking away and laughing. "Perhaps I should be thankful you did not turn out to be weak and subservient," she mused. "Your attitude causes me to believe you have gotten more of my blood in you than it appears."

I wasn't sure whether to take that as an insult. "Than it appears? Do I look more like my father?"

Her eyes fell upon me once more. "Very much so, yes. But I would not go so far as to call him your father."

I frowned. "Why? That makes no sense."

"He is a *man*, Kai," she replied, glancing over my male friends in disgust. "He is not worthy of such a title."

I tilted my head in confusion. "You have something against men," I stated. Between her words and how I saw them treated throughout Whispermere, it dawned on me as an indisputable fact.

"They are weak, filthy creatures," Nanya replied like she thought I would agree. "I am, frankly, offended you would bring three to my court. They are the first men who have been in this room since we built it."

"Why was it not women, then, who built this place?" I asked. "Why did you *need* men to build it for you?"

"Men built it for me because they are mentally weak," Nanya retorted in a hiss. "They will agree to anything if there is a chance for sex."

"That is why they are in servitude to you here," I replied, understanding. "You make them fall in love with you so they'll stay and worship you for the slight chance of being in bed with a goddess."

A smirk rose one side of her lips. "Perhaps you are not so daft."

"I am *not* daft, no. I have seen this situation before. There have been whores for as long as there have been people. It is your sexism that gives me confusion. Are you so angry with men because you desire them and your ego won't allow you to place the blame on yourself? The feast you fed us was *magnificent,* mother. Surely, you could find some sort of oblong vegetable that could satisfy your need."

Nanya watched me, silent, her lips pursed and eyebrow twitching. Her long fingernails still tapped patterns over her armrest. Finally, her golden eyes focused on those behind me.

"Leave us."

"They come with me wherever I go," I said, feeling as if I were on repeat.

"Then you will *all* leave," Nanya replied.

"Very well." I turned toward my friends. Everyone was flabbergasted at our situation, and I couldn't blame them. My mind swirled with repeats of our conversation, feeling foggy with an influx of information.

"Kai." It echoed off the chamber walls. I turned back toward my mother, who appeared angry but conflicted. "We will never come to terms with one another. I see that, now. But there are things I need to tell you, and I don't trust your friends."

I thought about this for a moment. The plea seemed genuine. "I will not be alone with you."

Nanya nodded. "Fine. Bring one friend. Tomorrow morning, I will send someone for you. For tonight, I've had rooms prepared for you in the levels below. Talk to the servants if you need anything—food, hot baths, bedding—they all know why you are here and have been instructed to treat you like me."

For a moment, I felt enough sympathy for my mother to almost like her. She had clearly tried to impress me on my visit. Maybe she'd had the same wishes for a relationship as I'd had. At this point, most of that had gone out the window. We were too different. She was not even a person I felt I could come to admire. I thought of all the men forced into servitude here, all for the slight chance of being with someone they thought they loved. It made me sick. There were many men in my life I loved or at least cared deeply for and admired. Bjorn, Terran, Silas, Cerin, and now, Theron...even imagining them being treated in such a way disgusted and angered me.

"Thank you," I finally replied, though my mind was elsewhere. My mother nodded, and then I turned away once more. I followed my friends back out of the long room, where a male servant greeted us at the door and led us down some floors to our rooms.

Five rooms were prepared for us, all blocks etched out of stone and each with its own lockable door, which I was thankful for given I didn't trust this place. Nyx insisted I take the farthest room away from the stairway so that if my mother or her servants tried anything, they would have to walk past all other rooms to get to me.

It was a relief to drop most of my things down onto the ground and have somewhere to keep them. I pushed most of my things under the bed: loot, extra purses of gold looted from the wyvern's lair, and a knapsack full of belongings. The bathtub was large and inviting, but I skipped on that for now. The others and I had plans to get together on the open part of the mountain peak tonight, for we had a lot to talk *about*.

I did take advantage of the personal toilet in the room, noting how the hole for it looked like it drained to the next floor down. It was nice not to have to squat to go to the bathroom for once. When I was done, I took the water bucket nearby and poured the liquid around the edges of the bowl, doing my part to keep it clean.

Next, I stripped my armor off carefully and laid it out to dry from my sweat on the floor. The servant who had led us here offered to do our laundry if we left it outside our doors tonight, which was a relief. My underclothes smelled of long days of travel, and I wasn't really willing to change into my clean pair until I'd had a bath.

Knock-knock.

I glanced toward the door, before grabbing my cloak and pulling it over me to prepare for the cold of the outdoors if it was Nyx telling me to come out with them. Holding the two sides of the cloak together in front of my undershirt with one hand, I opened the door with the other.

Theron stood just outside, alone. He appeared a little embarrassed that he'd caught me without my armor. When camping, I usually waited to take it off until I was in my tent, so he'd never seen me like this.

"I apologize for disturbing you, Kai. I can come back."

"Nonsense. I'm just relaxing." I glanced to the side of him where no one else stood. "Are we going outside?"

"Not yet," Theron replied, glancing down the hall to his left where the other rooms were. "I wondered if I could speak with you."

That was odd. Theron had never requested this before. It made me wonder if something was wrong until I remembered hiring him back in Sera and our deal for him to bring us here to Whispermere. My stomach ached. He probably wanted the remainder of his pay so he could be on his way.

I nodded and moved to the side of my doorway. "Come in."

Theron chuckled low as he walked past me into my room. "You are...unconventional."

I closed the door to give us some privacy before turning to face him. "Should I apologize for that?"

"No, not at all." He leaned his tall form back against the stone wall. Theron was usually quiet and did not speak unless he felt he needed to. Still, he looked hesitant to talk now despite having something on his mind.

"Are you leaving us?" I asked him, in case he didn't want to say it.

Theron's eyes flicked up to mine. "While that *is* what I wanted to speak with you about, that's not the option I'm considering. Your..." he trailed off, his hand grazing along the handle of his right blade absentmindedly, "...offer from Sera...does it still stand?"

"Both do. If you were looking to leave us, I could pay you here. If you wanted to stay, you are more than welcome." I observed him carefully, unsure which he wanted.

"You have said nothing about keeping me in your company, and you have hired Cerin on. I thought, perhaps, you had no need of me. Particularly after my failure with the wyvern." Theron slowly met my gaze again, looking humbled.

"I have said nothing about keeping you because I felt no need to clarify it," I replied. "I want you to stay, and the others feel likewise. If hiring Cerin makes you fear for your share of the gold, we can—"

"No, that didn't cross my mind," Theron admitted. "My back aches each day with what loot and gold I have made with you. More would be a burden, particularly with nowhere to spend it."

"I am sure our travels will take us to merchants in the future," I mused.

Theron noted my wording. "If you would have me, I'd like to stay with you for that."

"Then there's no discussion, Theron. You will be there."

The ranger smiled. "You treat your mercenaries as friends. One could get used to that."

"What mercenaries?" I retorted lightly, glancing around the room as if searching. "There are only friends here." I ducked to the ground, grabbing one of my coin purses. "I will pay you the remainder of your fee now, and then we will never speak of this *mercenary* business again."

Theron held out a hand. "Keep it, friend. Don't burden me further."

The coin purse stilled in my hands. "You would burden *me?*"

Theron laughed. "Out of all the burdens you have now, that is a good one to have. Make it up to me at the next tavern, then. We'll go drinking. Pick up the tab."

I smiled. "Very well."

Within minutes of Theron leaving my room, Nyx knocked at my door to ask if I was ready to go outside. We headed through the hallway and to the main level, where we walked back out onto the open half of the peak. The sun was halfway through setting, the red orb the majority of the way below the line of clouds before us. The sky ahead was a mix of corals, oranges, and bright pinks. Above, the dark, navy blue of the night was chasing soft lavenders toward the horizon.

Near the stone railing to our right, an all-female band was playing a happy ditty, utilizing a lute, flute, and two drums. Before them, some women danced together, while many others were enjoying the music while eating at cafe tables surrounded by hedge bushes and flower pots. Male servants served both food and drink to the women, while others scurried around the stone railing and the wall of the other half of the peak, lighting sconces.

We headed to where there were two empty cafe tables we could scoot together. It was close enough to enjoy both the music and the sunset, while we could still talk. Within seconds of sitting together, a male servant hurried over, asking us if we needed food or drink. Though we'd had our feast not long before, the journey had been long and short of cooked food, so we ordered some. Nyx, Theron, and I ordered exotic ales, while Silas and Cerin ordered natural drinks.

They brought the food and drinks out to us before we had even started our conversation. When the male servant turned to leave us, I reached out and grabbed his arm to stop him.

"I apologize, Miss Sera. I didn't know you had need of me." He turned to face me, though, of course, he did not meet my eyes. His voice trembled like he thought I would be angry with him.

"What is your name?" I asked him, ducking lower to look him in the eyes. He cowered back.

"My name is of no importance. Please, do not concern yourself with such frivolities."

"I asked for your name," I repeated with authority. "And please, look me in the eyes when you say it."

"I am Fri'er, but I may not look you in the eye. Forgive me." The man shook like I terrified him.

"Why are you here, Fri'er?" I asked, my voice calm.

"I serve people here. It is my job. I bring food and drink out from the cooks to the people who order them. I have done this for twenty years." It was a confused ramble. A single tear fell down the man's painted cheek and I wondered if it was due to his fear of speaking with me or his circumstances.

"No, I meant in Whispermere. What brought you here?"

"I must confess it was the offering of a place to stay for my work, Miss Sera. I was homeless on the outskirts of Comercio. There was a man asking for volunteers. Offered me a place to stay. Said it was beautiful. And it is. Whispermere is beautiful."

How could he have known? The man did not lift his eyes from the rock below us. "Do you like it here, Fri'er?"

He nodded enthusiastically. "Oh, I do, Miss Sera. Your mother is a wonderful woman. She keeps us moving and well-fed. She is so kind to us. So kind."

My brow furrowed. "You love her," I said because it was obvious and he wouldn't say it.

"Oh, I do. Very much. So much it feels like my chest will burst. But I am not special—we all love her here. Nanya is wonderful."

"You could leave, Fri'er," I commented, still attempting unsuccessfully to look him in the eye. "Work for gold. Buy a little plot of land and find a partner and family who will love you back and treat you right."

"No...no, Miss Sera. I cannot leave Nanya. The heartbreak alone would kill me before I could pass the gate."

I exhaled slowly before I finally looked away. "Thank you for your time, Fri'er. That is all."

The servant hurried away, and I faced my friends. They had been eating and drinking while listening to my conversation with the man.

"Whatever my mother is, her power is true," I said, watching as Nyx scooted her glass of ale toward me, and motioned for me to try it. As usual, we had ordered two different types. I took a sip of hers and squinted as the vile liquid tore past my tongue and down my throat. "That is rank," I blurted like a curse, pushing it back.

Nyx chuckled. "I thought you'd say that," she teased, before taking another swig.

"You don't believe she is a god?" Theron questioned, cutting some meat before him with a knife.

"She can call herself that all she wants. I will call her a god, sure, but it is only a race like any other. Gods can die. We've all heard the legends of gods fighting for power and killing each other. She called us mortals, but she is not *immortal.*" I hesitated. "The gods are not all-powerful beings who should be worshiped. They are an ancient race whose pride in themselves has never been challenged."

"It is a wonder that you believe that, given you would otherwise have been able to wield your identity as a weapon," Theron mused.

"I see what identity politics can do to people," I replied. "Like my mother. Her arrogance has swelled her head to where it is a tumor. She is one of the most sexist people I have ever met. She uses her race and her gender to control and hurt people. I *pity* her. She loathes men so much, yet she doesn't see the irony in resorting to her magic to get them to love her. Perhaps she is afraid that without her spell, they would find nothing about her to love."

"The only thing I liked about her was her dress," Nyx blurted, which caused me to laugh at the unexpected jab.

"Well..." I trailed off and shrugged when my friend glanced over. "Those heels were interesting, too."

Nyx lifted her mug in a toast. "Impractical, though."

"And the dress *wasn't?*" No one I had ever known wore a dress. They were reserved for those who didn't work and had the money with which to spend on a piece of clothing they could only ever wear to social gatherings of the wealthy.

"It sounds like she has something important to tell you tomorrow," Cerin pointed out across the table from me. His pitch black hair appeared almost like a deep red in the sunset's light.

"Yes, well...we'll see about that. I want to learn more about my father. Perhaps I can find him."

"Kai...don't expect a happy reunion," Nyx warned me. "If your father is a god like your mother, he might be just as awful as she is."

"He can't be a god," I retorted, though I understood her concern. "Nanya said she knows most of the gods. She would have known him. Instead, she thought he was mortal."

"That's assuming we believe her," Silas pointed out.

I sighed, frustrated with the excess of information swirling around my head and the lack of answers to my questions. "I don't know. Perhaps I'll just have to make sense of it when I talk to her again tomorrow."

Tomorrow. After half a year of traveling to get here, waiting another day for answers I still might not get was tortuous. Still, it gave me something to focus on so I could ignore my immense disappointment from meeting my mother. I wondered who she was my whole life. Now that I knew, it felt like the worse of two options. Perhaps I would have been better off not knowing.

Sixteen

"Your mother is waiting." The male servant nodded toward Nyx, who had waited for his arrival with me in my room. "Is this the companion you're bringing?"

"Yes."

"Follow me." He turned and we hurried to catch up, closing the door to my room behind us.

This time, we were led to the top floor of Whispermere, where there were no more staircases leading upward. We were likely at the peak of the mountain. At the top of the last steps, there was a thick wooden door. The servant knocked. This time, instead of footsteps, we heard my mother's voice.

"Come in."

The servant opened the door for us while waiting in the stairwell. Nyx and I walked into what must have been Nanya's personal quarters. It had a cathedral ceiling, mimicking the peak of the mountain itself. The first thing that demanded my attention was the gigantic bed just before us. It was large enough to sleep five people with room left over and clad in thick red blankets. A variety of red and dark gray pillows adorned it. White lace drapes flowed from a canopy above the bed.

There was a large porcelain tub in the room's corner. On the walls above it were mirrors that stretched from just above the tub to five feet above it. Vines of fresh red flowers adorned the borders of the mirrors. A globe of Arrayis sat near me to the right, next to a plush red velvet couch. Bookshelves aligned the wall before the couch, filled with a variety of texts. On a table before the sofa sat a tray, little bowls of sugar and tea leaves upon it.

Across from her library was Nanya's closet. She had floor to ceiling cabinets made of thick wood that appeared to be tinted red. I wasn't sure if it was a dye or if the wood came from a particular tree. In either case, both cabinets were full of clothing, their doors open. Most of her outfits were gowns, some completely sheer.

On either side of her room, someone had removed the stone walls, leading to two balconies carved right into the side of the mountain. The railings of her balconies were pure, clear glass, allowing it to seem like there were no walls at all keeping her from the sky. I couldn't imagine how hard it must have been to import glass up this mountain without breaking it. My mother stood on the balcony to our left, barely visible from through a sheer red curtain separating the outside from her room. A steaming mug was in her hand while she looked out over the morning sky.

Only when Nyx and I made no move to walk farther into her room did she turn to us. Nanya looked pleased to see that my companion was Nyx. It was the primary reason I'd picked her to come with me. I didn't want the men to have to withstand Nanya's sexism.

"Come," she said, motioning toward the balcony before her, where a small table and chairs sat overlooking the clouds. "We may sit and talk."

We made our way over to her where we sat at the small table overlooking the clouds. Glancing up, I saw that we were just meters below the peak of the mountain. With the glass as our only barrier to the sky, it took my breath away. It was beautiful here.

Nanya pointed out over the layer of clouds. "That is west," she informed us. "That is the way you came from. I haven't watched the sunrise in many weeks because I came to this balcony every morning. I would come here because I knew you were on your way."

There was a certain longing in her voice which broke my heart. She, too, had anticipated this meeting. I was sure by now that we had both disappointed each other.

Nanya took one last look out over the clouds before pulling out the one empty chair and sitting down. She was dressed in a flowing white gown. It appeared she had slept in it. Throughout my time in Whispermere, I had never seen her outside of the mountain with everyone else. I wondered if she got lonely.

"You do not approve of my ways," Nanya said, avoiding my gaze by continuing to look at the view through the glass. "But it is the way I have lived for nearly six hundred years. I will live like this for six hundred more."

"I *don't* approve of your ways, and I certainly don't approve of the way you run Whispermere or treat its people," I replied. "But I understand it is not my place to ask you to change."

"Yes, I know. As I cannot ask you to understand, or change, or do anything you do not wish to do." Nanya finally turned to face me. Much of the arrogance that had been in her eyes the day before was temporarily gone. "You are like me, Kai. Stubborn. A natural leader. Staunch in your beliefs. I respect that. It is the first time I have seen it in a long while. You angered me yesterday with your words. After some thought, I realized I welcome that. No one has dared to challenge me for a long time, and I have become bored."

"I was harsh with you," I agreed. "But I believe you deserve it."

Nanya laughed before looking away again. "There it is again. That spark." After a lengthy exhale, she said, "Go on, then. Tell me where you want me to begin."

"From the beginning," I said. "Tell me of my father. Tell me why I ended up on the steps of Seran University. Tell me how you know of my life and why assassins are sent after me. Tell me why I have the power I do and what I need to know about having the blood of the gods."

Nanya raised her eyebrows as if these were hefty requests. "Hmm. Your...*father.*" It was clear she still had her biases, but she continued after a moment all the same. "He appeared at the gate one day, seeking shelter on his way to Brognel. I happened to see him there and found him attractive, so I told the servants to let him in. He wasn't the most muscular of men, but I noticed he had rings on all his fingers, much like you. And a head full of the reddest hair I'd ever seen." She paused. "I think that is why I slept with him. My favorite color is red."

That would have been humorous to me if it hadn't been so sad. "He is a mage," I deduced.

"Was a mage, yes."

My heart split in two. "How did he die?"

"I'll get to that, child," Nanya replied, slightly annoyed. "So, he was a mage. A dual caster, in fact. Fire and life magic if I remember correctly. He told me about how he was more of a scientist of magic than a battlemage. He studied it. Made some discoveries. Claimed he had an entire town named after him for it out west."

My mind raced through possibilities. "Arturian Kilgor?"

Nanya snapped her fingers. "Ah. *Yes*. That's the name. That's your father."

I felt a little light-headed. One of the most applauded mages of all time was my father. The discoverer of the Kilgorian Law, something all mages knew by heart. We'd had painted portraits of him up in the Seran University. As a young girl, I had liked his paintings best because he had bright red hair like mine. If only I had known...

"Wait...Arturian Kilgor died forty years ago," I pointed out, remembering reading about it. "He was assassinated for his work."

"Is that what they taught you at the university?" Nanya asked.

"...Yes," I admitted, confused.

"Well, the date is probably correct. I was pregnant for a good many years. I didn't really know when I would finally give birth because it was untested."

"Gods do not give birth to other gods?" I questioned.

"Rarely. Many gods were created by the Ancients, not birthed. Gods can breed, but only with each other. At least, until you came along. In any case, I was pregnant by a man who was not a god. In total, I carried you in my womb for sixty years. As soon as I could get someone to come here and tell me who the father was, I did so. I sent a messenger out to your father to give him the news and tell him I would adopt you out. The messenger came back to me and told me your father insisted on

241

taking you. Arturian felt you would get magical abilities from him and wanted to raise you as his own."

"Why didn't he, then?" I asked, saddened. To know my biological father wanted me and was now dead was extremely upsetting. I'd always wanted a parent who *wanted* me.

"Well, first of all, the messenger said that Arturian was human. In the thirty-something years it had been since I'd seen him, he aged tremendously and was partially into his old age. I did not know when I would give birth to you. I could not promise him anything, and I knew that wouldn't sit well with him. He was a scientist—a man who sought answers. I knew he would be a thorn in my side." She paused. "Also, the other gods were angry with me for being pregnant. If I had the baby, and they *knew* about it, they would come to kill you. I couldn't have Arturian going around bragging about how you were a half-breed with the blood of a god."

I didn't like what I was hearing. "But the gods *knew* you were pregnant. They knew you were going to have me."

"Yes, but they thought I would kill you as an infant. I've never had any qualms about killing nuisances, and the others knew I wanted no children. It was a given I would kill you. Speaking of which, I had your father killed." She glanced at Nyx. "By an Alderi not dissimilar to yourself."

I swallowed hard. *"You* had him assassinated? For *wanting* me?"

"I did him a *service,* Kai," Nanya retorted. "The man was old and decrepit. He was going to die before long, anyway, and I didn't give birth to you for another twenty years. Arturian would have spent the rest of his miserable life wanting answers I could not give him."

I knew she had a point, but I was too upset to acknowledge it. I could not cry for my father because I did not know him; instead, I felt distraught and conflicted, and found yet another thing to resent my mother for.

"Why didn't you just kill *me*, then?" I asked. "Why did you have me and send me to Sera?"

Nanya shrugged and smiled. "Because I wanted to see what would happen."

"...That's it?"

"Yes. I'm admittedly proud that I'm the only god to ever breed with a mortal. I didn't know what to expect of you. I figured Arturian was right, that you would have magical abilities like he did. So I sent one of my servants to Sera with you where he hired a mercenary to take you to the university steps. Then, I waited." Nanya paused. "To answer your question on how I know so much about you, I have had servants and messengers relaying messages to me of your upbringing your entire life. I knew we were in for some trouble when you found out you could wield all elements when you were fourteen. You had Arturian's abilities, but it seemed as though they were amplified by my superior blood. Word spread to the other gods, who put two and two together and realized you were my child."

"So they decided to have me assassinated."

"Well, *yes*, but given your prestigious position in Sera, that was harder to do than they anticipated. They sent messengers to Sera, warning Sirius that if he didn't kill you, he would incur the wrath of the gods."

My heart skipped a beat. "My *father* Sirius?"

"Yes, dear. So when you were sixteen, Sirius hired the Alderi to assassinate you."

Time slowed. My heart pounded so hard that it throbbed in my ears and rattled my head. In my brain, I connected dots, followed timelines. I turned to Nyx, who looked just as shocked as I felt. "My *father* hired you."

Nyx looked taken aback. "Your father hired the *Alderi,* Kai. They just picked me for the job. I had no idea. They never told us the client. Only the target."

Nanya's eyebrows were raised when I turned back to her. "My, my. You keep odd company."

Nyx told my mother of our connection before turning back to me, noticing I was still quiet. "Kai, if I knew Sirius was the one who put the hit on your head, I would have said something. You *know* how much I hate him."

"I don't doubt you, Nyx. It is my..." I trailed off. I had almost said *father*, but given the new information, that left a sour taste in my mouth. "It's Sirius's actions that have me quiet." My friend visibly exhaled with relief beside me, having been distraught by thoughts of me loathing her. I tried to focus back on my mother. "I don't understand, though. When Nyx failed to assassinate me, he threw her in prison and hired Silas as my bodyguard. Why would he do that if he wanted me dead?"

"Sirius wanted you dead for a time," Nanya replied. "I don't know everything about your adoptive father save for what I've been told by those who have come across him. What I *do* know is that the attempt failed, obviously, and Sirius was angry at the loss of gold. Either he told the other gods to do it or he told them to fuck themselves because I haven't heard him attempt to hire anyone again. Rumors say he uses you as a bargaining chip for Sera, however."

I frowned. "How so?"

"You are the most powerful weapon in his arsenal, my dear, and one that cannot be replicated. In Chairel's talks with other countries, your name is thrown around as a benefit to allies or a threat to enemies. Since you were fourteen, Sirius rose to be Queen Edrys's favorite regent, and all because he has you."

"Had," I corrected in anger.

"Yes, well..." Nanya trailed off and then narrowed her eyes. "What did you tell him about your coming here?"

"I told him nothing. I just left. He would have eventually found out where I was headed because I told my brother." *Terran.* My heart ached with longing. How I missed him, and how I wished I could give him the information I had now.

"Be careful, daughter. I don't know whether Sirius would look to capture you or kill you, but I do know he would want to be in control of the situation either way."

I nodded. It seemed like my quest to find a loving parent had only made me realize the parental figures in my life were all terrible. *Except for Arturian,* I thought. But he was dead.

"Tell me what I need to know about having your blood," I said, next. Now that I knew the truth about my background and my so called *father,* I needed to know what I was capable of so I could do something about it. I didn't intend to stay quiet or docile about his wrongdoings against me, and open dissent had never gone over well in Chairel.

"Ah. Well, given you are a half-breed of the type which has never been seen before, I don't know for certain. I do know you will have a much longer life than any human, but since you are half-human, you won't live nearly as long as the gods. I already know that by looking at you."

"I think I look twenty-one," I replied because that was how old I was. Nanya made it seem like I looked older for my age.

"Yes, and you look it. I am six hundred and two, child, and it took me nearly sixty years just to look fully grown." Nanya hesitated. "Of course, elves come to maturity within twenty years like humans and have longer lifespans. I guess we never know, do we?"

"How old do you expect me to reach before old age?" I asked her.

"I would guess six hundred. I expect to reach two thousand years old or so, and it looks like you're aging at three times my rate. Like I said, though, a guess." Nanya shrugged.

Six hundred. The possibilities that came to my mind with all the time I hadn't known I had were varied and exciting. It should have occurred to me the day before that my lifespan would be longer given my mother's youth, but maybe it was too much for my brain to handle considering all the life changes I was going through. A burden the size of Arrayis lifted off my shoulders. I didn't have to worry anymore about which day would be my last for merely living and practicing my skills.

"There is one last thing I think we should discuss, daughter," Nanya went on when I had been lost in my thoughts. "I feel I already know your answer, but in my letter, I mentioned that you had possibilities open to you."

I nodded, though the letter was so vague in my memories now. I remembered that most of the message dealt with my powers, and not with the fact that we were mother and daughter separated by distance. The tone of it made sense, now.

I was sitting right next to my mother, but the gap between us wasn't any shorter.

"You have the abilities of a god, Kai. You may have human blood, but you also have mine." Nanya looked over me for a moment. "You have my eyes...the eyes of a god. For all I know, you are just a mistake of nature from two vastly different races, but it matters not, because you are here and there is only one like you. You *are* a god. I say that not because you are my daughter, but because I know of your powers."

I stayed quiet, waiting for her to finish. I knew I was more than human now, but I did not place such importance on my bloodline. I was used to wielding the six elements; knowing why didn't change how I thought of myself or my powers.

"Because you are a half-breed, the other gods want you eradicated. What you are and what you signify defies one of the greatest laws of our kind. I have faith, however, that we may reason with them."

"What are you suggesting?" I asked. I certainly had no idea how to reason with gods. It was hard enough to find one, let alone tell them apart from the crowd.

"I suggest that you join us, child," Nanya replied as if it were obvious. "Together, we could perhaps convince them to leave you be."

"How can I *join* you? I am already one of you, by your own words."

"You have our blood running through your veins, nothing more. I do not pretend to know what you intend to do with your life, but anything more than a quiet one will anger the gods. We do not live like mortals. If you were to live with me, here, or even create your own home somewhere peacefully, perhaps they will see that effort as making amends."

I couldn't help but feel insulted. "I have no need to make amends. I have done nothing to them. If they are angry with me for simply existing, they can come down from their high horses and fight me themselves."

Nanya sighed. "Were you named *Kai* for your ability to wield fire or your disposition? All you think of is fighting."

"No, I simply won't be controlled. If the gods are pretentious enough to sit comfortably at home while convincing the man who raised me to assassinate me, *I* am not the one who needs to make amends. If they were to ever try to finish the job, I will defend myself. Something tells me they'll be too lazy to do anything about it."

"Think twice. Many gods live secretly among the mortals and would come for you in a heartbeat."

"*Let* them come."

Nanya looked away, back toward the mid-morning sky. "As you wish. You won't be staying here, I imagine. Tell me: what is it that you will do now?"

I watched my mother's face with an even stare. "Whatever it is I wish to," I replied. "I won't go into details with you, for I know if the gods want me dead and blame you for my existence, you have the incentive to help them find me."

Nanya turned to face me once more, a mischievous smile pulling up one side of her sultry lips. "You have come to know me so quickly, daughter."

Seventeen

After two nights in the village that rivaled the skies, we headed back the way we came. I had updated the others on what information I learned from Nanya on our first morning in Whispermere since none of them were there to hear it other than Nyx. They listened and offered their support. There was nothing any of them could do to ease my disappointment over learning my true parentage. There was nothing they could do to erase the anger I felt toward Sirius for raising me with scorn for years just to try to have me killed. The only positive thing that had come of the whole experience was learning my lifespan was not as finite as I initially thought.

My twenty-second birthday came and went midway through our trek back down the mountain which was quite the experience. Occurring close to the end of High Star, I was used to celebrating it in the blistering heat of Sera during peak festival season. This year, it was spent fighting to breathe as a blizzard wind refused to stop blasting me in the face with snow chunks so frigid and biting they tricked our brains into thinking they were hot. I was sure that if we'd been able to hear each other over the weather, Nyx would have been lamenting the lack of festivities. She'd always treated me to a night on the town in Sera, which was as much of a present to herself as it was to me.

By the time we finally reached the warmer embrace of the Seran Forest, it was early Red Moon. The trees grew sleepy from the cooler weather, injecting their leaves and pine needles with spouts of reds, oranges, and yellows. Even the long grasses had a yellowish hue. Gray skies, thick clouds, and stormy weather replaced blue skies and sunshine. Other than having to sleep in the rain, I loved the cooler, stormier weather. Red Moon had always been my favorite season. Not only were the colors so vibrant, but fierce storms were abundant with energy for mages.

The group of us followed along the edge of the Seran Forest, using the same route back toward Sera as we had taken to get to Whispermere. It was here that I finally broke the ice with my plans. I'd had an idea swimming around my head since that last talk with my mother, and so far, I'd been pretty vague with my friends on what I felt the future held for us. As far as they knew, my personal mission was over and we were about to embark on the mercenary life once we broke free of the forest and could find work. It was part of the reason I hadn't wanted to bring up my idea. It was yet another personal mission, and they'd already done so much for me.

We were sitting around a campfire eating. It seemed like the most talking we ever did as a group was during these times. There was a break in conversation, a comfortable silence. I blurted it out to get it over with.

"I'd like to return to Sera."

I received four intense stares, three of which stated I was crazy, and one of which was Theron, who seemed intrigued to know my reasons why. Cerin was most upset, which I could understand, though it pained me to see the look in his eyes turn to angered disbelief when he glared at me. While we talked often, he was always reserved, despite seeming to want to befriend me at the very least. Cerin was internally torn between trusting me or not. And now, here I was, suggesting we do the same thing I said I'd never do.

"I am *not* returning to Sera," Cerin protested, his voice heightened. "You said you never wanted to go back."

"I don't *want* to go back, but I feel I *need* to," I replied, having a hard time keeping eye contact with him out of shame.

"For *what?* Your funeral? Mine?"

"I left two men I love in Sera who both unwittingly do the bidding of a man who tried to have me assassinated," I said, my voice teetering on the edge of a plea. "I want to take them with us. Or, at the very least, inform them."

Cerin didn't reply. He knew what Bjorn meant to me. He also knew Terran from his time at the university. Anyone who had seen my brother and I together had to realize I adored him. Perhaps my brother's work ethic left much to be desired, but he had forever been a welcome reprieve from Sirius's scorn.

"Kai, you *have* to know neither will come with us," Silas said from across the fire, his voice lacking energy. He had been quieter than ever since Whispermere, looking as if he were always treading a fine line between feeling depressed or conflicted. "Bjorn has worked for your father for forty years. He is human and fast approaching sixty. The last thing he needs to do is go on a trek with us avoiding your father's armies, which he *will* send."

"Sirius *knows* how much I love Bjorn. For all I know, he could have found out that Bjorn knew about me leaving or even that he's the one who allowed the messenger from Whispermere to meet me." I frowned at Silas, desperate. "He could have thrown him in the Seran dungeon or worse. This is the man who tried to *assassinate* me, Silas!"

"And he's the same man who hired me, is he not?" Silas retorted. "You're assuming that everything your mother told you is correct. Why would he have gone to such precautions to prevent further assassination attempts if he had tried it

251

himself? Why would he let Nyx live after hiring her? For all we know, Nanya may *want* you to pick a fight with Sera."

"Sirius knew I didn't know he was the client, you *idiot,*" Nyx spoke up in my defense. "It would have been incredibly stupid of me to befriend Kai rather than kill her if I knew her father had hired me. And besides, Sirius is no stranger to the Alderi."

"How would you know that, if you never know the client?" Silas mocked in return.

"Because it was after I escaped the underground that I started noticing certain people popping up dead, all of whom would have been convenient for him. Do you remember Dali Miri? The protester who always paraded around in Comercio four years ago yelling about how her child died of a simple wound because she couldn't afford a healer from Sera?"

I stared into the campfire before me, remembering that woman's story all too well. It was yet another instance of the civilians of Chairel stoking the flames of rebellion, but in Dali Miri's case, her protests had been cut short. "She got an activist group together that called for affordable healing services and lower restrictions on magic licenses," I said softly.

"Yes, she did. Her main target was Sirius. Called him out for things time and time again. Held him responsible. Spread the message. Then—" Nyx swiped a deep purple hand across her throat. "By an Alderi blade, no less. And I could go on with others, but that's not really the point, is it? Kai's mother was many things, but she *wasn't* a liar. Nanya admitted to throwing her daughter out to the wild for the fun of it and to the possibility of helping other gods come find her in the future. She admitted to not knowing why Sirius tried to get Kai killed before simply using her as a pawn. She admitted when she didn't *have* the answers. But that was one answer she gave, and it was the *easiest* to believe." Nyx squinted her black eyes at Silas. "Perhaps if you didn't have your Celdic nose shoved so far up Sirius's ass you would see that."

There was silence, then, and my heart beat so hard I was sure the others could hear it. Nyx and Silas had always had their differences, and sometimes they'd argued, but Nyx had never gone this far. Perhaps she was fed up with him hurting me no matter how unintentional it was. She'd been angry with him for his words to me in the wyvern's lair all that time ago. I had told her about it after the fact and made her promise not to mention it. Maybe keeping quiet had allowed that anger to boil over.

"Your undying loyalty blinds you," Silas finally retorted, his voice trembling with held back anger.

"My loyalty to who?" Nyx asked, genuinely confused.

"Kai." When he said my name, I felt my heart drop. There was a pain in his voice...along with regret, and rage.

"If you are *not* loyal to her, maybe you need to move the fuck on," Nyx seethed.

Silas hesitated a moment, thinking through his words before saying them even when this angry. "You are helping her go down a dark path, Nyx, and you will come to regret it. Kai's decisions will get you killed. She is now a practicing necromancer and going back to Sera is a death sentence. For *all* of us." His intense green eyes moved to mine. "You used to want to help people, Kai. I don't know when you strayed so far from the path of righteousness."

Now it was *my* turn to be angry. "How *dare* you suggest I've changed, and all for practicing necromancy! It is for the sole purpose of *helping* those I love that I want to go back to Sera! Don't you think I'm *aware* they could catch us? Is it not a selfless act to risk my own well-being to go back? Your opinion of me must be so low as to suggest I'm on a *dark* path, Silas. Well, let me tell *you* what I think of you." I hesitated, before standing. The tinges of my vision were stained a blood-red. "You are a pretentious *coward* who is more concerned with telling me how to live my life than supporting me. I don't ask for your agreement. I ask for your support. It *sickens* me that you are so concerned for yourself that you would leave Bjorn and Terran to whatever fate Sirius has decided for them."

I walked off into the night, leaving the silence behind me. I needed to breathe. I needed to figure out what the hell was going on in my life. Just a year ago, Silas was one of my closest friends and greatest supporters. Life, then, seemed so much simpler. Maybe I hadn't known just how good I'd had it. Perhaps I had been in fear of an early death and avoided dealing with Sirius. But at least I could bask in ignorance to his true intentions, and I wasn't losing friends, and I could continue fantasizing about how great the mother I'd never met could be. That seemed like the better alternative.

I collapsed in the grasses when I was far enough away from the campsite not to hear Silas and Nyx's continued bickering. I focused on breathing, one inhale before a long exhale, over and over again, trying to clear my head. I'd hated bringing up my idea to the others, but I couldn't get past the sickening feeling that Bjorn and Terran were in danger. Perhaps not Terran—my brother was, after all, the heir to Sera.

254

But Bjorn...I had spent the better part of a year on the road, which was the longest I'd ever been from him. I longed for his strong embrace, the same one that comforted me as a child. Now that I knew both living parents of mine were awful, I longed to ask his permission to call him my father. After all, Bjorn was the only person in my life who deserved the title. It was a wonder he'd never had a brood of kids he could call his own; he was one of the few who would've been great at it.

There was a *swish* in the grasses behind me as I heard someone approach. I didn't turn to see who it was. I kept my eyes on the night sky, attempting to find peace in it.

"If we are to return to Sera, we have to keep our identities hidden." It was Cerin. Somehow, he was the last person I expected to follow me out here after the anxieties I'd just put him through.

"Yes..." I trailed off, my anger turning to sadness. It was the first time the consequences of my actions really hit me. The city in which I'd spent my childhood would no longer have my friends or me. My throat felt thick with tears I refused to shed. I didn't want to live in the city like I once did, but if I had, I couldn't.

"You have to realize that Sirius knows what I look like," Cerin continued. "I'm his most-wanted criminal. I've found death warrants with my face in the pockets of his men. They could either catch me or criminalize you for being with me. They don't yet know what I have taught you. You, *alone,* are safe."

"I will not run from you hoping to get a lesser sentence, Cerin," I replied, my voice thick with emotion. "If they want you, they must get through *me.* If they want *me,* I will not use your crimes as a shield. If we are never seen by anyone other than Terran and Bjorn, it will be for the best."

"The key is doing that successfully," he said. "If you do nothing else at all, I plead you to think twice about those you trust before you do this. It takes just one stab in the back for everything to unravel."

My stomach ached at his warning. "You do not trust me? Or Silas?"

"I don't trust many. Silas's loyalties are unclear to me. I've heard your love for your brother and Bjorn, but I have no reason to trust them, myself. Please understand that I must be leery." Cerin hesitated. "They love you, I'm sure of it, but they are both close to Sirius. Terran doesn't stand to gain anything with you, but a kingdom has been promised to him. As for Bjorn, who is to say he will not sabotage us simply because he wants to do what he thinks is best for you?"

I exhaled so hard it whistled through my teeth. "Bjorn trusts my judgment. He may not leave Sera with me, but he will not sabotage us. I would bet my life on it."

"And indeed you will," Cerin replied softly.

In the days that followed, we planned our visit to Sera. It was a place none of us wanted to re-enter, but hopefully by working together, we wouldn't have to stay long or be found out by those who would do us harm. Cerin possibly trusted me more than he let on given his begrudging acceptance to follow me there. Silas was clearly not happy with our return, and he seemed even less happy over my reasons. I understood he was scared. Given his position of royalty, if he was found out to be in the company of necromancers, no matter how unintentional, it could ruin him.

Nyx wasn't happy about returning, but it was nothing she wasn't already used to. She'd always avoided the upper tiers of the city if she could help it. Theron was the odd one out; besides his relations to Cerin and me, he had no reason to fear Sera. It was for this reason that we chose him as our leader in the city when we would eventually get there. Theron was the least recognizable of us. When securing rooms in an inn, the names of Sera or Galan would never be uttered.

We reached the outskirts of Sera when the second moon of Meir was high at the center of the sky, exchanging the coolness of Red Moon for the chill of Dark Star. It had taken us nearly two seasons to reach Whispermere, but only a few weeks over one for the return trip. We'd had fewer detours and stops this time around, not to mention that we were much better at traveling together than when we started.

As I stared at Sera still a day away in the distance, I hoped we would be as good at working together for this than we had been at traveling. My home made for a beautiful view, each tier of it lighting up the mountainside. With Meir dominating the sky to the city's east, it was easier to see its buildings and architecture, and even the smaller things like the guards upon its walls on their nightly strolls.

Still, it seemed so intimidating now. My eyes lingered on the tall stone towers of the Seran University, that put even the highest buildings in the lower districts to shame. Sirius and Terran were there, and to get the attention of one without the other would require good fortune and teamwork.

Bjorn. I couldn't see the barracks from here, but knowing I was so close to him and couldn't just run the rest of the way to see him killed me. I had to believe he would leave with me. Bjorn was growing older, yes, but I believed he would rather be on the run with me than work the rest of his life under Sirius. Thinking back on it now, I wished I would have asked him to join us when we'd left.

There was nothing I could do to change the past. I could only hope that this time in Sera I could make up for my past mistakes.

Eighteen

Walking into Sera was downright anxiety-inducing. We entered at night when the streets were empty save for Seran soldiers and people of ill repute. Cerin and I wore our cloaks so that we could hide our faces in shadow though the soldiers at the gate could not have cared less when we came through. The men had been amid heated political disagreement about a trade deal Sirius arranged with Nahara in my absence.

Nyx and Theron led us through the shadowed and broken cobblestone streets of the poor sector. Ramshackle homes built out of equal parts stone and wood rose up on either side of us. Sometimes new apartments were constructed haphazardly over the roofs of existing houses from a lack of space. The city did not pay to keep these streets lit like the upper sectors, or even to keep it well-guarded. I glimpsed shady dealings down thin, dark alleyways, and heard the cries and coughs of sick children whose parents were most likely unable to pay the exorbitant prices of the mages who lived so tortuously close to them. Somewhere, a dog barked, its hoarse warnings echoing off of stone walls. Then, with a squeal, it was silenced.

It was a far cry from the merchant and wealthy sectors higher up in Sera. I hadn't been down to see the poor neighborhoods often when I'd lived here, and now I remembered why. Theron and Nyx knew this area much better than me and led us through it with purpose and direction.

We traveled down side streets until we turned down a broader road that served as a shopping strip for the poor. A small market sat beside some shops advertising homemade goods and a tavern, which was the brightest place in a reasonable distance from any direction.

The tavern was on the corner of the intersection of two main streets and built out of large, untrimmed whole trunks of trees. It was three stories high, and light from within spilled out its windows over the cobblestone streets in rectangles. Laughing, talking, music, and the sounds of drunk people dancing were muffled behind its walls. A sign hung over the door between its two street-facing walls, a carving of a mug of ale and a stack of coins lying just below the words, *The Hung HorsemINN: Your Secrets are Safe With Us!* Given the reputations of taverns and this particular inn's tongue-in-cheek sign, I doubted that was the case.

Nyx opened the door with a push and then a kick of her boot and led the group of us in. The enclosed walls amplified the music and conversations. This was a place for the poor and destitute to come and spend their wages on things that would only maintain their lifestyle, but nevertheless, the people were laughing and having fun. If I were here in better times, I may have joined them.

As Nyx led us to the bar, we passed couples making out at corner tables, and men passed out in pools of spilled alcohol. To our left, a man who had gotten too into dancing while drunk fell, causing belly laughs from all who saw it. Above my head and through the floorboards I heard a particularly hyper bed spring.

"Ah, Nyx! Long time no see, love!" The man who spoke from behind the counter was a Celd, his long brown hair pulled back in a high ponytail, allowing the tips of his ears to glow in the nearby candlelight. He had three thick scars running horizontally across his face like it had come from the swipe of a paw, and a long pipe stuck out of his lips, smoke rising slowly from it. When I approached the bar, I could smell a mix of herbs, many of which were likely illegal.

"Heeey, Linden," Nyx greeted, glancing back toward us.

"There are a few lonely guys here tonight. Could point them out to you, if you're interested," Linden offered. "And don't forget, if you want me for the night, I won't even charge." He wiggled his eyebrows and took a puff of his pipe.

"Not here for that tonight, bud," my friend replied. "I need..." she glanced back toward us again. "Five rooms."

"You brought your own, ey?" Linden's eyes scanned over us all. "You don't need five rooms for that."

"I need five rooms. Don't argue," Nyx replied impatiently.

"Hm. Okay, okay, I won't ask." Linden stooped down below the counter and pulled up a book. As he flipped through it to the current date, I found myself surprised that he kept records at all here. "I hate to say it, but I only have three rooms left for the night." With another cheesy grin toward Nyx, he said, "Mine's got room for one more." He glanced at me. "Or *two.*"

I jerked a thumb back toward the front door. "The inn...was it named after you?"

That caught his attention. Leaning over the book on his forearms to smile flirtatiously at me, he replied, "Why yes, Nyx's beautiful fire-haired friend, it was. I can prove it to you if you'd like." Another wiggle of the eyebrows.

I chuckled. I found this man oddly charming in a goofy way if a little desperate. "I will believe it is as you say, Linden."

The Celd's eyes beckoned in mine. "Nyx, be a dear and introduce me to this vixen, for I fear chasing for her affections will be difficult otherwise."

"For fuck's *sake*, Linden, put your dick back in your pants and do your job," Nyx hissed.

"Ah, the lady protests," he complained lightly, standing back up. "You want the three rooms, then?"

"Yes, *please*."

We waited as Linden marked it down in his book and took the coin from Nyx. He then gave us three silver keys. "Your rooms are 18, 19, and 20. Up the stairs and down the right hallway, all the way at the end." Even as we walked away, the horny elf sneaked an alluring smile my way.

We decided that Nyx and I would sleep in the same room, and Silas and Theron would sleep in another. Cerin would be alone in the room between the other two. After a good night's rest, we would send Theron out in the morning to the barracks to find Bjorn and give him a message from me to both him and Terran. From there, we would just have to wait and hope they came quickly unless they gave Theron a letter in return.

The next morning, I had my message written by Nyx and given to Theron so even my handwriting could not be recognized in the case it was seen by someone else. I deliberately kept the note vague so it would mean nothing to anyone who came across it if they were not one of the intended recipients. I hoped the message relayed just enough to get them to come.

Bjorn/Terran,

Urgent. Please come at the earliest convenience. Messenger will tell you where. It has been nearly a year since I left for Whispermere. I have much to tell you both.

With that, Theron was off, and all we could do was wait. I had given him a visual description of both Bjorn and Terran, though it was imperative that he reach Bjorn. It would be much harder for him to get an audience with my brother.

Theron returned some hours later and informed us Bjorn received the message and promised to pass along the news to Terran. He told me Bjorn could not make it that night due to an influx of new recruits keeping his schedule full. Bjorn promised he would find the time for me.

Over the rest of the evening, as the sun crawled across the sky and dipped back below the horizon, we waited in our rooms. I didn't want to risk being seen by anyone who knew me. Theron and Nyx took turns waiting in the bar since Bjorn and Terran were told to meet them there to be led to me. Just when I'd all but given up hope to be visited on the first day, a knock came at our room's door.

I opened it. Terran stood on the other side, a range of emotions running through his sharp features. He immediately grabbed me into his arms.

"Sister, thank the *gods*. I never thought I'd see you again."

Ale and sage. It was so comforting to me. I pulled back from his hug and tugged him inside the room Nyx and I prepared to share for a second night. Terran and Nyx said awkward hellos before I sat my brother down on the edge of the bed.

"I've missed you greatly, Terran. I have so much to tell you." I swallowed hard and sat beside him. "You don't need to fear for my life, brother."

"What have you learned?" he asked, intrigued.

I tried to rush through most of our journey, though I kept Cerin's name out of it. I knew Terran might remember him, and if so, it was possible he knew why he'd fled the university. I told him of my mother, and my disappointment, and finding out I was no longer just human.

"You have made friends along your journey," Terran commented at a point.

I nodded, thinking of Theron. "I hired Theron as a mercenary before we left here. He has become a friend."

"You chose well." Terran hesitated, before asking, "Who else?"

My stomach twisted into a knot. "No one else. I have Nyx and Silas with me."

Terran frowned, his dark brown eyebrows dipping toward the center of his face. "There is a man here, clad in black. He has the room next to yours."

I wasn't sure how Terran could know that. Cerin had done such an excellent job of staying hidden in his room. "Yes, well, there are many rooms here with people in them I have never seen, brother."

Terran nodded and looked away. "I love you very much, sister. I hope you remain diligent with those you keep close to you."

My heart pounded in my ears. Surely he knew nothing of Cerin being here with me. We had been so careful. "As I hope you do as well. I have one last thing I need to tell you."

Terran glanced back over at me. His eyes held a certain distance. I felt sick with confusion; I didn't know what had caused it. "What is it?"

"Sirius—father—is the one who hired the Alderi to assassinate me six years ago," I said, keeping intense eye contact with him so he could see my honesty. "He was—"

"Kai, *Kai*, listen to you!" Terran looked perplexed. "I understand your relationship with father is strained, but to suggest such a thing! Who has fed you these lies?"

"My mother told me this. She knew those who requested it of him."

"She may be the woman who birthed you, but you knew her a total of what—two days and nights? She fed you *lies*, sister. Father has always had plans for you. He loves you—"

"Don't *lie* to me, Terran. You don't like what I'm saying, but do *not* attempt to change my opinion with lies."

Terran stared at me a moment. "Don't be the pot that calls the kettle black."

I was quiet, thinking back over our conversation. Terran knew more than he let on. I didn't know what it was—whether he knew Cerin was with me, or if he thought I was just lying about the assassination attempt—and not knowing drove me crazy.

Terran stood up, facing away. "Forgive me, Kai. I must leave."

"Please, Terran...do me a favor. Believe in what I am saying to you. Sirius has put my life in danger before. I know he places you in much higher regard, but still..." I trailed off, watching as he stopped just before the door. "I fear for your safety."

Terran held a hand over the doorknob. I watched his shoulders rise and then slump with a defeated breath. "I fear for *yours,"* he replied, his voice barely above a murmur.

Just like that, my brother left, and I felt worse for having seen him. Something had changed between us from when I'd left and now, and it wasn't just because of what I'd learned. Maybe it had to do with Cerin. Perhaps it had to do with Sirius spreading lies about me in my absence. I wasn't sure what it was, but it made no sense.

"Something about this stinks to the heavens, friend," Nyx murmured when Terran's footsteps had been gone for several minutes.

"I don't understand it at all, Nyx. We've been to Whispermere and back. We have come across no one from the Seran Army, and we have made good time. Even if someone had followed us, surely we are back sooner than they could have been?"

"That depends on if their mission was to kill us or just report back," Nyx mused.

I was silent. That was all too possible.

"We need to leave as soon as possible. I would not trust even Terran," she murmured.

That broke my heart. I didn't want to believe my brother would turn against me, but I couldn't discount it. I'd left Sera while he had always tried to get me to find a place in it. Terran had always accepted the path in his life assigned to him. Even if Terran still loved me like family, at some point with Sirius and I having drastically different political opinions, he would have to choose a side. If I were in his place, I would have chosen the same.

"I need to talk to Bjorn first," I finally insisted. "I cannot leave without seeing him. I need to make sure he's all right and has the option to join us."

Nyx sighed. "Then I hope he comes tomorrow because the longer we stay here, the more dangerous it is. Theron and I will need to keep a close eye on anyone coming upstairs in this inn tonight. The last thing we need is for them to capture Cerin."

"Yes, *please* do that. I would appreciate it." Anxiety laced my voice. So much was happening and unraveling in what I thought had been a simple plan.

"I will talk to Theron," Nyx promised.

The night was long, for I could not sleep. Every noise stirred me, and there were a few times throughout the night when I got up to investigate the hallway to ensure Cerin was safe. I did not believe that the gods were almighty, but I wished I could pray because sitting around doing nothing did not sit well with me.

When a knock came at the door the next morning, a lack of sleep kept me sluggish. I hurried to the door nonetheless, hoping it was Bjorn on the other side. I wanted to leave Sera today, and ideally, I wanted him with me.

The door opened, and I felt nauseated for the umpteenth time in the two days since I'd been back in Sera. For it was not Bjorn, but an official messenger from the Seran University who awaited me on the other side.

"Kai Sera," the young man said, holding up a summons from Sirius's court. "I hereby notify you to come with me for a meeting with your father, Sirius Sera, and his court, effective immediately. He requests you bring Silas Galan and Cerin Heliot. No one else."

There was my heart again, forcing my brain out of my head with the pounding of my blood. "Cerin Heliot is not here," I stated, trying to keep my voice from shaking. "I can bring Silas Galan."

The messenger read along the back of the summons he still showed to me. "You are harboring the necromancer Cerin Heliot and are required to bring him." The young man's eyes raised to meet mine over the scroll. "It says here that you might try to lie, and that your ties to him are proven."

My nostrils flared, and my mind flew through thoughts at a mile per minute. "I *was* harboring Cerin, yes. He grew suspicious of my intentions here and fled during the night. There is nothing I can do. If Sirius requires his presence, I suggest he send his men east of Sera."

The young man looked flustered and confused, reading through the summons again. "Well...I guess just bring Silas Galan and yourself, then. I'll request he send his army after Cerin Heliot when we arrive." He hesitated. "We must leave immediately, Miss Sera. I have armed soldiers waiting outside the inn for us."

Thump-thump. Thump-thump. I turned to Nyx, who watched with a look of horror. I could not portray what I wanted to her without the messenger overhearing me. Instead, I stared at her, before flicking my eyes to the left, toward Cerin's room. She made no mention of noticing the move, but I knew she did.

"Sirius will not hurt me," I said to her as I slowly exited the room. "He desires my powers more than my death."

Nyx nodded, even as she stood from the bed. I didn't know what she was planning, but I saw the options racing through her black eyes before I could see her no more. Passing Cerin's room without so much a glance, I knocked on Silas's door.

The Celd's face appeared before mine a moment later. His eyes flicked from me to the messenger.

"Silas," I said, my voice low. "Sirius has summoned us."

Nineteen

Walking to the Seran University surrounded by armed guards was humiliating. While not all the citizens of Sera knew me by my appearance, those who did spread the message through the crowds that had gathered on the main road. I heard the hum of collective whispering. There were likely both true and untrue things being said about me. I wondered if I was liked enough to have sympathizers, and then I realized it didn't really matter. None of these people had any control over the politics in Sera; they barely had control over their own lives under Sirius's rule.

I had never been so scared to walk through the gigantic two front doors to the university, even back when I'd anticipated past arguments with Sirius. I had told Nyx he wouldn't hurt me and though there was a possibility of that, I wasn't sure it was true. Even if he refused to hurt me, I had multiple people I cared about who did not have the powers he desired.

They led Silas and me through corridors that were immediately familiar and up twirling staircases that led to Sirius's personal court. While I had been in the room before, I didn't know the people who made up the court. Sirius kept me far from his political sphere growing up, if only because he hated spending time with me. Only Terran had been given such access.

They opened a thick wooden door before us, and the top floor of one of the university's towers presented itself, holding a variety of people. Some were vaguely familiar like I'd seen them before. Some were complete strangers. There were two whom I loved.

Terran. Bjorn. My brother avoided my eyes. That was the moment I knew he had been the one to lead Sirius's men to me. I had such heartbreak I felt I would fall. I wavered on my feet and even whimpered his name. One soldier grabbed my arm to still me.

And Bjorn. He sat a few seats away from Sirius at the round table. His eyes watched me with nothing but love despite appearing conflicted. The first time I saw him since leaving Sera, it was as a criminal.

"Where is the necromancer?" Sirius demanded from the soldiers at our sides.

"There was no one else, sir," one of them replied. The messenger who had led us here had already left, having apparently forgotten his promise to send Sera's armies after the false lead I'd given him. Perhaps the messenger just feared having to face Sirius. I couldn't blame him.

The man I had always known as my father glared at me. "Where is Cerin Heliot?"

"Probably halfway to the ocean by now," I replied shortly, refusing to look away in intimidation.

"He fled?" Sirius replied, before looking to Silas.

"As far as I knew, he was at the inn with us as of this morning," Silas replied.

My heart dropped into the bile of my stomach, and I glared over at the Celd but said nothing. Silas refused to look back at me, but I could tell this was hard for him. Regardless, I didn't care. Nothing but hatred swelled in my chest for him then.

Sirius nodded. "Very well. I should have known I couldn't rely on Kai to give me the truth."

"As I could never rely on *you* to be honest with me, *father.*" The last word was a hiss of mockery. "You could have admitted it was *you* who tried to have me killed when I was sixteen, rather than waste your army's time and resources trying to find the one responsible."

Bjorn frowned at my accusation but said nothing. Terran cringed. Surely, he thought I was crazy at this point.

"*Or* I could admit that I have retroactively wished the attempt succeeded, or that I hadn't spent so much money on something that gave me no return." Sirius stared at me evenly. "You are *nothing* but trouble."

Terran stared in horror over at our father. "Father, you didn't! She is telling lies!"

"Sometimes, Terran, you must do what you feel is right for your city. It's a good lesson for you to learn." Sirius paused and refocused his attention on me as Terran looked pained by this new development. "I have no intention on speaking with you on matters you are not here for. This is *my* court, not yours. You will bring me the necromancer, and I will not charge you for harboring him all this time. This is as merciful as I will ever get with you."

I stared at him but said nothing. I had no intentions of betraying Cerin and dragging him here to his death.

"Kai, do not act like a child. Respond."

"I will *not* bring you Cerin," I replied, each word sounding stronger than the last. "I didn't think you were so stupid, *father*. My lack of response served as my answer."

"And with your answer, you prove your own stupidity," Sirius sneered. "If you will not bring me the criminal, I will let *you* serve his death sentence."

"*Sir,* if I may," Silas interjected desperately.

"What is it?"

"Leave Kai be," the Celd pleaded. "I will bring you Cerin myself."

"No!" I turned to Silas and grabbed him by the arms before two soldiers violently pulled me back and held me still. *"Don't* do this," I pleaded with him, my chest heaving. "You *know* how much he means to me. He saved my life, Silas! You cannot—"

"For the love of the gods, *shut up,"* Sirius huffed impatiently. "It is no wonder you won't turn him over. It seems my dear daughter has become a necrophiliac." It was clearly meant as a distasteful joke, and some at the table laughed. Bjorn and Terran both appeared ready to dig their own holes to be buried in.

"That's not what that means, you ignorant *fuck!"* I screamed at him, tears of anger in the corners of my eyes. I could not be the reason for Cerin's death. Not after finding him after all this time. Not after he trusted my judgment to come here with me. Not after his kindness and his teachings.

"Silas Galan, you are free to leave," Sirius said, ignoring my insult. "You may request the help of my guards near the inn. Just let them know you act in my command."

One stranger at the table wrote something on a small piece of paper and handed it to Silas. "Take this and show it to the guards. This is official parchment."

Silas nodded, still avoiding my gaze. "Thank you, sir. I hope to be back with him in the next few hours."

I heard Silas leave the room behind me. Anger consumed me; I shook so badly in my boots their buckles rattled. The only thing I could hope for was that Nyx and Theron were escorting Cerin to safer ground and wouldn't be there by the time Silas arrived.

"You haven't changed much," Sirius griped to me. "You are so obsessed with unconventionality and the macabre that it undermines any potential you could have had. You should be thankful Silas has the intelligence and foresight to make up for the things you lack."

"Sirius, your insults are unwarranted," Bjorn protested, his voice reserved. Somehow, he'd sounded calm when confronting his superior.

"And your comments are unnecessary," Sirius replied coolly.

"Terran," I blurted out, desperate for answers. "Why would you do this to me? Cerin hasn't harmed you. He saved my life. *This* is how you repay him? Ratting him out to our tyrant of a father?"

Terran still stared down at the table, ashamed. "We knew of your relationship with him before your return to Sera, sister. I needn't have said a word."

I switched my gaze to Sirius. "You had men follow us?"

"The people of Thornwell were talkative once the Twelve torched their homes," Sirius replied nonchalantly. *The Twelve.* No wonder we hadn't seen them. They observed us from a distance in the air on their griffons. "They continued on the way to Whispermere, as we knew that was your destination. They found you just before the Cel Mountains. Lo and behold, dear daughter is consorting with a necromancer who has eluded us for years and is the murderer of *many* of my men."

"If you hadn't have sent them with orders to kill—"

"He is a *necromancer*. By simply existing he offends the laws of Chairel."

"And he is *kind*. And a healer. He saved my life and prevented one of my friends from becoming a cripple."

"I don't care if he is a god's gift to humanity and throws annual tea parties. He is a *necromancer.*"

I thought about arguing that so was I. I decided that offered no benefits to me during this conversation. My anger slowly turned to defeat.

"I tire of your despicable words and your uglier face, *father.* If you are going to put me to death, just do it already."

"As much as I would love to, Silas's actions have spared you," Sirius replied. "You are free to go."

His soldiers loosened their grips on my arms, and I spun to the door. Perhaps, if I hurried I could catch Silas before he had Cerin arrested.

"Oh, and Kai?" *Sirius.* I turned around, facing the man who raised me for what I hoped was the last time. *"Never* expect to be invited to join my armies or be considered part of Seran royalty ever again."

"I would sooner eat my own vomit than consider you family," I retorted, before continuing out the door.

Sera was a blur of colors and people as I ran through the city, my eyes biased for the Celd who was my target. I wanted to kill Silas for his betrayal, but every second I took to get there was another second of danger. I wasn't sure how I would stop him. Perhaps I could hurry past him and to the inn where I would help Cerin escape.

By the time I reached the inn, my heart shattered my ribs with its incessant pounding, and my inhales drew knives against the flesh of my lungs. I had not seen Silas, so I feared for the worst. At the same time, I hadn't seen Cerin being escorted to the university, either.

I hurried through confused stares in the inn and to the second floor where Silas and Theron talked quickly with each other at the end of the hall. I heard rustling and ignored Silas for the moment to hurry to Cerin's room, busting open the door and catching him amid packing.

"Cerin, we must leave," I warned, hurrying to him. Even as I was confused over the current events and wondered why Silas had no soldiers with him, I also felt relief wash over me to see Cerin okay.

Cerin turned and held his left hand out toward me, his right at his scythe like a threat. His silver eyes were hostile and distrusting. "I'll only warn you once. Do *not* come closer."

I stilled with distress halfway through his room. "I'm not here to hurt you, Cerin, but to escape with you."

Cerin shook his head manically. *"Don't* pretend that's why you are here." When I didn't move, he went back to packing, frantically stuffing his things in his knapsacks without any organization.

I thought of Silas out in the hall. *"What* did he tell you?"

"Don't act dumb, Kai." Cerin didn't stop to look at me even as he shoved his feet into his boots. "You are a talented actress after all this time of encouraging me to trust you, but I see through your manipulation now. I should have never trusted you, and I regret ever coming back to this *fucking* city."

"What are you *talking* about?" I breathed, exasperated. "We need to leave Sera *now*, Cerin, and together. Going alone is

276

suicide. They will recognize you at the gate!" I hesitated, waiting for him to reply. When he didn't, I said, "Silas will lead Sirius's men to you. He—"

"Well, *that's* funny, because he said the same of you." Cerin glanced up between grabbing his things off the floor. "You finally admit to some truth. *Leave me be,* Kai. Either way, I am dead if I stay here. I'm better off alone."

I stared at Cerin, my eyes trembling in their sockets, the anger having come back to me. I was losing *everything.* I'd already been on a quest that had been nothing but a disappointment and caused me to grow apart from a friend I'd had for years. Now, I was losing what little I'd gained and then some. Terran, Bjorn, Cerin. They would all be gone from my life.

"I *plead* you to reconsider, Cerin," I begged, my voice thick. "I've never lied to you. I thought we had grown close. I care for you immensely." I choked up. Embarrassed, I sniffed away the emotion that wanted to escape.

"I also thought we'd become close, Kai," Cerin replied, his glare much softer now that I had devolved into tears. "If anything, I don't blame you for sacrificing me to save yourself. I blame my own weakness that I have when it comes to you." He hesitated and ripped his eyes away from mine for the last time. "That is why I must go. I can't trust you, nor can I trust myself when I am around you."

The room was nearly empty, now. Cerin was almost gone. Again. Maybe forever, this time. I was so torn from heartbreak and anger from so many different things, and Cerin wouldn't listen to me. I did the only thing I knew to do; I went to the next target on my list.

"*Silas!*" I was yelling it as I exited Cerin's room, my eyes finding the Celd still in the middle of a conversation with Theron. They quieted after overhearing my banter with Cerin.

My former lover looked up at me and prepared to defend himself as I shoved him into the corner of the end of the hallway.

"*Tell him!*" I screamed directly in Silas's face. He grimaced, holding his head back from mine. "*Tell him the truth!*" Silas stared back at me silently, not allowing my anger to get to him. I heard Cerin exit his room and hurry down the hall. I wasn't sure where Nyx was, and Theron had his hands on my shoulders preparing to pull me off of Silas, though he allowed me more leeway than he should have. Perhaps he knew of Silas's betrayal.

I jerked my head around, watching as Cerin hurried down the inn steps and out of sight. My heart ached as he left, and even more as I heard the inn door downstairs open and squeak to a close. I turned back to Silas, and despite my anger, burst into tears.

"I regret ever befriending you," I sobbed, nearly falling forward into his chest before stopping myself, disgusted.

"Let him go, Kai," Silas replied, despondent. "It is for the best."

"You betrayed us," I replied, unable to keep the seething pain from my voice.

"I *saved* you," Silas retorted. "And I gave Cerin a fighting chance. I did not bring the guards to him like I promised your father. I may tell Sirius that I missed him, but they could still hold me responsible. I did it for *you.*"

I breathed shallowly, letting those words sink into my head painfully. It made sense, save for one detail. "You lied and told Cerin I was the one who would have him arrested. I will *never* forgive you for that."

"You don't have to," Silas replied, his voice pained. "I wanted him to run from you, Kai. Better him run from you than to have the entire world running after you. For as long as you are with Cerin, you are a criminal."

More anger rose to replace the last bout. "That is *not* your decision to *make!"* I protested. "You are trying to control my life by deciding what is best for me. I'm a grown woman, Silas, and we are no longer together. Leave me free to make my own decisions and mistakes."

Theron released his hold on me. He was likely surprised to hear such personal conversation. He hadn't known until today that Silas and I had ever been romantically involved.

Silas pulled away from what had been a mutual gaze. He looked heartbroken. I could tell, then, that despite everything, he still felt immensely for me. Perhaps jealousy had helped shape his intentions. Maybe learning of my longer lifespan had caused him to want to rekindle a relationship with me again. But it was too late. We were headed down two very different paths.

"I'm sorry for intervening, Kai, and I am sorry for my harsh words to you in the past," Silas finally said, his apology genuine. "The trip to Whispermere changed you, and it frightens me. A year ago, I would have never imagined you would want the things you want now. I knew of your obsession with necromancy, but I always thought it was only a morbid interest. You are willingly crossing legal lines left and right, and I don't know what to make of it."

"You are so worried about what is *legal,* Silas, that you are blind to logic. Necromancy is practical and can be used honestly. You've seen that with Cerin."

"Cerin is one exception in a long list of others who have used it for ill," he replied. "And besides, your father and all of Chairel—they don't care about your arguments. You'll be treated as a criminal for as long as necromancy is illegal."

"So I will make it legal," I stated.

Silas blinked at me a moment. "You cannot do that, Kai. You have no political power."

"Then I will take it." It was a promise. The anger I felt at Sirius throbbed through my veins, combining with my everlasting distaste for the stringent magical laws of Chairel. If I would no longer be welcome in my homeland, the least I could do was build my strength to take it and change it. I'd studied rebellions and war my whole life, and now I knew I had the power and lifespan to work toward such a goal. I could change everything about Chairel I didn't like, from the prohibition of necromancy to the stringent laws that caused magical services and healing to cost a fortune. If only someone had the power and ambition to change it before me, I wouldn't have had to go through such turmoil now.

With these thoughts running through my mind and filling me with the purpose I'd always longed for, I backed away from Silas and glanced at Theron. "Where is Nyx?"

"She went to secure different lodging," Theron replied. "She told me you weren't willing to leave without speaking to Bjorn."

I nodded. I had told her that. Now that Cerin had gone off on his own, I almost regretted saying it. I wanted to go after him, but that quest would have to be put on hold. Speaking to Bjorn came first. It was, after all, one reason we had come here to begin with.

Nyx came back to the inn hours later, just as the sun had started to set. Silas, Theron, and I waited for her at the bar since we needed to free up the rooms for other guests.

Nyx hurried up to me, her eyes wide. I remembered then that Cerin was at the inn when she left. Maybe she thought they had captured him.

"How did they capture Cerin?" Nyx demanded in a panic.

"They didn't. Silas lied to him and got him to leave on his own," I explained, my tone bordering on depressed.

"No," Nyx protested, before reaching into a pocket of her armor and pulling out a folded piece of paper. She slammed it onto the bar before me, rushing through pulling it apart so I could see it.

On the parchment was a spot-on sketch of Cerin's angled face. At the top was a hole, like the poster was nailed to the side of a building before Nyx tore it down. Across the bottom of the sign in thick black ink, it stated:

CAPTURED! Cerin Heliot.
Charges: Necromancy, 226 counts of murder of Seran armed forces, 12 counts of abuse of a corpse, evading the law, practice of magic without a proper license, refusal to follow official court summons.
Sentence: DEATH.
Execution: Guillotine, 13th of Dark Star, 417, at Seran University Court. Public welcome.

The paper shook. I wasn't sure why until I realized I was holding it, so I let it go. It drifted to the bar below me. "Nyx..." I murmured, my voice weak.

"What?"

"What is the date today?" I asked, my eyes on the execution date.

"The tenth," she replied, sounding just as forlorn as I felt.

I stared at the sketch of Cerin, imagining him sitting in a dark dungeon cell with nothing but a straw mat on which to sleep. I felt broken. I'd warned him this could happen. Too many soldiers knew his face, and perhaps even knew of his presence with us here before they had summoned us to the court. Even still, I felt responsible. I felt *Silas* was partially responsible.

I swallowed hard, feeling fear for the second time in what had been a long day. "We have work to do."

Twenty

"Nyx, what did you find?"

Nyx spread out a hastily drawn map onto the bed. I reached out and held down a corner when the paper rolled back up. My eyes darted around the markings my friend had made on it with charcoal.

One dark finger pointed to the top right of the map where Nyx drew a line from the center of the parchment to the border. "This is a river that flows all the way from Sera to the Servis Ocean," she explained, swiping her finger upward to the ocean. "There's an underground stream that flows from the mountains and into Sera's water system, and they reroute it from there to take sewage to the ocean to dump. Here," she added, pointing to a circle at the end of the river closest to Sera, "is a sewer gate that separates the underground river from the above ground river. It is the same gate I used to enter the university six years ago on my mission to kill you."

"Does it require a key?" I asked.

"Oh, my *dear,* you don't need keys when you have me," she teased. "They haven't changed the lock. It's still as easy to pick as the first time. I tried it tonight—obviously, because I got inside." Nyx swiped her fingertip to a set of boxes farther up the line underground. "These are water treatment rooms. Water is heated here to purify it in these huge vats. When I was there, there were maybe four, five people working. The vats are big enough that you can avoid the workers just by using clever timing.

"There are steps here," Nyx continued, moving her finger along, "that will take us to the castle storage. Ales, dry foods, all that fun stuff. There was no one here when I was just there, but since it's directly connected to the kitchen, we'll eventually come across some chefs or other types of food service workers."

"How easy is it to avoid them?" Silas asked, standing beside me, watching over the map with crossed arms.

"Easy for me. For three or four people?" Nyx shrugged. "We'll do what we have to do."

"We cannot kill innocents," Silas protested.

"And we'll try not to," Nyx replied, looking up to him. "We can let them go, tie them up. It doesn't really matter to me. But if someone gets feisty, I *will* defend myself."

I didn't want this to turn into another moral argument. We didn't have the time. "Go on," I prodded.

"From the kitchen comes a hall," Nyx went on, dragging her finger horizontally across the map. "At the end of this hallway comes the dead end of another. The same hall that leads all the way out to the university's entrance and gathering room."

I nodded. "I know where that's at." I pointed at where the two hallways dead-ended into each other. "The dungeon is here," I said, tapping my finger at the end of the hallway.

"Right," Nyx agreed. "This'll be our biggest issue. Getting from the kitchen to the dungeon and defeating the guards. One of them—if not many of them—will hold the keys to the cells. The two hallways we need to travel to get to it are busy and lead to areas with lots of foot traffic. The probability of being caught in the act is high. If that happens, one or two of us will have to go into the dungeons alone while the others fight just outside to hold them off. Thankfully, once we have Cerin out of his cell, it's a straight shot from the dungeon back through to the sewers, where we'll be away from the main gates of Sera at the front of the city. Our only resistance should be from the castle itself."

"You did a good job getting all this info," I complimented, thankful for her.

"Oh, it was fun. It's been awhile since I've gone creeping around like that. Nearly forgot how much of a rush it gives me," Nyx admitted. "Besides, Cerin's one of us now. The only regret I'll have is not being able to see Sirius's ugly face when he realizes he's escaped."

I swallowed a lump of anxiety. *If he escapes. If we pull this off.*

Silas turned toward the door of our room, perhaps going to his own. The inn Nyx had found for us to stay after The Hung HorsemINN wasn't any better regarding location or clientele, but it had worked last night. We would stay here tonight but had no plans to visit again. Tomorrow was the twelfth, and it would be the last day we could help Cerin escape before his execution. The day of our attempted jailbreak would also be the last day we ever expected to be in Sera given our attempt would make us outlaws from the city for life.

"Silas?" I asked.

The Celd stopped but didn't turn back around.

"Off to bed so soon?"

"I am going to get a drink," he replied, before leaving the room and shutting the door behind him.

When I pulled my attention back from the door, I found Nyx watching me with her intense black eyes. As we heard Silas's footsteps disappear down the hall, she said, "He won't be with us. You know this, right?"

I ground my teeth together in worry. "I have figured it, yes. Has he said anything to you?"

"You know Silas doesn't speak to me alone if he can help it," Nyx replied, her eyes falling back over the map, studying it distractedly. "Besides, I think he resents me for our arguments near the Seran Forest."

"I'm surprised he hasn't left us yet," I admitted. I had gone through many emotions over the past few days when it came to Silas. Over the past few moons I'd fallen out of love with him, but I still greatly treasured him as a friend. Our argument at the inn after the incident with Cerin irrevocably harmed even that. On the one hand, I couldn't change him or the strained relationship we'd ended up with. On the other hand, I heavily mourned the loss of someone I thought would always be there. It was like mourning a death because that is what it was. The death of a close friendship, and the death of an entire chapter of my life.

"I think he feels guilty over causing this," Nyx suggested. Though she missed our argument, I'd told her everything that happened. "If he hadn't lied to Cerin about you to get him to flee, we would have planned our departure much better, and he'd probably be with us now. What we're planning on doing is pretty dangerous, and it might end in loss of life. Silas will feel partially responsible for that. He might be struggling with deciding to help us or not."

Two sets of boot steps came up the hallway, so the conversation between Nyx and I tapered off. A knock came at the door.

"Come in," I called out.

The door opened. There Bjorn was, nearly filling in the doorway with his bulk. Out of all the people I expected, I hadn't expected Bjorn, especially after all that had happened. Just his presence made me immediately happy, like all was suddenly well.

I was in his arms before I even had the recollection of jumping up from the bed. Bjorn held me close to his chest, nearly crushing me, and I didn't care. I welcomed it.

Bjorn kissed my hair. "I am so, *so* sorry, my girl," he murmured.

I laughed, but it was thick and awkward from through a sob that otherwise would have stayed hidden. "For what?"

"For everything, love. For not being able to come sooner, for having to hear of your adventures through Terran before you could tell me. For all the awful, *awful* things your father said to you." Bjorn pulled back from me, and his hazel eyes switched back and forth between my own. "And for not realizing his true nature. If I had known he tried to have ya killed, I would have scooped you up myself and taken you far away from here."

How I wished he had. "He's not my father, Bjorn," I stated.

Bjorn nodded, his large hands rubbing my upper arms affectionately. "I wouldn't let him have that title either, my girl."

"Since the title is open, maybe you could take it," I offered. It sounded so juvenile. I was an adult woman; looking for a father figure shouldn't have been a priority. Still, I justified it by reminding myself that I'd always *had* that father figure. I just hadn't asked him for permission to call him as such.

Bjorn slowly came to understand my meaning, and he pulled me in for another hug, just as tears welled in his eyes. "I feel like it's been mine for years. I stole it a long time ago."

I laughed through tears as we hugged again. "Nobody stopped you," I teased him, light-heartedly. We hugged for so long, both crying into each other's clothing, that even Nyx had tears in her eyes as she watched us embrace from the bed. It was the first time I'd ever seen her come close to crying.

It was a long time before we parted, but when we did, Bjorn dropped a thick brass key into my palm. I looked up at him through hurting eyes. "What is this?"

"The key to the dungeon, love," he replied.

Bjorn couldn't have known how much that meant to me. Or maybe he did, and that's why he did it. Either way, I expected Bjorn to love me no matter what because he always had. I did *not* expect him to support my choice in companions, or to automatically assume we planned to break into the same dungeon he helped to regulate.

"How did you know we were planning this?" I asked quietly.

"Because I know you do what you believe is right, and I believed you when you argued for Cerin in the court. You won't let that man die if you can help it. Plus, he saved my girl's life." Bjorn smiled at me.

"Have you spoken to him?" I asked.

"I did. Briefly, between guard shifts. I told him who I was, but he said he recognized me from years ago. I thanked him for his service to you and told him how you fought for him in front of Sirius's court at the risk of your own life."

"What did he say?"

"Not much. He broke down and cried. Said he was sorry. I wasn't sure if that was directed to you or me."

I nodded, understanding. Cerin likely was depressed if he thought his last words ever to me were negative. "Did you tell him you would help him escape?"

"No. I don't want to do anything to sabotage you or him...and besides, I don't know his mindset. Prisoners can get loopy before they die. The last thing I needed was him rambling about escape." Bjorn hesitated. "He has my permission, by the way."

I frowned. "For what?"

"To marry you. I could tell you were falling in love with him when you spoke of him at court." Bjorn paused, noting my shocked face. Nyx laughed hysterically at the situation behind me. Bjorn frowned with innocent bewilderment and asked, "Am I incorrect?"

I couldn't help but chuckle out of both embarrassment and because Nyx's laughter was contagious. "I...I mean, I care for Cerin. Deeply. But nothing has happened between us yet. He doesn't trust easily. I want to pursue something with him, but..." I trailed off and smacked Bjorn's wrist playfully. "Not *marriage*, Bjorn!"

"I apologize, love." He chuckled heartily. "Maybe I should have said nothing at all. You don't need my permission, anyway. You wouldn't wait around for it if the time came. You've always forged your own path in life."

"It's what causes me the most trouble," I lamented.

"Speaking of getting into trouble, there's one more thing about the escape," Bjorn said. "I can't control the soldiers throughout the university, but I know the schedule of those who work the dungeons. Tell me when ya plan to go, and I'll do my best to clear it of guards."

I frowned. "How will you do that?"

"Easily. Tell the soldiers working that their relief is coming early, and tell the soldiers on the next shift to come in later."

I nodded. "Okay. Well, we plan on going tomorrow evening. We'll enter through the sewers about sunset." I hesitated. "If there are no guards, how will we open the cell?"

"There's always a set of keys hanging on a peg above the desk," Bjorn replied. "They're on a metal loop. The keys are in order of cells from end to end."

"And the desk is..." Nyx trailed off, attempting to remember from her own stint in the dungeons.

"As soon as you go through the dungeon door and to your left," Bjorn answered.

Nyx snapped her fingers. "Ah, that's right."

"I want to ask you something," I said to Bjorn, watching as Silas passed by in the hallway, back from the bar.

"What is it?"

"Will you leave Sera with us?"

Bjorn exhaled, the breath whistling through his lips. "I am sworn to serve your father—" he paused, thought over his words, and continued, "—*Sirius* until I am sixty. I have three years left to go before my retirement. Leaving before then would be a dereliction of duty."

"Let me rephrase, then. Would you come with us if we return to Sera to fetch you in three years?"

Bjorn chuckled. "In a heartbeat, child. I am getting up there in years, and given all this *god* business my life will be but a speck of yours, but I'd come with ya. Considering this little jailbreak of yours will have you running from the law, I'd suggest you go south to Nahara for a few years."

"You think we'd be safe there?" I questioned.

"As safe as you're gonna get without crossing the ocean to another continent."

I nodded. "Thanks, Bjorn."

"Anytime, love." Glancing back to Nyx, he commented, "Now, it's getting kind of late, and you have a big day tomorrow, don't ya? Maybe I should head back to the university."

I grabbed him into another hug. "What big day tomorrow?" I murmured, in jest.

"What? *Oh,* I don't know. Must've gotten confused with something else." Bjorn was grinning when we separated. "I love you, Kai. I am so proud of you, ya know that? Even with all this *necromancer* business." He wiggled his bushy eyebrows. "I mean, he *is* a good-looking necromancer. *That's* a plus."

I gave him a goofy smile. "You might want to leave before I refuse to tell you I love you back."

"Yeah, yeah, all right." Bjorn slowly backed out into the hallway. "I'll see you in three years, girl. Red Moon. Don't leave me hanging, yeah?"

"Never." I swallowed hard as he walked away. "I love you! And I'll miss you!"

Bjorn turned near the end of the hall. "I'll miss you too, love!"

"I'll only miss you this much, though," I replied, holding two fingers out about an inch apart.

Bjorn laughed heartily as he disappeared out of sight. A little piece of me went with him.

"I kind of regret not going to see him more often," Nyx commented behind me. "He's a good man."

"Yes," I agreed. "He is."

I had just closed the door and sat on the bed again when another knock came at the door.

"Yes?" Nyx called out, feigning irritation.

"Kai, may I speak to you?" *Silas.* Given the tone of his voice, I felt a pang in my chest. Nyx and I exchanged glances.

"I'm coming." I got up and opened the door, where Silas stood distraught on the other side. "Are you okay?"

"Can you come out here a minute?" he requested, his eyes flicking back to Nyx.

"Yeah." I closed the door behind me. Silas walked down to the end of the hall where a large window overlooked the cobblestone streets outside. I followed him, watching as he averted his eyes to the city. "What's on your mind?" I asked him softly. I wanted to make this easy for him. I figured I knew what he had to say.

Silas's forehead creased as his eyes watched the stars flicker over the city's skyline. "This is the hardest thing I've ever had to do," he murmured, his Adam's apple bobbing as he swallowed emotion. "I thought I was done making hard decisions when it came to you, but somehow, this is hardest."

My eyes fell to his hands, which were twitching as he stared out the window. Silas spoke about his decision almost two years ago at this point to break our romance and revert it back to a friendship. He regretted that now that we knew his reasons for doing so weren't applicable.

"I keep hoping that you've read my mind and that you'll decide for me, but you won't. I respect that, in a way. You are letting me be free to make decisions as you wanted me to do for you." Silas hesitated before a shaky exhale blew through his lips. "I still love you, Kai. I always will. I know I've given you reasons to believe otherwise, and I'm sorry for that. I am not asking for you back. I understand we're beyond that. I know you feel for Cerin. I know the reason we went to find him was that you were seeking love that I refused to give you, and that this all, in a way, is my fault."

"Silas, you made your decisions. I've made mine. Don't place blame on yourself for doing what you felt you needed to."

"But I've done many things I felt I needed to that have caused you distress and trouble. Our differing opinions on things are affecting our actions and causing problems between us, and..." Silas trailed off, his voice broken. "I would rather be a fond memory to you than a recurring problem."

There it was. He'd finally said it. I had expected this, but there was no way I could have prepared for it. I fought back tears as I followed his gaze out the window because looking at him was too hard.

"Please say you understand," Silas said, the words hopping over hiccups.

"I do. I understand completely, and I'm sorry," I offered, going to hug him. I let myself cry, then. It wasn't like Silas hadn't seen it before, and I wanted him to know that this was hard for me, too. I felt his arms come around me and hold me like it was the last time. It probably was, but to acknowledge that would be too much.

"I'm sorry for all the trouble I've caused you," Silas murmured just above my ear. "All I've ever wanted to do was protect you and help you. I know that by leaving, I cannot do any of those things and it kills me."

"It's not your job, Silas. Not anymore." Tears streaked his armor below my cheek as I held onto him. "You've focused on me for far too long. I want you to be free. Find something you can throw yourself into and do it. I know you can."

"I will, and I'll dedicate it to you," Silas said, before pulling back from me. We gazed at one another for a while, committing each other to memory. "You may not believe me when I say this, but despite our disagreements, I wish nothing but the best for you. Your quest to save Cerin, your desire to legalize necromancy...they are daunting tasks, but I know you can do it. If *anyone* can, you can."

"Thank you," I murmured. That meant so much to me. "And thank you for your decisions at Sirius's court. I've thought about it, and it was a selfless thing to do. My anger would not allow me to see it at the time, but you saved my life and tried to save Cerin's."

"It means a lot to hear you say it," Silas admitted, his hands longingly rubbing at my own.

"Where will you go?"

"I think I will return to Celendar," he answered. "I haven't seen my family in quite some time. It'll be nice to be in the forest again." He paused and smiled softly at me. "You would love it, Kai. Trees that rival the mountains. It puts the Seran Forest to shame."

"I will visit someday," I promised.

"I hope you will. Be sure to ask for me, and I will give you a tour. Show you the sights." Silas hesitated. "After I get reacquainted, myself."

"I will hold you to it," I replied. Letting my fingers slip from his, I said, "Be careful, Silas."

His sharp green eyes were sad in mine. "You too, Kai."

It was the second time someone I loved would walk away from me that night. I didn't plan on either goodbye being permanent, but sometimes you make plans, and the gods will only laugh.

At times, literally.

The skies were a blanket of dark periwinkle blue that hugged the snowy Seran Peaks. With a discerning eye, one could see the stars twinkling, eager to join the night. Meir loomed in the sky behind us, shining brighter as the day ran off and made way for the darkness. The second moon headed back to the horizon, preparing to complete its second run over Chairel for the year. As I watched the sky, the first snow of this year's Dark Star fell, drifting lightly down from the heavens in white puffs.

Water rushed by my boots through the Seran canal, carrying sewage from the city off toward the Servis Ocean. Nyx had mistakenly called it a river during our plans.

A mixture of sewage and water poured out of a large pipe that came out of the underground. Filling in the circle of the tube was a thick black iron gate that Nyx was unlocking. The iron had rusted and corroded near the bottom of the bars, at times discoloring the water that ran through it to copper.

Despite being sewage, the water didn't smell too bad or look too thick and awful. It seemed to run clear past Nyx's boots as she stood on the edges of the pipe. Of course, we were still outside. It was possible that as we followed the pipe underground to the water treatment plant, the smell would overwhelm us.

Click. Snap. The iron gate creaked as Nyx slowly opened it, pulling her body to the left side of the pipe to leave a way for its arc. Theron and I hopped the short distance from the side of the canal to the tube, hurrying through the gate. Sound became condensed in the pipe; the water rushing by us sounded ten times closer and louder in here.

Nyx followed us as soon as she could hurry around the gate, closing it slowly behind her.

"Does that need to be unlocked for us on the way back?" I asked, my voice barely over a whisper. I hadn't needed to be so cautious; the entrance we'd just come through was outside of Sera's wall and north by quite a distance. Still, I didn't want to sabotage anything about our mission tonight. Nyx was used to doing things silently. Theron was great at it, too, given his tracking abilities. I was the only one I needed to worry about. I had been quiet enough to avoid confrontation a few times over our journey to Whispermere, but I would need to travel silently today.

Nyx shook her head, putting her hand on a lever just inside the gate. "This opens it from this way," she replied.

I nodded. Theron and I waited to the side of the pipe, letting Nyx pass by. This was both of our first times going this route, and we would rely on the assassin to take us the right direction since she'd been here before.

We slowly made our way through the rushing water, pushing through the resistance of the current and following the pipe's path toward the underground of Sera. The water breached my boots and soaked my clothes and leather armor, adding to my weight and discomfort. It was freezing. While the Dark Star weather hadn't yet gotten as cold as it was known to, this water had initially come from underneath the Seran Peaks. It was mostly runoff from the snow of the mountains, and its path underground ensured its temperature stayed low.

The pipe angled to the right after a while. It wasn't long after that when I heard a distant humming. Up ahead was a faint light at the end of the tunnel, shining down from above. As we approached it, I realized we were beneath Sera. As Nyx hurried below the light, it was revealed to be a grate that led to the water treatment room. Nyx pulled out her lock picking tools, going to work on unscrewing one side of the grate. As Theron and I watched, she stopped, quietly moved to the side of the grate, and held one finger to her lips.

I listened intently to the ground above, though I could hear very little over the rushing water beneath my boots and the humming in the room over us. I did notice when the light coming through the grate dimmed into shadow as someone walked around above. Then, the shadow passed, and after a few seconds, Nyx continued unscrewing the grate. Finally, it swung down, and she took a step up the ladder built into the wall of the pipe, poking just the top of her head up. A moment later, and Nyx hurried up into the room above.

Theron and I waited in silence for a few moments. Then, one blackish-purple hand lowered into the pipe and made a "come here" motion. I went up the ladder next, and the ranger followed closely behind me.

We were in the corner of a tall room made of thick stone, and it was dimly lit. A large, floor to ceiling object rose just beside us, humming. It must have been one of the vats Nyx had told us about that heated water for use. As she closed the grate behind us, I looked above our heads where a scaffolding bordered the room to allow access to the top of the vats. Thankfully, no one was on it right now.

Nyx passed me, moving to the left of the vat, crouching amongst the shadow until she became a part of it. I followed her slowly, trying to find a method to squat that wouldn't completely kill the circulation to my legs. My boots were still mushy inside from the water of the sewers, and I knew we had to be tracking water across the floor. But this *was* a water treatment room, and what our tracks were behind the vats and in shadow.

I was so thankful to have Nyx. The woman knew what she was doing.

Theron tapped me on the shoulder from behind, and I glanced back. He nodded forward, where Nyx had hurried across the gap between vats and motioned for me to join her. As quietly as I could, I scurried across. Theron soon followed.

We circled the second vat around the outside, sticking between it and the thick stone wall. Nyx waited at the edge of its shadow, watching the room ahead. Though dimly lit, it was still much brighter than where we were. I could hear people talking in the room, but the echoes of their voices made it difficult to discern their direction.

Then I saw the origin of the voices, watching as two workers crossed from left to right ahead, amid a conversation about what the plans were this year to keep the pipes from freezing during the harsh weather. The conversation slowly teetered off to our right as Nyx waited ahead. Then, with a quick motion behind her to follow, she hurried forward.

Once we were out from behind the vat, the water treatment room opened to our right, but Nyx headed left, scurrying up some stairs that led to a doorway. She glanced both ways before checking on Theron and I as we were coming up behind her. Without a word, she hurried through the door and went right, where stairs led upward.

At the top of the stairway, Nyx hesitated and fell back to a crouch from her dart up the steps. Ahead in the storage room was a lone woman sorting through dry goods for the kitchen, her back to us.

I felt my heart pounding in my chest. I didn't want to hurt her. I hoped there was another way.

Nyx made the decision for me, darting out silently from the stairway and grabbing the woman, her right hand clasped over the worker's mouth, her left arm keeping her still.

"Do *not* scream," Nyx murmured in her ear, turning to face us and motion toward a big canvas bag of produce near their feet. Because I didn't know her purpose, Theron entered the storage before me, untying the rope that held the bag shut at the top. "We are not here for you."

The woman's eyes widened as she breathed heavily against Nyx's arm. She stared at me in a state of shock. I realized that she probably recognized me from passing me in the hallway or serving me before. As Theron set to work tying the woman's hands together behind her back and sitting her down on the ground, I rummaged around in my coin purse.

"You didn't see us here," I murmured, dropping two gold coins in the pocket of her apron. It was equal to her pay for a fortnight, but it was just a fraction of what I had on my person. "For the inconvenience."

The woman nodded frantically, bewildered.

Theron came back over to the woman, tying a long piece of canvas he'd cut off a produce bag around her head, keeping it between her lips.

"There might be a ruckus," I told her. "Wait until it dies down. *Then* yell for help."

She only nodded.

We left the storage room behind us, moving along the counters of a kitchen during its after dinner downtime. Thankfully, most of the workers had been on the other side of the kitchen washing dishes, so our path to the last hallway before the dungeon was clear. The doorway ahead beckoned to us, a cobblestone wall from across the university hallway teasing us that our job was nearly finished.

Then, our plans rapidly unraveled. A kitchen worker entered the doorway from the other side, carrying a tray of half-eaten food and coming to a stop when he saw the Alderi before him.

"*Guards! Assassins!*"

The call vibrated against the walls and in my eardrums. Nyx sprung from her crouching position, throwing her twin daggers forward and into the gut of the man who'd set the alarm, before slicing them out to his sides. The man fell backward into the hallway, his intestines spilling out of the wound meant to silence him. His tray fell over his corpse, glasses and ceramic plates alike sliding off it and crashing to the stone floor beneath, shattering into pieces in an expanding pool of blood.

It was too late. There was now pandemonium. The kitchen workers were screaming and in a frenzy, arming themselves with knives they had available. Somewhere in my head, Nyx's voice echoed as she told them they would not die if they left us be. Some listened, some did not.

Nyx whipped her head to look at me. "*Get Cerin!* The guards are coming. With luck, we might avoid most of them."

Theron followed me as I ran out into the hallway. It wasn't until we were at the dungeon's door that I saw the guards, running from the university entrance toward me and unsheathing their weapons.

"Unlock the dungeon, Kai. I'll hold them off." Theron drew both of his swords, preparing for battle.

Even as I pulled the key Bjorn had given me out of my pocket with one hand, I prepared a shield for Theron in the other. Only after it connected in an egg-shape over him with its energy field glistening in the lights of the hallway did I focus on the door. I shoved the key into the lock, failing to open it right away from my nerves.

"Sister!" I stopped. Looked to the left. Behind a rush of soldiers on their way to us was Terran, his eyes wide with a variety of emotions. He was dressed in full armor and wore a deep green cloak on that matched his eyes; it was the same one I bought for him for his twenty-fifth birthday just four years ago.

I said nothing. I only stared back, the brass key rattling in the lock. Time was too short. With one last glance toward my hand which held the key, Terran turned back to the rest of the workers and tourists alike in the entrance to the university.

"Bjorn has betrayed us!" Terran screamed, his hoarse voice echoing off of the cobblestone walls. My heart sunk into my stomach, and then I remembered that only members of Sirius's court held sets of keys made of brass. All other soldiers, guards, and workers used aluminum keys. By process of elimination, Terran figured out the culprit with little more than a glance.

The dungeon door clicked open. I rushed inside, slamming the wooden door shut behind me. I heard Theron and the guards come to a clash outside, even as my eyes darted down the line of cells, looking for Cerin.

302

"Kai?" There he was, five cells in, sitting in a lump on the dirty dungeon floor. Cerin wore nothing but a flimsy tunic and pants given to the prisoners, and the clothes practically hung off his lean form. It was a combination of that and the bags beneath his eyes that proved how weak he'd become from sadness and a lack of good food over the previous days.

Cerin stood quickly, his pale hands running up the bars imprisoning him. "Why are you here?" he asked, glancing toward the door to the hallway where there were muffled sounds of fighting.

"To get you out, of course," I replied, grabbing the ring of keys from the peg Bjorn told me about.

"Oh, *thank* you," Cerin breathed in a rush, leaning his forehead against the bars in relief as he watched me hurry to his cell with the keys. "I can't apologize enough for misjudging you. I should have known—"

"Shh," I murmured, trying to remember the order of the keys. "There will be time to talk later."

Five cells in. Five keys from the—

Crack! Something flew from the direction of the dungeon door, as big and hard and heavy as a stone, and hit me directly in the hand. The ring of keys flew behind me and skipped across the floor, the scraping noise coming to a stop only when the they hit the bottom of a chest against the wall. I stared at my hand, seeing stars from the pain dancing before its shattered bones. I was in a state of shock for the moment, not yet knowing what had happened and too dazed to figure it out.

"Leave him, Kai." *Terran.* My brother stood just inside the dungeon door. A stone hovered above his left palm, but his

303

right was empty. Considering my limp and broken hand, I figured I knew what it had held just moments ago.

"Kai, let me heal you," Cerin insisted from within his cell, his arms coming between the bars.

In a daze, I walked over to Cerin's cell, moving my shattered hand toward him. Terran watched, conflicted, as the necromancer mended the limb that he had just broken.

"I will let him heal you, but I will *not* allow him to leave with you," Terran stated, his eyes on my hand to avoid my gaze. "You need to leave Sera, sister, and take your friends with you. Father will *not* take kindly to another slight."

As my hand healed, the pain lessened. The dazed, pained phase of my brain was over, and the situation became clearer. Cerin finished treating me, and I flexed my fingers, ensuring they worked right.

"This is not a slight," I retorted. "I am merely fixing his injustices."

"He is a *necromancer,* sister!" Terran exclaimed, perplexed.

"A necromancer who once saved my life and just healed the wounds you gave me," I retorted, just as baffled by his argument as he was of mine.

"I do not *care* what he does—" Terran stopped, frustrated. "There is no getting through to you, is there? You have already caused the death of someone you love, sister. Will you bring about your own demise over a necromancer?"

My heart thudded against my chest, my mind on his selective words. "Whose death have I caused, brother?"

"They're preparing to execute Bjorn for treason, Kai. In a time of weakness, he has aided you in this—this—" Terran

304

waved a hand toward Cerin, a look of disgust and anxiety on his face. *"Quest."*

Time slowed. In this one moment, there were five people I cared about, all of whom were at risk. It was as if I would never get a break. Eventually, if this terrible luck of mine continued, someone I loved would be hurt, and there would be nothing I could do about it. I was playing catch-up with the injustices of fate.

And there, barring me from protecting people I cared about, was yet another person I loved. I stared at Terran for what felt like ages but was really only seconds. I understood his position. He was Sirius's son and was raised to take his place. Thus, he now stood as my opposition, and I had to treat him as such. Though he was a grown man seven years older than me, for a moment, I saw him as a boy again. The boy who had been good to me. The boy who was a ray of sunshine in the darkness that ran through Seran royalty. The fun-loving, optimistic older brother who I had always looked up to and admired.

I swallowed the lump that had formed in my throat, and it scraped painfully down my esophagus. "I love you, Terran."

Air magic swirled in winds above my palms as I recited a spell in my head. My brother's eyes widened as he realized what I had chosen to do. I released the magic, and as the gust of wind rampaged past the cells toward Terran, he threw his own magic to the ground. A wall of earth stretched from the ground to the ceiling before him, blocking the wind, particles of dust and debris flaking off where it hit.

"Do not do this!" Terran screamed from behind his defensive wall.

305

"Leave me be, and I will let you go," I demanded, water swirling in balls above my palms.

"I cannot," he replied, his voice thick with desperation and sadness.

I said nothing, only thrusting my arms forward to unleash a torrent of water. It gushed from my hands, rushing toward the dungeon door with the force of a raging river. Water rammed into Terran's earth wall, turning the dirt into sludge and swirling behind it. My brother screamed in surprise as the water engulfed him, his wall melting into a thick mess of mud into the cracks of the dungeon floor. The water rushed back and engulfed my own feet and flooded the cells of the prisoners. Some convicts who had been sleeping now stirred.

Panic hit me, for I knew Terran could drown. I continued to expel water from my hands, aiming for the doorway. Now that the earth wall had all but melted completely, the force hit the dungeon door, tearing it open at its hinges until it slammed back against the hallway wall. The rampaging water broke through and into the corridor beyond, carrying my brother with it as he struggled to stay afloat. Outside the dungeon, Nyx and Theron both fought soldiers, though everyone scattered as the room released its water over their feet like a rush of vomit.

I dispelled the water magic. Terran sputtered to breathe from down the hallway. The water from my spell sunk into the cracks of the floors and walls, and the farther it flowed, the lower its level. I hurried to grab the cell keys that I now found in the back corner of the dungeon due to the water's current moving them.

"Kai, they will execute Bjorn!" Nyx yelled through the doorway at me, even as she fought. Thick blood dripped down her arm from a gash in her shoulder.

"I know," I shouted back, still in a panic. Cerin exited the cell quickly beside me, going to the nearby chest.

"Kai, keys," he pleaded. I threw them to him, watching as he found the right key to unlock the chest. In it, he found the things they had taken from him, save for his gold. He rushed to pull his armor on over his jail clothes and equip his scythe.

I hurried out of the dungeon, my boots squishing through water that had spread from my spell. At a distance down the hall, Terran watched me, seemingly unwilling to continue our fight. I was fine with that. I didn't want to hurt him. He knew I was much more powerful than him and had access to a wider variety of spells from all elements. To continue to fight me would be daft.

"Where did they take Bjorn?" I asked Nyx in a rush. I gave her a shield while Cerin mended her wounds.

"Out front, University Court," she blurted in response. "Same place they planned to execute Cerin."

"Let's grab him and go," Theron shouted, amid a sword fight with a guard. Many were dead at his feet, and blood mixed with the water puddles in the hall, tinging it red. The ranger, however, was not unscathed, and couldn't go on like this forever.

"It is a trap."

The voice was so low, I barely recognized it as Terran's. I looked his way, but he refused to make eye contact with me.

"*What* is a trap?" Nyx retorted impatiently. More blood escaped her wound just before Cerin finally closed it.

"They will execute Bjorn, but they're doing it now to draw you and the necromancer to the courtyard." Terran finally looked up, caught my eyes. His were broken and depressed. "Father's armies are in the streets. Archers align the roofs and walls around the courtyard. He will kill you all." It wasn't a threat, but a statement. Even after I'd fought him, my brother looked out for me.

"If he looks to kill Bjorn, he will *have* to kill me first," I replied. Cerin leeched from the last guard in the hall with us, and the man fell, his life force drained. The hallway was now eerily quiet. Thanks to Terran, I knew why. Sirius amassed his armies for us in the courtyard, so he had pulled them from the university.

"Sister..." Terran's eyes glazed with tears as we turned to leave. "Be safe."

Twenty-two

Outside of the Seran University's two thick, large front doors, the courtyard was full of people. They quieted once the light from the large chandeliers of the university spilled out over them, calling their attention to my presence.

If we had expected to be attacked right away, we were quickly disappointed. The only weapons thrown at us were the glares of Sirius's soldiers, which gathered as Terran had predicted. Overhead, snow flurries still fluttered down from the sky; the precipitation gathered as dust in the crevasses of the ground below, and in the corners of curbs and walls. The sun had set some time ago during our trek through the university, leaving the stars to blink at us between soft collections of ice crystals.

The others followed me as I made my way through the crowd. Surprisingly, they parted for us. On the wooden platform where Sirius held his executions, the man I now called father and the man who had once unjustly held the title were in an unfortunate position. Bjorn was on his knees, his thick hands tied behind his back, and his head in the cup of a guillotine. Sirius stood beside him, his hand on the rope which he planned to use to end Bjorn's life.

My mind fought for a strategy. If I went into this fighting, all it took was a flip of Sirius's wrist, and I would lose my father. I knew, however, that Sirius planned on me dying here, along with my friends. He had to know I wouldn't go without a fight; my rebellious nature was, after all, one reason he loathed me.

When I reached the front of the crowd, a line of soldiers blocked me from moving closer, their swords and shields held before them. I wondered how many of them I knew. I wondered how many of them Bjorn had trained before they ended up standing guard at his execution.

Movement waved by my peripheral vision, up along the shadows of the rooftops and the nearby city wall. I knew archers waited up there, ready to loose arrows into my flesh. Cerin and I had prepared before leaving the safety of the university by ensuring the four of us had life shields to fend off physical attacks and wards to fend off the spells of Seran mages. The protections couldn't last forever, but they would help enough during the initial attack to give us a fighting chance.

"Let him go," I called out past the soldiers to Sirius. Bjorn couldn't see me, but he jerked his head in its holder when he heard my voice. "He has done nothing wrong."

Sirius sneered back at me. "He is guilty of *treason.*"

"I stole his key," I lied. "He did not give it freely."

"Did you also sneak into the university, *become* him, and then give false directions to dungeon guards?" Sirius smiled cruelly as he watched my panicked reaction to his words. *"No,* you did not."

I shook in my boots. I wanted nothing more than to hop over these guards and get to Bjorn, but I knew that would only cause him to be executed more quickly.

"This—citizens of Sera, is what happens when you consort with necromancers," Sirius shouted, his voice traveling over the crowd, while pointing at Bjorn. "Even the most loyal are not immune. For if you sympathize with those who would deal with the dead, you will find yourself among them."

My nostrils flared. I glanced back to Theron. He carried a bow. He had seldom used it during our travels to and from

Whispermere since Silas had been with us. Now, he was my only hope. I moved my eyes toward Sirius upon the stage. Theron understood and slowly went about switching his weapons.

"Since dear Kai is here to witness the consequences of her actions—let us get on with it." Sirius glared down at Bjorn. "Do you, in your *unfortunate* position now, regret your illegal activities?"

"No. I regret ever serving you," Bjorn replied, his voice somehow calm from his position.

Sirius gritted his teeth. "Give us your last words so that I may end you."

"Give 'em *hell,* Kai."

I swallowed hard as he spoke to me, my throat thickening with emotion. "Bjorn—!"

Just then, Theron lifted his bow. Just as quickly, the soldiers took note and sprung to action, shouts of attack ringing out from multiple voices. Time slowed, and I watched in horror as a soldier grabbed Theron's bow, causing the arrow to fly off target, passing by Sirius's face as he realized what we meant to do. Soldiers surrounded us, and the clash of metal rang out.

There I stood, my ears dulled, preparing a spell even though I had no time to cast it. Sirius pulled the rope of the guillotine with little more than a careless flick of his wrist. As the blade fell, reflecting the moonlight back toward the crowd from its thick steel, Sirius hurried off the stage, preparing some sort of spell from his palms.

Thump-thump. Thump-thump. The energy was building in my hands, but the spell wasn't complete. I watched despondently as the blade hit flesh, cutting through the spine and throat of the only father I loved and meeting with its wood

311

holder whilst dripping with his blood. Bjorn's head rolled away from the guillotine, coming to a stop with his hazel eyes facing the crowd. Gasps and cries echoed out from the people watching, perhaps because they had once known him. Worked with him. Joked with him. Behind the execution machine, his body slumped to the side, blood spurting violently from his neck.

Thump-thump. Thump-thump. I dispelled the air magic I'd been building with little more than a shrug. In both hands, I accumulated fire. I stared into Bjorn's lifeless hazel eyes, wholly removed from myself. Somehow, I was aware that Bjorn's death irrevocably changed me. Somewhere within myself, I tore my own heart out with broken nails.

But right here, right now, I wanted everyone dead. They would pay for executing a good man. The people would pay for coming to watch. All of them. *All* of them would pay.

I rose my hands to the sky, two glowing orange orbs casting light over those fighting beside me. The hissing and crackling of flame spit protests as it begged me to unleash it. Even still, I funneled even more energy into the two spells, seeking maximum damage. *Maximum* impact.

Sera had carved an irrevocable scar in me today, one that was both senseless and brutal. I would return the favor.

I felt the life begin to drain from my body. The fireballs in my hands now trembled with immense power, pleading with me to release them.

Not yet. It's not strong enough.

Just as I became light-headed from draining my own life, I released the spell, forcing the energy into the sky. It was then that I noticed a soldier had stabbed me through the gut. My blood dripped off of his sword near its handle as he pulled the blade back out. I hadn't even felt it through my rage. Thrusting both hands at him, I leeched from his life force, regenerating the energy I'd lost. The man fell in seconds, drained of his life. I turned to another soldier, absorbing his energies. Another, and another, and *another*.

Even as the skies darkened above me, preparing to unleash the fire spell, I readied another with the life force of a dozen men. I let my stomach wound drain blood over my leather armor, paying it no mind. I would heal it later if we made it out of this mess. There were thousands of soldiers here. That was an abundance of energy I could use to wreak havoc upon Sera and all Sirius held dear.

Then, came terrified screaming. From multiple directions and just as many voices, people finally looked up to the sky to see what I had summoned. A high-pitched whistle cracked through the air, and the noise loomed louder and louder. I looked up to see my spell in action and was pleased to see a fireball the size of a large barnyard animal hurtling toward the earth, the air whistling past the flames as it fell. The courtyard of Sera glowed orange, and the people scattered.

BOOM! It hit in the midst of the crowd. Bodies flew up around the fireball like it had splashed into water, some flying over the courtyard wall and into the merchant's sector on the other side. Bits and pieces of people flew everywhere like bony confetti and fell into mismatched piles like the pieces of a bloody jigsaw puzzle. I heard pained screaming and saw grown men running from the point of impact burning alive. Just feet away, some fell from the jolt of the debris alone. The fireball had been so powerful it upended the courtyard's expensive cobblestone, throwing bits and pieces of it into the crowd like blunt force shrapnel.

I heard fanatical laughter and realized it was my own. Though the people scattered, maybe they had expected that to be the only meteor. Looking up into the sky, I saw at least seven more, and all from my first spell. Using the energy I'd leeched from dozens of men, I prepared even more. I released the next bout of fire magic into the sky and prepared for my personal Armageddon.

The next fireball crashed into the side of the university's tallest tower, the one which held Sirius's office. It caved the smoothed stone out of the corner at impact, solid rocks falling to the university below, some breaking straight through the roof from the gravity of its height. As I watched with glee, the remaining two walls of the tower could not hold its weight. Crumbling echoed from above, and the tower leaned before admitting defeat. The stones which had once held it up popped out of the sides from the pressure. As the tower fell, it crumbled into pieces. Some of it collapsed more of the university's roof, while even more fell into the courtyard, crushing the flesh of dozens into stone like they were merely insects.

Each fireball that fell jolted through my skeleton, the force of its impact loosening the stones from buildings, walls, and ground alike. I could hear screaming, some of which came from my friends and companions. I attempted to ignore it. Most of the soldiers and citizens of Sera had fled. Those who could, anyway. As for the rest of the soldiers, I sought them out of the crowd and stole their lives from them with death magic, only regenerating what I lost.

Those who ran from me ran in fear. *Good. Let them fear me.*

Ahead, the courtyard wall exploded into pieces from another ball of fire. Somewhere behind me, yet another crashed through a wall of the university. Sera was literally breaking apart, and I loved every damn minute of it.

I took a moment to heal the wound in my gut from earlier, not even looking at it as I did so, my eyes feasting on the destruction surrounding me, disbelief and elation consuming me as I realized just how powerful I was. After my skin closed, I put both palms toward the ground and recited a spell Cerin had taught me.

Tendrils of black magic raced across the cobblestone, burying themselves in the recent dead. Dozens of mutilated fresh corpses rose, shambling off to chase after those who fled. Pounding on the doors to the university behind me shattered the air, and I realized the dead were after even those who would keep themselves safe inside.

"Kai!" Cerin screamed at me, alarm in his eyes. He was warning me to stop. Maybe the energy I'd used to raise the casualties helped to clear my mind because I could hear him at least. That's when Bjorn's corpse shambled through the courtyard, his head only attached to his body via my own magic.

I dispelled the necromantic spell with a new feeling of horror, and Bjorn's body fell, his head separating from it once more. A ripple traveled from my stomach to my throat, and I bent over, vomiting straight onto the cobblestone.

"Kai, you have made your point! We need to leave!" Theron shouted, wiping the blood from his face with a forearm. An arrow stuck out of his upper arm after at least one archer hit

315

their target. I heaved over the ground, vomiting once more. Now that the anger subsided and the abundance of energy from leeching escaped me, my mind cleared. My display shocked me. The image of Bjorn's reanimated corpse would forever haunt me, forged with the knowledge that it happened due to *my* spell.

"You killed innocents," Cerin informed me with a gasp, directing my attention to where the first fireball had impacted. Amongst the rubble were civilian bodies of all shapes and sizes.

Vertigo overcame me until I swayed over my feet. "I'm sorry," I breathed, uncertain of what else to say. All around us, there was silence. The only sound was the burning from my destruction. Everyone had fled.

"We need to get the *fuck* out of Sera." I looked over, seeing Nyx for the first time in a while. A burn ran down the side of her face, the purple skin bubbled up with liquid. The leather armor beneath that protected her right arm was scorched off, and the skin was dark and bloody with burns, though not as bad as her face.

"What happened to you?" I asked, frightened. I was sure I knew, but I didn't want to face it.

"What could've happened to all of us if you continued raining your fire," she replied shortly.

"I'm sorry." I moved to heal her.

Nyx jerked her face away from me. "We *need* to get moving, as I said. The people have fled, but now that it's quiet, they'll come back out."

"Okay," I agreed. Nyx hurried toward the courtyard entrance and ran beyond. We all followed her, eager to leave the wreckage behind us.

We hurried as quickly as we could out of Sera, going through the front entrance rather than traveling back the way we'd come underneath the city via the sewers. We only came across resistance from two soldiers near the front gates who were quickly dealt with by Theron and Nyx. Right now, I didn't want to kill another person. The shock of my rampage was still fresh in my system.

Once we escaped the city's walls, we did not even stop to breathe. Somewhere, in Sera, plans were being made to take us out. I knew that, and I welcomed the challenge. I wasn't sure if I had hit Sirius with one of my spells, but I hadn't remembered coming across his own. It was possible he'd hid like a coward while I wreaked havoc on his people. Even if I'd somehow killed him without knowing, Terran and those loyal to Sera would plan their revenge.

I glanced back at Sera when my inhales torched my lungs. We were making good distance from the city, but even from here, I could see that my rampage had broken it. The university's main tower no longer rose high above the walls to rival the mountains, and fire spotted the city. Overhead, thick clouds of smoke cast the stars out of the sky. My power—the power of the gods—was *immense.*

My seething anger at Sirius and the ways of Chairel fueled ideas of rebellion. Thoughts of building armies to undo everything Sirius had ever accomplished and change the magic laws of Chairel fluttered around flirtatiously in my mind, but getting there would be one hell of an arduous journey. I would soon have a country seeking out my head. Just days ago, I would not have agreed with them on how I was a criminal. The only charges they could have gotten me on were necromancy. Now? They could try me for murder.

I felt disoriented by my own actions. Cerin had warned me of the high from leeching. I had experienced it before, and it was the most overpowering feeling I'd ever had. That combined with boiling rage had affected my actions tonight. I hoped Bjorn would still be proud of me.

Bjorn. My stomach sliced in two. I could not save him. All I'd wanted to do in Sera was ensure he and Terran were safe. If I'd known things would turn out like this, I might have refused to go at all. Silas left us, Bjorn was dead, I'd unintentionally hurt Nyx, and I picked a fight with Chairel, which had the strongest military in the world. In what once was a quest to gain something, I'd only lost so much more. But losing these things only filled me with the purpose I'd always desperately sought.

I promised myself I would find the willpower to take a stand against Sirius and Chairel once the upset of the night calmed down. I had so many reasons to now. I'd always hated Chairel's restrictions on magic, but Sirius's mistreatment of Cerin and me was unforgivable, and Bjorn's execution proved to be the final straw. Many rebellions had formed in my home country over the centuries, but all of them failed. After learning about my heritage and seeing the extent of my power tonight, I felt I could be the first to succeed and change history. Sirius had once hired assassins to kill me because he hadn't wanted to incur the wrath of the gods; little did he know that the only god he had to fear was *me*. My wrath against Sirius would be relentless. I'd spent my whole life studying war and the decisions historical legends made that formed and changed our world.

Sirius's actions tonight gave me a reason to work toward putting my name in the history books to be beside the best of them.

"Give 'em hell, Kai." Bjorn's last words to me echoed over and over again in my head, filling me with more of the purpose I'd always longed for.

I will, I promised with gusto.

"Where to?" Nyx asked, the words cracking into my thoughts. She turned to face us briefly beneath the moonlight during our rush through the grasslands of Sera.

I thought of Bjorn and his words to me back in better times. "South. To the deserts of Nahara."

Coming up next in *Earth...*

In Kai Sera's rage after the brutal execution of a loved one, she has decimated one of the most prized cities in Chairel in a show of magical prowess, and now the country seeks her head. Kai and her companions flee to the unfamiliar land of Nahara, where she must convince its leaders to ally with her in a rising rebellion against her former home.

Nahara is a strange and dangerous land full of giant beasts, and it has a culture that values the bloodshed of gladiators in its coliseum. If any country will join Kai in waging a war with political goals that include legalizing necromancy, it is Nahara. But convincing them may not be easy—for Kai must first prove her power against foes who have yet to be defeated, and when it comes time to battle with Chairel, her ideals will force her to oppose those she loves.

Teaser of *Earth...*

The attack came after the darkness of night fell over us near the end of Dark Star, just as the year 417 came to a close. Our trek after leaving Kilgor took a detour from Caravaneer Road, though we were still going in the same direction. We planned to visit Comercio, as it was the last settlement we would come across before the remaining trip to Nahara. Caravaneer Road led there because it connected all major cities to Comercio, but we wanted to avoid traveling on the road. The closer to Comercio we traveled, the more populated it would be. We didn't want to risk being seen or recognized before making it to Nahara.

We were amid setting up our tents in the middle of the grasslands that appeared to stretch for miles in every direction. As always, it made me feel unsafe. Though Dark Star would soon make way for the warmth of New Moon, for now, snow still blanketed the earth. Our mish-mash of cream and brown-colored tents stuck out like a sore thumb amongst the fields of white.

Tonight, I found I had reason to fear, for our pursuers found us with little problem.

At first, I heard a distant beating which vibrated with power in the air. The noise was unfamiliar to me, but I knew it was not any of my companions, and we were far from the main road, so it couldn't have been a caravan or pack animal.

My friends and I quieted. We all froze in the middle of finishing the preparations for camping, because to move felt like it would call attention. Even as the unfamiliar beating came closer and got louder, I hoped for innocent explanations.

FWOOSH. FWOOSH. FWOOSH. FWOOSH.

My golden eyes rose to the sky. Up ahead, patches of the stars in the night sky blackened, squelched from their places. My heart picked up its pace, and my hands dropped the bag I'd been carrying. Keeping my eyes on the sky, I recited two identical air spells in my mind, and felt the energy building in my palms.

FWOOSH. FWOOSH. FWOOSH. FWOOSH.

Theron grabbed the bow he'd put just inside his tent, and pulled the quiver over his shoulder, preparing an arrow. Nyx watched the sky, holding her daggers, looking as if she was trying to think of a plan. She had nothing but melee.

Cerin had his mind set on raising the dead, two growing orbs of black casting shadows over the snow at his boots. He watched the skies with trepidation. Out of all of us, he was the only one to have experience with such a foe, as I was certain I knew the identities of our airborne pursuers.

FWOOSH. FWOOSH. FWOOSH. FWOOSH.

Perhaps in my ignorance, I waited to attack. I did not wish to kill anyone I didn't need to. There had been a time when Sirius used words before attacks. If I didn't immediately attack, it was possible only words would need to be exchanged with our pursuers. It was hard to tell if this could be the case; despite the stars which had darkened to black in the sky, I could not see our followers. I could not tell if they were hostile.

Then, through the loud vibrations of the beating in the air, came a whistling. I recognized the noise, but could not switch to life magic in time to prepare a shield.

Shik!

"Gah—!" Cerin jerked back from the force of the arrow that sunk deep into the soft flesh between his neck and shoulder.

324

The pain didn't stop him from releasing the death magic. Black tendrils raced across the snow in dozens of directions.

"All right, you sons of bitches," I grumbled, thrusting my hands toward the sky, releasing the air magic. More stars fled the sky as thick storm clouds gathered above us. Now, not only did the beating in the air vibrate through the sound waves, but the sky itself groaned with such pressure that the ground trembled. Even as I prepared another spell, small veins of lightning lit up patches of the sky with anticipation. A flash of purple light confirmed my worst fears.

Sirius had sent the Twelve. The entire dozen. In the sky above us, twelve griffons of various shades hovered heavily in the air, their wings manipulating the air with a laborious effort. Though I had seen the Twelve's griffon mounts a select few times, it was always at a distance. The creatures were magnificent in both size and beauty; they had the heads and wings of birds of prey, only at many times the size. Large, waterproof feathers glistened back from their elongated necks into the thick fur of the lower body, which was double the bulk of horses. The four thick paws of each creature hung heavily below their bellies, razor-sharp claws extending outward between toes as a threat.

On top of each griffon was the form of its rider, each wielding different weapons and intent on leaving here today after the death of my friends and I. Many of the riders were people I knew. Bjorn had trained all of them at the beginnings of their individual military careers. They would be magnificent fighters, and they outnumbered us.

But I fully intended on making it out of this alive. Despite my sorrow for it, I would be the death of the Twelve.

325

Made in the USA
Columbia, SC
14 August 2022

65320173R00195